FLIRTING

WITH A

NEW LIFE

MW01028518

PRAISE FOR FLIRTING WITH A NEW LIFE

"This was the most wholesome, funny, feel-good book ever. The plot culminated into the perfect ending, one that had me cheering for Kelly (and also simultaneously very emotional). The final message was like a salve to the wounded heart to anyone who has ever been hurt by someone they love. I found myself relating to the ex-experiences, and the crazy world of dating (I never want to be back there. Ever). And it came full circle! I love when books come full circle."

—Goodreads reviewer, Kat

"Excellent read! I loved the characters and the story line and am hopeful that this becomes a series. Kelly, the main character, reminded me so much of a very dear college friend and I did not want the book to end. I couldn't help but laugh out loud at Kelly's quirky choice of words. The characters were so well developed and so relatable. I absolutely loved this book!"

—Goodreads reviewer, Chris

FLIRTING

WITH A

NEW LIFE

a novel

Jill Cullen

"Isn't Life Great?"
&
Jill Cullen

MONROEVILLE, PA
jillmmo
2024

if you enjoy this book, please consider
giving it a positive review. &

ISBN: 9798865488033
Imprint: Independently published

Cover design by: Heather Mihalic
Printed in the United States of America

for Eilish and Finn

A Beginning

I am capable of taking care of myself—at least I think I am. I mean, I'm 34 years old. I have a five-year-old, and I'm capable of taking care of him.

But trying to navigate my current life, I can't help but think about that stupid boy in high school—what was his name? Chad Somethingorother?—who had told me that there were two types of people in this world, people who were meant to work and people who were meant to be taken care of by others. He then said, in a not so nice way, that I was one of those in the second category. We were dating at the time, and I don't think he was trying to be offensive, but him saying it really irked me. Maybe it was just because it was a man—well, a 17-year-old man (a-hem)—who was telling me that I couldn't do something. Being reared in a feminist household, that hadn't sat very well with me.

But you know what? Within 10 years, I really wished I could have tracked him down to ask, "How the hell did you have me so pegged at 18?" Seriously? It wasn't like he was even my boyfriend. We had only gone out a few times, but he just knew.

I needed to be taken care of by others.

It seems I still do.

And thank God there are a number of people in my life ready and willing to take care of me.

ONE

The Sister

And there I sat in my dining room (my very white and boring dining room). Across a large oak table and on the other side of that day's pile of junk mail, sat one of the people who liked to take care of me, my older sister Kim. Because she had always been the math whiz of the family, she was helping me figure out a budget. I'd been cursed with being the creative genius of the pack—well, if you can call two kids a pack. We both had bold personalities, so it always seemed like there were many more of us than the actual two in number.

I was recently awarded a grant for my creativity, my writing. A few months earlier I'd started to panic about how I was going to continue to make ends meet. That prompted me to research some writing grants and apply for all that matched my qualifications. I was awarded only the one. But, fortunately, it would buy me a little more time before I'd have to find a day job. I was a fiction writer with three publications to my name, a book of short stories that came out shortly after getting married and then two novels that were still selling okay. While I appreciated the royalty checks that would come in from time to time, there was no dependable amount, and my current day job of being a stay-at-home mom, well, it didn't really pay much unless you count hugs and messes. My son Evan was great at both!

Anyway, while I was noticing how white the dining room walls were and trying to resist the urge to reach for a department store coupon poking out from under the pile of junk mail, Kim was going on and on about how if I could just stick to this budget that she had created for me, I could make my grant last for about six months. I had just taken a sip of coffee and literally spit it back into the mug.

"You've got to be kidding me, Kimmy! Nothing stifles my creativity quicker than a strict timetable with such a short amount of time to finish my book. Can't you somehow figure out a way to squeeze out another—" I rubbed my eyes with my thumb and fingertips from my right hand for a few seconds and looked at her, "—year or two?"

She looked up at me over her glasses and took a deep breath through her nose. Her dishwater-blond hair was pulled up into a clip in the back and strands from the sides were hanging down around her face and bangs. She looked a bit wild at that moment, but I held back my laughter. I mean, she had just spent a couple hours helping me. It would have been rude to laugh at her.

She took another deep breath and then opened her mouth. *Here it comes*, I thought and braced myself. "So I just sat here doing this math for the past two hours with Evan teaching my three-year-old to say shit for what reason? Kel, there's only so much money to work with. I'm an accountant, not a magician."

She was so like Mom when you pushed her too far. They both had no patience for my sense of humor or creative nature. My dad had always been a little more accepting of my creative, albeit scattered, mind. While he hadn't been a perfect father, he'd come pretty darn close, mainly because he was kind and patient and, well, not as structured.

Things with both my mom and sister were very scheduled, very matter of fact. They're great qualities to have... if you're not me. It was just that I couldn't have lived that way. I had always been the kid who had taken four hours to do an hour of homework because I kept getting distracted by any number of minute details that meant nothing to the assignment. My mom had probably wanted to kill me several times growing up. She hid it well. I mean, she had tried to hide it at least.

My ex-husband Sam had found those scattered qualities in me endearing, and that was probably part of what had made me love him so fiercely—he had accepted me as I was. It didn't bother him that it could take me a whole day to clean out one desk drawer because I had to stop to read every old letter and look at every old picture. Well, he hadn't cared at first. Eventually, it felt like everything I did annoyed him. Funny how that happens when you're no longer in love.

"Shit, Mommy," Kim's daughter, Meredith, called from the other room. I pressed my lips together for a second so that I wouldn't laugh.

"You know what? Six months'll be perfect," I said then smiled and winked at her. "Let's go and get some dinner." I raised my eyebrows. "My treat."

She threw her hands up in the air. "Your treat?"

"Okay, your treat?" I said quietly.

She got up and walked into the living room, and I heard her say, "Time to go, Meri. Let's clean up the toys you played with."

I sat at the dining room table for a couple minutes longer. God, I needed to paint these white walls! They were driving me a bit crazy. I needed to accept that this was my new life and move on. It was; wasn't it? I needed to get my photos hung. I still wasn't fully unpacked from my move, and it was creeping up on a year of being in this house. While it had been great to live with my clutter in boxes in the basement, my house didn't feel completely like home. But I hadn't been ready to unpack the past, and I wondered if I'd ever figure out a way to get there.

I reached across the table and grabbed Kim's budget, well, my budget. I took a deep breath and blew it out. "Okay, creativity, you've gotten me this far. Don't fail me now," I mumbled and threw the budget back on the table. I grabbed my coffee and wandered toward the living room, which was a bit more settled into.

I had painted the living room walls Autumn Harvest, which was really just a pumpkin orange color. I was still deciding if I liked it every time I walked into the room. My gut said *yes* (it looked great with my hand-me-down brown and green furniture), but my head screamed *you've got an orange living room!* every time I entered it.

I had my favorite print, *Flaming June*, hung above the fireplace and a few photos of Evan and other family members in various locations. This room felt a little more like home—at least what home had become after being dumped from a 13-year long relationship.

Wrapping my mind around this new definition of home wasn't

coming easily for me. I missed having a family that was more than just Evan and me. I missed the sense of security that having a husband had given me—albeit a false sense of security obviously. And I even missed him when I was ignoring the bad memories and romanticizing the good.

But there had been a lot of good. Like the day we had brought Evan home from the hospital—that had been a good day, the best even. Sam had driven home so slowly while I sat in the backseat beside Evan. I'd been so scared that I was going to break him and kept saying stuff like, "I can't believe they just gave him to us. This is crazy!" and "Are you sure this is legal—to just keep him... here with us?" But Sam had kept his cool and kept reassuring me by saying stuff like, "You got this!"

Later that day, I had just finished putting a diaper on Evan and held him up. "See that!" Sam said. "Look at you! You're a natural." Sam squeezed my shoulders.

The diaper fell off.

I shook my head and laughed. Looking at Sam, I said, "Am I really?"

Sam took Evan and laid him down on the changing table. "I mean," he shook his head and smiled at me. "It was a good solid attempt, Kelly." We both laughed. "The effort was definitely there." He smirked at me and laughed.

"I don't think effort alone is going to keep us all dry," I said as Evan peed all over himself and Sam.

"Little bit of effort each day," Sam said. He started to take off Evan's clothes. "You wanna grab me some warm washcloths, and I'll wipe him down?"

"Absolutely," I said as I walked out of Evan's room toward the bathroom. "You do the work," I called toward the room. "I'll be your assistant." I warmed the water against my wrist and wet the washcloths.

I walked back into Evan's room and found him with his clothes balled up over his crotch. Sam pointed and laughed. "It's my shield."

"Get those yucky clothes off my baby," I said and started to wipe his tiny body with the washcloth. I leaned over and kissed Evan's head. "You are the sweetest boy, and I love you so much, Little Man."

Sam had grabbed some clean clothes from Evan's drawer and brought them over as I was drying Evan off. Sam set the clothes beside Evan and grabbed a new diaper. I stepped back. "Tag-team baby. You're it," I said and poked Sam's arm.

"We make the best team," Sam said and smiled at me. "I love you, Kel."

"I love you too." I kissed him on his shoulder and then hugged him from behind as he finished dressing our baby. "We do make the best team." I pressed my face into his back and squeezed.

There had been so much good—but a lot of bad too, especially toward the end. The day before he left me we were celebrating my birthday with dinner and cake at my parents' house. It seemed like seconds after we were done with the cake, Sam was heading out the door to go and meet up with his new friends that he'd started hanging out with right after his best friend Jason had died suddenly. I'd walked with him to my parents' front door so that I didn't have to bring my family into the dysfunction that had recently become our marriage and quietly said, "Can you please stay?"

"No, I'm gonna go. They're expecting me." He stuck his hands in his pockets and then pulled out his car keys.

"Sam," I said. Where had he gone? Where had my husband gone? Over the past several months, he'd turned into, well, a stranger. "What about what I expect?"

He looked at me for a couple seconds. "That's not fair," he said. "I'll see you later." He leaned toward me for a kiss.

Fair? I turned my head. "Don't," I said firmly—although my voice breaking gave me away—and walked back to the dining room.

Once Evan and I were home and he was tucked into bed, I spent the rest of the night trying to call Sam and only getting his voicemail.

When we finally talked the next day on my actual birthday, he had told me he was leaving. He claimed that one of the reasons that helped solidify his decision to leave was that I wouldn't kiss him good-bye the night before. He always had been good at deflecting blame on me.

I closed my eyes and took a deep breath. I held it for a few seconds before blowing it out. I shook my head and walked into the living room.

Kim and Meredith were on the floor putting blocks back into a bucket, and Evan was jumping on the couch and holding what looked like the pizza cutter. "Whoa there, Little Man." I grabbed the cutter out of his hand. "What're you doing with this?"

"I like it." He smiled at me. He knew that I couldn't resist his cuteness. That was part of my trouble. I was too much of a pushover and always had been. But at least I was aware of it. And he was adorable with short, wavy, messy brown hair, brown eyes, dimples on both cheeks when he smiled. Also he had these great pouty lips.

"I know you like it." I set the pizza cutter and my coffee mug on the table and wrestled him down onto the couch so that he would quit jumping. "And, by the way, I believe the last time I checked you're not allowed to jump on the furniture."

"Yes, I am." He wiggled away from me and ran upstairs to his room.

"No, you're not!" I yelled because having the last word was very important when you were in such an immature battle of wills. I laid my head down on the couch and looked at my niece. "Thank you for always being so good, Meri." Meredith was darling and dainty—long platinum blond hair usually tied in a bow, bright blue eyes. She had an endless amount of perfect little outfits and looked like she had stepped right out of a magazine.

Meredith smiled at me and laughed. "Evan's bad," she said.

I laughed. "No, Evan's not bad." I looked at Kim and then back at Meredith. "He's just misunderstood."

Meredith looked up at her mother and shrugged. Then Kim pulled her daughter to her feet. "Will you give Aunt Kelly a hug good-bye, please?"

I sat up to get my hug. Meredith tripped on the coffee table on her way to my arms and fell into me. "Shit," she said. I burst out laughing but quickly stopped.

Looking at Meredith, I said, "Sweetie, promise me that you'll try not to repeat anything that comes out of Evan's mouth. I love him, but he has a potty mouth to beat no other." She nodded her head, and I hugged her. I squeezed my niece to me and covered her ears. "You better let her come back over," I whispered to Kim who shook her head and pursed her lips.

"Hey, Evan," I called. "Aunt Kim and Meredith are leaving. Come and say good-bye."

"Good-bye!" He shouted from his room.

I raised my eyebrows. "Close enough."

I could tell that Kim was ready to go because of the fact that she was already halfway out the door. Her exits were usually on the abrupt side.

"See you guys later," I said as she shut the door. I sat there for a couple minutes and looked out the front window as they got in their car.

The Son

I went up to Evan's room and found him sitting buck-naked on his beanbag chair and looking at books. "What! Why?" I said.

He giggled.

"Aren't you cold?"

"No," he said.

"Fair enough. But," I paused, "Daddy'll be here soon, so get dressed after that book." I smiled at him and shut his door. I wandered into our third bedroom—my office—and sat in front of the computer.

I had better get started on this whole creativity thing if my book needed to be done in six months. Was that even going to be possible? Considering the looming deadline, I guessed that I'd find out sooner than later. I knew I needed to focus on the writing and not the deadline. But that was almost scarier. Why was I scared to death about the idea of actually writing? I didn't remember ever feeling like that in the past. Although actually finishing something on a schedule had never mattered so much. Writing had been fun. And if I were lucky enough to create something someone wanted to read, that was a bonus. There had been no pressure when Sam and I were still together. Writing had come easily. Everything felt easier then. I guess I hadn't realized how lucky I'd been in that regard. Add that to the reasons why I hated Sam because he left me—left us.

I wiggled the mouse. First things first I checked social media. It was just a habit, but I felt like I couldn't possibly be creative if there was any chance that I had any unread messages or new notifications. Maybe I was just stalling, but I was a social being and didn't want to feel left out. There was nothing though. And I had half my friends' posts blocked, anyway, because they posted excessive religious or political or boring stuff that I usually didn't feel like dealing with, so the process took all of a minute to check. "So much for that."

I opened the file to my novel and scrolled through a few pages. I really enjoyed my characters and had a good feeling that this really was going to be my bestseller. Thank God for this grant and for not having to get a real job for a bit longer—even if, according to Kim, it was only six months. And knowing Kim, she probably told me six months, but it was really more like seven or eight. She would be clever enough to factor in the time it would take to find a job after the six-month deadline was up. Plus, if I were frugal, I could somehow stretch it out to at least six and a half or even seven months before starting my job hunt. Maybe if I started to sell some of my stuff on eBay, I could even get a good year out of not working in the traditional sense of the word. The idea of it all was just too freaky to me—the working thing.

I think that was a good part of my writer's block. *Is that even the right phrase?* Writer's block. Writer's block? It's not writer's cramp or writer's freeze. It had to be block. Anyway, no wonder I was freaking out. I didn't even know what I had.

The doorbell rang.

And then there's Sam.

I got up and walked toward the door and thought about how strange it was that we used to live together and now he was ringing my doorbell and waiting for me to open it. This man had watched me give birth to our son. Why was he outside waiting for me to let him in? I still couldn't figure out why he thought this was the best decision for our family.

The Ex

"Daddy," Evan shrieked as he ran down the stairs and beat me to the door. That kid could be fast when he wanted to be. He threw his arms around Sam. "I love you, Daddy!" Sam picked him up. I was glad to see that Evan had put his clothes back on. I mean, his joggers looked like they might be on backwards, but at least they were on.

Sam and Evan were pretty much twins. Evan had gotten his dark hair and brown eyes from Sam. Forgetting that I was starting to hate Sam, I smiled at the two of them as they hugged.

"I love you too, Ev. I've missed you."

I stopped smiling and remembered. *Of course you missed him. You hardly ever see him—hardly ever call.*

Sam looked from Evan to me. "How are you, Kel?" He held his right arm open to hug me.

I hated the fact that we always had to still hug and act like we were friends. We weren't friends. A friend wouldn't leave me alone to rear our son while he went and had a mid-life crisis of sorts. I wasn't bitter about it.

Okay I was, but I didn't want to be bitter and was trying not to be. So that was something. That was at least a start.

"I'm good, Samson." I hugged him quickly and made sure to keep my head turned far enough away that he couldn't kiss me. We had recently stopped the kiss hello and goodbye on the lips. Soon enough we'd probably stop the fake hugging too. Honestly, I wasn't quite ready for that yet though, and since Sam usually initiated it, he probably wasn't either, which always brought me back to wondering why he left us.

I picked up Evan's weekend bag and handed it to Sam as I took Evan from his arms. I held Evan really tight. "You are the sweetest boy, and I love you so much, Little Man. You have a great weekend with Daddy. I'll see you on Sunday."

We nuzzled noses for a second. "I love you so much too, Mommy." Then he kissed me three times and then held on for one more really tight squeeze. I loved feeling his little arms wrapped around me as he tightly hugged my neck. It was the best feeling in the world. If nothing else good came from my marriage, this did.

"That one will last me the weekend," I winked at him as I put him on the floor. "I love you." I kissed my hand and tousled his hair.

"So you guys don't want to stay for dinner tonight or anything like that," I said and looked at Sam, who was already waiting with the door opened.

He shook his head. "Um, maybe I'll take a raincheck," he said quietly.

"Bye, Mom," Evan waved at me then grabbed Sam's hand and looked up at him. "Where are we going, Daddy?"

"Bowling!"

"Awesome!" Evan yelled. I hated Sam even more at that moment for the fact that he got to be the fun parent—the one of us who swooped in every other weekend and once during the week and did all the fun things that I didn't get to do on my limited budget. Of course I'd rather be consistent than fun, but from my five-year-old's point of view *Daddy's fun,* and *Mommy makes me clean my room.*

I shut the door.

"Awesome!" I imitated then leaned my back against the door. "Whatever." *I'm so mature!* God, I would have left me too…

I stood there with my back to the door for a long time. I wanted to get something done. I wanted to have a productive weekend and feel like I had accomplished something. I normally had all these grand plans (this running list in my brain) of what I was going to accomplish when Evan left for the weekend. I was going to write, of course. I was going to paint a room or two—or at least get some pictures on the walls. I was going to unpack boxes and put things away. I was going to clean out my closet. I had so many ideas and projects that all seemed doable while Evan was home. But the minute he walked out the door I couldn't do any of it because all my will walked out with him.

I stood there with my back to the door and pressed my palms against it. I leaned my head back and closed my eyes to squeeze in a few tears that were forming. I didn't want to cry again. I was sick of crying. I cried way too often and not at all enough. And I hated myself for the second feeling. I swallowed hard, took a deep breath, and walked to the dining room.

The Best Friend

I picked up my phone and called my friend Lisa who I've known since grade school. "So what are you up to?" I said.

"I'm hanging out with Phil and the kids. What's going on?"

"Sam just picked up Evan, and I need to get out of the house. Do you mind if I come over?"

"Not if you don't mind spending your kid-less evening with children," she laughed.

"It wasn't my idea to have a kid-less evening, remember? Sam left me."

"Point well taken. Did you eat yet? We were just about to have some stir-fry. I'm making it now. You're welcome to join us."

"Thanks. I'll be right there." I ended the call and picked up my budget to look at the amount allotted for food. If I ate dinner at friends' houses at least three—maybe four—nights a week, maybe I really could stretch this thing out another month or two... *Would that be wrong?*

I tried not to think about Sam and Evan and what they may be doing on my drive over to Lisa's. That always made it worse. The idea that they had this home life away from me was crushing. I shook my head. "Just let it go, Kel," I said quietly and turned on the radio.

About five songs later, I pulled into Lisa's driveway. Her house was gorgeous, and it was at least double the size of mine. It was red brick with beautiful navy-blue shutters. The yard was perfectly manicured with shrubbery. I got out of the car and walked up the steps to the front stoop.

Lisa and Phil had three kids—Julia, Olivia, and Jennifer, seven, four, and two respectively. Evan was in love with all of them. For a five-year-old, my son was very much into girls.

As I walked in, Jennifer shouted, "Keh-yee's home!" And all my bitter, angry feelings about Sam vanished. Isn't it amazing how children can do that?

Dinner was awesome! Lisa always made the best food, and I always made the best yummy noises when eating her food. She was the ultimate homemaker. Her kids were perfect—three strawberry blond princesses. Her house was perfect. Her meals were perfect. Of course I knew better since we had been best friends for years, but from the outside that was how it appeared.

After dinner Julia and Olivia did a dance show for me while Jennifer sat on my lap and played with my hair and jewelry. I loved every single moment of it.

Then, I'm not exactly sure why or how this happened, but Lisa insisted that they call some of the neighbors who often got together in the evening. She kept saying to me that she wanted to show off her hot single friend. Lisa had been drinking wine with dinner, and when she had a few, she often would throw caution to the wind. Corny a phrase as it was, it truly described tipsy Lisa.

And next thing I knew she was barking orders at Phil to put the girls to bed and at me to put on some lip gloss because the neighbors were coming over, and she wanted me to be her hot single friend— no more joking about it.

She handed me lipstick and lip gloss. "Put this on."

"Lisa, this color would look hideous on me," I laughed.

She winked at me as she shoved the lipstick tube into my hand and folded my fingers around it. "My friends are coming over, and I promised them a hot single friend. Just put it on."

She meant business. She killed me when she was tipsy! She really was too much sometimes, but that was why I loved her so much. I looked at her in the mirror that we were standing in front of and thought about how *she* was basically my hot friend. Lisa had the waif-like body of a supermodel even after giving birth to three children. At about 5'10" she was a few inches taller than I was and her hair was cut in an adorable, wavy chestnut bob. I looked from her to me as I noticed the similarities and differences in our appearances— chest-length, highlighted blond hair on me versus her chin-length, dark hair. All my features were smaller than hers except for my eyes. Sam used to joke that when we first met, my eyes had jumped right off my face and punched him. "There's no way I couldn't have noticed her!" I'd heard him say that about a hundred times over the years. Lisa and I both had blue eyes and tiny frames, but her extra height and glamor made her look more like a model whereas I just looked like her quirky little sister trying to tag along as she got ready for a date. That idea made me laugh. "What are you doing? Stop staring at me," she said and pointed to the lip gloss in my hand. I put some on and was pleasantly surprised that it didn't look as hideous as I had originally thought it would, and it did take my look from little sister to friend. She handed me my glass of wine, which also added to my grown-up look. "Now finish this, so we can get you another glass."

"What has gotten into you aside from a few too many glasses of wine?"

She took the lip gloss and put some on. "Nothing. Just the wine." She winked at me in the mirror, and we both laughed.

So Phil—who would now be known by me as "Wonder Dad"— put three girls to bed without a fuss in record time. After the first few weeks Sam had rarely helped out with one child. Rarely, hmm. Let me edit that. Sam had never helped out with Evan's bedtime. And I think the only reason that he had probably ever even given the boy a bath was because now he was responsible for Evan every other weekend, and I was pretty clear on the fact that Evan needed a bath some evening during those visits. Although some Sundays Evan would arrive home riper than a black banana, so I wasn't totally sure that Sam had actually bathed Evan yet.

Anyway, Wonder Dad did an awesome job. Where had I gone

wrong in my judgment of Sam when I'd met him? He seemed like such a great catch. Of course, when I was 20, a great catch was just someone who made me laugh, could keep up in a conversation, and was a good kisser, I suppose. Sam fit those categories fine.

I sighed.

It was kind of a shame he turned out to be so wrong. We'd had a lot of laughs. The highs were very high, but then there were the lows. And there was also the fact that in the end he'd fallen out of love with me and stopped trying. I wasn't sure in which order.

Lisa and I sat on their back porch and drank wine and waited for the neighbors to arrive. Lisa's porch was like a mini retreat. I always felt like I had wandered into a design magazine pretty much anywhere in her house, especially on the porch. The porch furniture had plush tan cushions with green and burgundy throw pillows. There were large pots with plants peppered throughout. On the coffee table there was a smaller potted plant beside a lantern with a candle burning in it. When had Lisa even gotten a chance to light that thing? *See? Perfect!*

Phil joined us just about the same time that the neighbors started to show up. I guess everyone on this street put their kids to bed and then came out to party. I thought that was a bit odd and slightly unsettling, but who was I to judge? I couldn't even keep my marriage together, and they all seemed to arrive as couples. So they all had that advantage on me.

Susan and Brad lived across the street. They looked to be in their late 20s and were perfectly put together. It almost felt like they were trying too hard though. Natalie and Ben lived next door, and they looked to be in their early 40s. While what they were wearing was fine, it felt like they'd begun to stop trying as much. I mean, Natalie was in yoga pants. Gail and Chris had a 10-month-old named Riley in an infant carrier. I never did figure out if it was a boy or a girl. They were early-to-mid 30s, and probably Gail was the least focused on her looks. She was in leggings and an oversized sweatshirt that read "Fries Before Guys." I laughed out loud then quickly coughed a couple times to cover. I wasn't sure if that was her pre-baby style or just the result of being a newer mom.

Lisa asked them all what they wanted to drink, and she and I went to the kitchen. "Why does it matter that I'm your hot single friend?" I said when we were out of earshot. "I'm the odd person out here at this couples' party. In fact, I think I should probably just go home."

She grabbed my arm. "No, no, no. You're staying," she laughed. "I'm drunk. I don't know what the hell I'm talking about."

I rolled my eyes at her and grabbed a couple bottles of beer, a bottle of wine, and some glasses and followed her back out to the porch.

The neighbors started to have a few drinks and some conversation about other neighbors that I didn't know. I sat and sipped my drink and tried not to feel awkward. Then Susan suggested that we played a card game that required pairing off into couples. I chugged the rest of my drink and jiggled my empty glass. "Excuse me for a second. I'll be right back." I stood up and walked into the house.

About an hour later Lisa and Phil walked in laughing, and I

looked up at them from my magazine. "Hey there," I said. I'd been flipping through a *People Magazine* and tossed it back onto the coffee table. Lisa and Phil came over and sat on either side of me.

"I thought you went home," Lisa slurred and laid her head on my shoulder.

"Nope," I said and patted the top of her head. "I'm sleeping on your couch tonight." I hadn't really drunk that much, but when I walked inside earlier, I just couldn't bring myself to leave and go home alone.

"Good idea," Phil said as he headed toward the stairs. He threw me a blanket from the chair he passed on his way.

"Thanks, Phil."

Lisa kissed me on the cheek and then stumbled behind Phil. "Wait for me, Babe."

I sat there for a while and held the blanket while listening to the sounds of the house—of my friend and her husband getting ready for bed. I could hear Lisa giggling and Phil talking in a whisper. I couldn't understand what he was saying, but it felt like love to me—two people who lived together and took care of children. I sat and listened until it was completely quiet upstairs and the only constant sound was the ticking of their wall clock. I put the back of my left hand up to my lips and closed my eyes. Then I slowly sank down into the couch, pulled the blanket over me, and listened to the ticking for what felt like forever as I fell asleep.

TWO

The Girls

What seemed like a couple of minutes later—although it was light out, so it couldn't have been—Julia, Olivia, and Jennifer were sitting on the floor in front of the TV and eating cereal. I laid on Lisa's couch and watched them.

Jennifer was laughing really loudly. "Sh-h-h," Olivia pushed her over, and Jennifer rolled to the other side and sat back up like one of those wobble people and continued right along with her laughing just out of reach of her sister.

"Julia, make her stop," Olivia insisted.

"Get over it, Livy." Julia took a long drink of her juice and stood up and carried her bowl and cup into the kitchen. She walked back into the living room and placed her hands on both sides of Jennifer's face and rubbed Jennifer's cheeks in a few circles. "You're such a sweetie pie," Julia said in a high-pitched voice.

Jennifer giggled even more.

Julia turned to Olivia and shrugged. "I tried."

Olivia started screaming at the top of her lungs, and I winced and realized I was feeling the beginnings of a migraine. She turned around and noticed that I was awake and stopped screaming. "Kelly's awake," she whispered to the other two.

Jennifer quit giggling and jumped to her feet. She crawled up on the couch beside me. "Hud," she said while squeezing my neck.

"Girls, leave Kelly alone," Lisa said as she rubbed the top of her head and walked down the steps. "I swear they get up earlier on the weekend than they do during the week."

"Evan's the same way." I sat up and wondered what he and Sam were doing this morning as Jennifer crawled into my lap.

"Jenn, put your bowl on the kitchen table if you're done eating," Lisa said.

"No, Mommy. Sissy do it."

"Jennifer Joy, do you need the naughty chair?"

Jennifer screamed loudly, but the threat of the dreaded naughty chair must have been enough to scare her into doing it. After a couple seconds of screaming and a quick look to her mom, she quickly got off my lap and picked up her bowl. I took that free moment to stand up and stretch. My back and neck were stiff from sleeping on the couch. And even though I hadn't drunk that much, my head was killing me probably a little from the wine, but mostly from the migraine coming on—and maybe the screaming too. My stomach was queasy. Alcohol definitely affected me differently these days.

"Lisa, I think I'm going to get going. Thanks for dinner and everything," I said and hugged her.

She laid her head on my shoulder. "You're welcome any time. We love you." She pulled back and looked me in the eyes.

"I know. I love you guys too."

I hugged and kissed the girls and headed to my car.

The drive home was painful. The glare from the sun was intensifying the pain in my head, and bouts of nausea had me holding my car's garbage bag in my lap for most of the ride. When I got home, I ran to the bathroom and power puked into the toilet which splashed the toilet water back up in my face—what a lovely way to start a day.

I took some migraine medicine before getting into bed and cried for about the millionth time since Sam had left me. Along with everything else that went wrong anymore, the migraine was his fault. Why not? My life started sucking royally after Sam left. Everything bad was his fault—end of story.

After a short pity party, nap, and the medicine kicking in, I felt much better.

I got up to work on my book. I didn't really want to, but I felt like I should at least try.

I sat at the computer and looked around my office for a few seconds and noticed the beige carpet and white walls. I hated white walls. I had two diplomas hanging over my desk from college and high school. I wasn't sure why I'd done that. They'd never hung in any other house I lived in, but maybe I subconsciously put them up as a reminder that I had, in fact, finished something at some point. To the left of my desk was a window looking out on the front street. Beside the window was a bookshelf filled with books that included my previous publications—another reminder. On the wall beside that was a fairly empty closet. To the right of my desk was a table with a lamp and a couple photos of Evan and the two of us when he was a baby. The room felt so unfinished to me.

I hoped that *unfinished and empty* wasn't going to be a new running theme in my life, but I laughed at the idea that everything around me seemed to reflect how I felt inside lately. I needed to change my frequency.

Sam used to always tell me that if you smiled for a minute, you could turn your day around. I have to admit that the times that I've tried it, it sort of worked. I mean, you start off with a big cheesy grin and you feel silly for smiling. After a while, that silly feeling amuses you, and you actually do feel better. The problem lately was that I didn't necessarily want to change my frequency because then I had to admit that this was going to be my new normal. I didn't want to be okay with this. If I were being honest, a part of me was still holding out hope that Sam would realize what a huge mistake he made and come back. I mean, he'd gone through something horrible and wasn't acting like his old self. When he remembered who he was, wouldn't he want his family back?

"There was so much good, Sam," I said under my breath. "Please remember that."

I thought about the last great day that we'd had together as a family. We had driven to a fall festival and spent the afternoon walking around in perfect autumn temperatures. Part of the time Evan had ridden on Sam's shoulders. "I'm so big," Evan had said several times. "I can see for miles." Sam and I had gotten a huge kick out of that for a couple reasons. One of them was that our almost four-year-old was using that odd expression. But more amusing to us was the fact that since we were sort of in a valley between two hills, you truly couldn't see that far at all.

Evan had said it a few times, and the look on Sam's face when we made eye contact was a look that you could only share with someone who you know gets exactly what you're feeling in that moment. No words needed to be spoken. Sam was truly my best friend, and I was so happy to be there with him, with our family. I felt so lucky and so happy that day that when I think about it, it makes me feel so cheated now. How could Sam take all of that away from me? I mean, I still had Evan, yes, but I didn't have that best friend.

A week after that festival Jason died in a car accident, and it hit Sam hard. Part of it was that he was supposed to meet up with Jason that evening. Sam had canceled earlier in the day because I wasn't feeling well. I hadn't asked him to stay home, but I knew Sam blamed both of us for Jason's accident. Jason had made alternate plans and died on the way to them. Even though he'd been driving in the same exact direction at the same exact time that he would've been traveling to meet Sam if he hadn't canceled, Sam still blamed himself. It wasn't rational.

Sam's behavior got more and more irrational leading up to his leaving. I felt like it was a phase at first and used that idea to excuse bad behavior. I figured he'd eventually process the death, snap out of his funk, and stop blaming us for it. But instead he left.

I pushed off the floor and spun around in my chair a few times. Then I turned back to face the computer, wiggled the mouse, and opened my novel. I re-read a bunch of pages, and then just sort of stared at the section that I wanted to work on. The novel was about friends during different phases of their lives. There was a love interest who had originally been based on Sam, so it made for a strain between him and the main character. I mean, I knew she wasn't me. But writing in the first person about this character who was in love with someone who was very similar to Sam... Well, it was getting to be hard for me to do in a genuine way. I should probably kill off this Sam-version of a love interest and have her meet someone new. Did I even have the energy to deal with all that pain and resolution?

Another part of the problem with the writing was I knew what I wanted to say, but my brain felt so cloudy that as much as I tried to put it down in words, I just came up with a bunch of crap each time. But maybe I didn't know what I wanted to say anymore since I was mentally debating about whether or not to kill off the love interest. I guess I knew where the original version was going. The version that I had started writing before Jason had died. And now I had to figure out a whole different version—all with a cloudy brain that felt too slow to process information at a normal pace. All this was a huge problem for a writer, on a tight schedule, with a grant that was going to run out in six months or a bit longer if I got creative with my budget—ironic that I was starting to try to be creative with numbers when I couldn't be creative with words anymore.

Maybe a shower would help me think, so I stood up and walked into the bathroom.

The shower did help me feel a little less anxious, but afterward I couldn't go back into my office.

I couldn't.

Being home alone felt too heavy. I hated having Evan gone. That's not the way it's supposed to be when you have little kids. They're supposed to be home with you, and it felt too empty in the house without him.

I went downstairs.

The Other Best Friend

I opened the front door and walked out onto the porch. My friend Dana and her husband Greg were walking their dog Pepper past my house. They lived a couple streets over. "Hey, Newmans!" They looked over and waved. Dana held up her poop bags, and I laughed and shook my head. "It's too late. It doesn't matter!"

"It does today though." Dana smiled at me. "You'll never let me live it down!"

"You're right! I won't."

"Taught her a good lesson though," Greg called to me. "She never forgets anymore."

"Good!" I laughed.

They were several houses over at that point. I sat down and thought about the day that Dana had forgotten her bags and how I had gotten to meet her.

We were moving into this house only about six months ago. After Sam left, I decided to move out. Sam and I had just bought and moved into a house, and he left on my birthday a couple weeks later. He'd been doing a lot of knee-jerk reaction things leading up to him leaving, but that one floored me—especially because it was my birthday.

Anyway, I couldn't afford the payments on that new house. For Evan's sake, I didn't want to suddenly get a full-time job because his world had been turned upside down enough. He was used to me being home. Sam gave me child support, but it wasn't enough that I would have been able to live in that house without having to find a job right away. So my dad, my brother-in-law Doug, Lisa's Phil, and a handful of other friends were moving my stuff into my new house (or, I should say my newest house as it was my second move in about five months).

Up to the chaos of my moving day walked a petite redhead with a gorgeous smile and the prettiest blue eyes I'd ever seen. She was walking a big black and white mutt. They walked over to me and offered us her assistance. Not sure how that was going to happen as she now had a big barking dog on the other end of the leash. The dog was about as big as she was. "You look like you have your hands full," I told her.

"She's always like this," she said. "I've learned to handle her and a number of other things at the same time." She laughed. Her laugh was so full—filled with delight or mischief. She smiled at me, looked around, and shrugged.

I was immediately enchanted. "I'm Kelly. I'm the person moving in here, by the way."

"I'm Dana. This is Pepper." We looked down at Pepper and noticed that she was in the middle of taking an enormous dump in the middle of the yard. "Oh, that's lovely, Pepper!" Dana stuck her hand in her pocket. "Great! I forgot my bags. Do you have something I can use to clean that up?"

I looked around and threw out my arms, "I wouldn't even know where to begin looking. I mean, maybe there's a shovel somewhere that we can at least move it." Pepper had managed to poop right in the middle of the path from the back of the truck to the front door.

"You've got too much going on here. I'll be right back." Dana made a mad dash down the street with Pepper. That was the fastest I've ever seen her move. And that was when I learned that even though we live close, we're not next-door neighbors. Even with her running, it took a good while for her to get there and back.

I went into the house to look for something to scoop it up, and in the meantime several of the movers stepped in the pile and tracked dog poop all through the house.

Dana was a trooper though. She ran home—again. This time for pet carpet stain and odor remover and helped me scrub my floors after everyone was done moving the stuff in. She also helped me scrub the bottoms of everyone's shoes while they ate pizza. If there was one thing I could say about Dana, aside from how tiny and charming she was, she was thorough! By the end of the day, we felt like old friends, and I've pretty much spent the last six months getting caught up on the time I never got to spend with her for the first 34 years of my life.

Anyway, after sitting on my porch and thinking about that for a while, I went inside, watched some shows, and fell asleep on the couch in front of the TV.

Before Evan came home on Sunday, I had already cleaned my bathroom and kitchen and dusted and vacuumed the rest of the house. I'd also taken a two-hour walk. I liked to walk because I'd found that was truly the only time when I didn't have to think...

about anything.

I did this thing where I counted the steps until 100 and then started over again. It was very meditative. I don't know how many times I got to 100, but it was enough to clear my mind.

Then Evan came home. "Mommy!" He squealed and jumped into my arms. He kissed me three times and gave me the tightest hug around my neck.

"Oh, I missed you so much, Evan!"

"I'll see you later, Kel," Sam said and squeezed my shoulder. I nodded. Then he patted Evan on the head. "Bye, Bud."

"Bye, Daddy," Evan said while still holding onto my neck with all his might.

I walked us over to the couch. "So did you have a fun weekend?"

"Yes. We went to the movies. And we went bowling. And we ate at McDonald's. And we played at the park."

Way to show me up there, Sam! "What movie did you see?"

"It was wickedly awesome with these robots and these space guys, and they had this big fight and all this shooting!"

Great! "Hmm. And bowling was fun?"

"Yeah, it was super cool! And Daddy could really roll the ball down fast and hard and knock 'em all down! Boom!" He made a big explosion with his hands. "And I rolled the ball down, and I knocked down pins too. It was so much fun!" Evan sank back into the couch and sighed.

I smiled at him. He stared at me for a few seconds and then leaned into me and hugged me. "I'm glad you're home, Evan."

He let go of me and leaned back into the sofa. "When's Daddy coming home?" he said.

I looked at him for a couple seconds.

"I want Daddy to come home," he added before I could answer him.

"Daddy is home, Evan. He's at his home. We don't live there anymore."

Evan looked down at his hands. "I don't think that's fair."

I bit my lower lip and blinked back a few tears. I reached over and pulled him back to me. "I know it's hard, Ev. I'm sorry it's hard." I rubbed his head and took a deep breath.

Evan cried for a couple minutes. "I miss him," he said quietly.

"Of course you do." I held onto him tightly, pressed my lips together, and shook my head. I took a few quick breaths in my nose.

After a couple minutes Evan leaned back into the couch and rubbed his belly. "I'm hungry," he said quietly.

"Me too. Let's see what's in the kitchen." I stood up and reached my hand out to him. He took it, and we walked into the kitchen.

We looked in the fridge first and found some leftover mac and cheese. It looked a bit green, so I tossed it. Then we found some yogurt cups and ate those while I put a frozen pizza in the oven.

After dinner I put Evan in the tub in case he hadn't been given a bath by his father over the weekend. He played for a good long while. I sat and flipped through a magazine. When I was almost to the end of the magazine, I said, "Just a couple more minutes, Ev."

"Okay, Mommy. I'm almost finished shaving my legs." I looked up, and, sure enough, he was using his toy razor to shave his legs. I ducked my head back behind the magazine so he wouldn't see me giggling. "Okay, there. I'm all done, Mommy."

"Good." I grabbed his towel as he pulled the plug to drain the water. "Good job, Sweets." I wrapped the towel around him and pulled him out of the tub. "You smell so much better! Let's get you dressed." I rubbed the towel on his hair to dry it a little and then kissed the top of his head.

Evan ducked away from my kiss, threw off his towel, and ran across the hall into his bedroom. "Ah, yoo-hoo, where does this belong?"

"What?"

"You know what," I said and rolled my eyes. Then I added, "Your towel," in case he actually didn't know what.

"Since you're still in there, why don't you take care of it?" *Since I'm still in here...* He almost had me on the cuteness factor with that one, but I had to stand my ground—especially since he had just gotten back from Sam's house, or he would never listen to me again.

"Better idea, you come in here and take care of it."

He walked back in buck-naked with his Cookie Monster slippers on and shook his head at me as if I were the laziest creature ever created. He sighed loudly, picked up his towel, and hung it on the hook. It slipped off, so he bent over and put it on the hook again. It stayed this time, so he turned to me, slapped his hands together a few times, put them on his hips, and tilted his head to the left.

I nearly peed my pants. "Good job, Ev. Go and pick out your jammies."

Hands still on his hips, he slowly walked across the hall back into his room. The towel dropped back to the floor, so I picked it up and put it back on the hook for the third and final time.

THREE

The Time Capsule

After taking Evan to school, I went home to get a few things done. His school pictures had come in, so I went to the basement to find a frame.

Of course, the box that was labeled "Pictures" was on the bottom of the pile. I dug it out and opened it up. I pulled out a few pictures and looked at them—family photos of Sam with us. We looked happy. I shook my head. "And then we stopped being happy. At least you did, Sam, so now the rest of us aren't either."

I picked up one of Sam and me that was in one of my favorite frames. It had been taken the day we found out we were having Evan. We were looking at each other with excited, nervous grins on our faces. It would be a lovely memory if he hadn't broken my heart. And on some level it still was a lovely memory in spite of that fact. The excitement, the fear, the hope that we felt had been real. The *we* that is now just he and I had been real. And even though *we* are finished, I still have the memories. And since I couldn't just erase 13 years of my life, I was trying to hang onto the beautiful memories and figure out how to let go of the ones that made me cry.

I shrugged and looked from the image to the frame. "This'll work… I guess." I closed the box and put the boxes back in some sort of order.

In the kitchen I got the paper towels and started wiping the frame. I grabbed the glass cleaner from the cupboard and turned the frame over to take the back off. Under the back was an envelope. "Ah, no," I said. I knew what it was before turning it over.

When things had been good, Sam could be quite romantic. He had a habit of writing me notes and hiding them with the hope that I would find them years later. That had been the case many times. He would write on the envelope "Time Capsule #1" et cetera.

Over the years I had found #1, #2, #4, #6, and #7. Time Capsule #7 had been written about six months before he had left me. I assumed #7 was the last. The last several months together after Jason died were not great, and he probably hadn't written any more.

I had found #7 about two weeks before he actually left. It was very sweet, and although he had been quite a jerk leading up to his departure, the letter had sort of fooled my heart into thinking he was still with me emotionally—even though he must have checked out by that point. But the renewed hope I'd felt when reading the letter and his insistence of buying the new house enabled his departure to blindside me two weeks later. I shuddered at the memory.

Anyway, #3 and #5 were still unaccounted for. "Damn it," I said and turned over the envelope. *Time Capsule #5*. "Of course."

I set the envelope on the counter and continued with the frame. The glass came clean nicely, and I got Evan's new school picture and put it over the one of Sam and me—hiding that picture—and put the frame back together.

I dug around in my junk drawer to find a nail and hammer. I found a piece of wall space in the dining room that looked like it needed a five-year-old boy's picture to hang there. He was a cutie. I still needed to paint those white walls. Maybe the next weekend that Evan was with Sam I would tackle that project. *Maybe not.* I should be writing and not painting—at least for the next six months—if I could even remember how to write.

I walked back into the kitchen to put away the hammer. *Time Capsule #5* was sitting on the counter. Part of me had hoped that it would have magically disappeared—like the person who had written it. I laughed at the image, but wasn't that what had happened to him—or at least to us. One minute we were a couple and then... poof. Gone.

I started to walk past the envelope and out toward the living room, but I grabbed it at the last second as I passed by.

I went to the porch and sat on the glider. I pushed it back and forth a few times and stared out toward the street. I didn't really have to open the letter. I could just as easily destroy it and go about my day.

Could I?

I wished I hadn't found it. I wished it hadn't been written. I wished that I had never met Sam. I wasn't sure my heart could handle any more from him.

And at the same time I wanted to read it to prove that there had been a time when he loved me deeply, and I hadn't just imagined that or made it up or was remembering it all incorrectly.

I looked at my watch, but there wasn't time to prove that until later. School would let out soon for Evan, and I didn't want to show up a hot mess. "I hate you, Sam," I said as I put the envelope in my purse and grabbed my keys.

"You look... confused," Kim said as I walked up to her at the preschool. Meredith attended the same preschool as Evan.

"Oh, yeah?" I blinked my eyes a few times. "I guess that's a good way to describe how I feel right now." My voice broke.

She raised her eyebrows at me. Then she hugged me.

I felt some tears and blinked a few more times. "Okay, don't." I pushed her away. "I can't cry here." I turned away from the other parents, wiped my cheeks, and sniffed.

She turned with me and rubbed my arm. "I'm sorry," she said quietly.

I nodded my head and squeezed my lips together until the feeling of breaking down had passed. Then I looked at her. She had that face that everyone had right after Sam had left—that look, like someone had just died. That had been one of the worst parts about Sam leaving—everyone tiptoeing around me so carefully and whispering in the next room about how I was handling everything. I had tried to put on such a happy face to make all that stop. I hated being pitied. That was almost as bad as the fact that my husband had actually left me. Hadn't he promised to love me forever? I know I had.

I sniffed again and turned back around. "I'll be okay. I can do this."

"I know you can." She fake punched me in the arm. "You're tough. My bets are always on you."

The kids started walking up the steps, and we turned to look at them.

Evan was the caboose today, and he wasn't doing a very good job of it. He was dragging way behind the line. *Come on, Ev. Get your act together.* I knew they were about to correct him.

"Evan, catch up with the class," his teacher said.

I knew it.

He started to walk a little faster, but I could tell something wasn't right with him.

Meredith was dismissed. "I'll see you later," Kim said. "Call me if you need me."

I nodded my head.

Finally after what seemed like at least five minutes of torture. "Evan, you can go to your mom."

He walked quickly to me and melted into my arms. "I'm not coming back here," he said quietly into my ear.

I held onto his shoulders and looked at him. "You okay?"

He nodded his head, grabbed my hand, and led me quickly down the hall and out of the building to our car.

Once he was buckled into his seat, he said, "I'm not going back there. I hate Jacob!"

I was getting settled in the driver's seat, but I turned to look at him. "What happened? Why would you say that?"

"He's mean. I don't want to go back there."

"Did he hurt you?"

Evan crossed his arms across his chest and closed his eyes. "My feelings," he said. Tears came out, and my heart broke.

"Oh, Evan," I said. I got out of my seat and got in the back seat beside him. "I'm so sorry he hurt your feelings. Can you tell me why?" I unbuckled his seat and scooped him into my arms.

"He said I couldn't be in his club because I don't sound like a cat." He sniffled loudly. "But I do, Mom."

"Ev," I hugged him.

"I do sound like a cat, Mom. Listen." He meowed and purred.

I almost laughed, but instead I pressed my lips together and nodded because clearly this had been a really rough day, and the last thing he needed was for his mom to laugh in his face. "You sound like a good cat too," I said. "He's wrong, Honey." I rubbed his head and scratched him behind his ear. "My little kitty." I nuzzled noses with him, and he giggled a little.

He nodded his head and climbed back into his seat.

After I fed Evan and had him settled in front of the TV for a much-needed nap, I grabbed my purse and took it to my bedroom.

I sat on my bed and pulled out some lip balm and put it on. I grabbed all the old receipts and pulled them out along with a church bulletin and a flier that someone had handed me outside the grocery store a couple weeks ago.

I put my hand on the envelope. Part of me wanted to be strong enough to throw it away without reading it. Part of me wanted to read it and have it not really affect me much. I knew I wasn't capable of doing either of those things.

I pulled it out of my purse and looked at it. I imagined Sam at a time when he had written this—and still loved me. I opened the envelope and pulled out the paper. *Kelly, our little man is here.* I closed my eyes but not in time because tears still ran down my cheeks. I set the letter on the bed beside me and pulled my legs up to my chest to rest my head on my knees. Sam and I had been such a good team that day. Nothing had gone as we had planned for the birth, but we were such a good team—so in sync with each other. Even one of the nurses had mentioned what a great team we made. Thinking about that day and about where I was now… It didn't make sense. It wasn't possible that those two people, only a few years later, weren't together.

I folded up the letter without looking at the rest of it, put it back in the envelope, and put it in my purse. I couldn't look at it alone.

FOUR

The Zoo Trip

I didn't have any extra money to blow but was sick of just entertaining Evan by hanging at the park or walking the neighborhood streets. I decided to take him to the zoo to mix things up a little. Plus, if I were being fully honest, those neighborhood activities gave me more of a chance for my mind to wander and think about the fact that I wasn't writing and should be and then worrying about all of that.

I figured looking at exotic animals would be a good distraction, and I would also have to supervise Evan a little more thoroughly than I did at the park (again where my mind could wander to my lack of creativity). So we got there and paid and headed up toward where the animals began. Evan, of course, was running way ahead. "Get back here, Ev. I don't want to lose sight of you!"

Eventually, he tired out a bit and started walking right next to me—which helped since my left knee kept hurting if I walked too quickly. It also gave me the opportunity to take a picture of him acting like each animal. He had a really good impersonation of the monkeys. There was another kid with his dad (I assumed), who happened to be going through the zoo at about the same pace we were. I noticed the dad watching Evan's animal poses, and, after a while, he was trying to coax his son into some of the same poses. That kid didn't want to play along though. The dad seemed to be very amused by Evan, so, of course, I really started to pull out the ham in him. With each animal, the pose got to be more and more elaborate, and if anyone was game in being a goofball, it was my Evan. Finally, we were standing right next to the guy and his son, and while Evan was posing like a gorilla, he let out a very loud Tarzan-sounding howl and pounded on his chest.

"Your kid's hilarious," the man said.

"He is," I said.

"I can't get Michael to do anything but smile, and I can barely get him to smile on command," he said.

"Aww." I looked down to where the kid was hiding behind the man's leg. "He's adorable though."

Evan bolted on ahead. "Come on, Mommy!" he shouted.

"I'm being summoned. Good luck with the photos."

"See you later," he said as I headed toward Evan's call.

We got lunch and were sitting at the outdoor tables talking about which animals were Evan's favorites of the ones we'd seen so far. "Daddy!" Evan squealed.

Can't be...

But sure enough I heard Sam's voice. "Evan. Wow, gosh. What're you doing here?" Evan got up and ran in that direction, so I had no choice but to turn around and look.

And... There Sam was getting up from a seat a couple tables over. He was with a woman and some children. "Nice," I said under my breath. I nodded my head and waved. "Hi, Sam," I mumbled. I had no desire to meet that crew. I turned around and pulled tiny pieces off the corner of my napkin and tried not to cry.

"Do you mind if we join you?" I looked up and saw the dad and son from earlier. "I can't find an open table, and we already bought our food. I hate to impose, but it's going to get cold, and he's really hungry too."

I pushed aside some of Evan's mess. "Oh, please. Have a seat." We were sitting at a table that could have comfortably seated five or six, and it was just Evan and me—well, just me at the moment. "I'm Kelly, by the way. And Evan, my son, was here." I pointed behind me toward Sam's table. "I guess he found his dad over at another table." I paused, "No comment."

"I'm Jack, and this is Michael." Jack looked over my shoulder toward them… and waved. Yes, the level of awkwardness was growing by the moment. "So you didn't know his dad was going to be here?" Jack said.

"Not a clue." I circled my pointer finger around my face. "As you can see, I'm thrilled. He and I get along fine. I just hadn't planned on running into him today—along with whomever that woman is and her kids. Considering all that, I assume he's just as thrilled to see us too."

"Gotcha," he nodded and sat beside Michael who was already starting to eat.

"So if he comes over, let's just pretend like we've known each other for longer than a minute."

Jack laughed. "Your son might give us away."

I let out a nervous laugh. "He's five. What does he know?"

"Here they come," Jack whispered and looked down at his

burger then picked it up.

"Kelly, nice to see you," I heard Sam say from behind me.

I turned around. "What a coincidence you being here, Sam. I'm surprised you're not at work." I looked around him toward the woman and her kids and then looked up at Sam. "It's a beautiful day though, right?" Sam was holding Evan. "Oh, I'm being rude. This is Jack and Michael."

Sam and Jack both said hello but didn't shake hands on account of the fact that Sam was holding our son, and, well, Jack was holding a burger.

"Do you mind if Evan walks around with us for a bit?" Sam said. "He asked if he could."

I looked at Evan, and he had his hands pressed together begging and his mouth was whispering, "Please, please, please…"

Yes, I mind. Without Evan I was kidless, alone at the zoo. But what was I going to say? Clearly, it was what Evan wanted, and that was always important to me. "You want to, Ev?" I said because I hoped maybe I had misunderstood the whole silently begging thing, and the answer would be no.

"Yes!" he shouted, and Sam winced and pulled his ear away from Evan's mouth.

"Okay then," I said to Evan and looked at Sam. "Where do you want to meet up?"

"Can I just bring him home tonight?" Sam said.

Wow! He had some nerve. If he had wanted to, he could have taken the day off work and pre-arranged to spend the day at the zoo with *his* son.

"You do realize I paid money to spend the day at the zoo with my son." I stared at him for a beat and then waved my hands in the air. "Never mind. It's fine. That's fine." I didn't want to fight, not in front of Evan who clearly wanted to spend the day with his dad. Of course he did. He was so starved for that man's attention.

"You sure?" Sam said.

"Yes," I stood and looked into Evan's sweet face and kissed him. "You are the sweetest boy, and I love you so much, Little Man. I'll see you later. Have fun."

"I love you, Mommy," he called as Sam walked him back to his table.

I blew him a kiss and sat back down. I took a deep breath and looked up at Jack who was looking at his sandwich. "I can't believe you had to witness that when all you wanted was a place to sit to eat your lunch."

Michael seemed unfazed at least.

Jack looked up at me and smiled. "It was a little," he paused and cleared his throat, "uncomfortable." He put his burger down. "I think the lesson learned here is never ask a stranger to sit with her."

I rolled my eyes. I wasn't in the mood for jokes.

"Also," he said, "I'm sorry that happened. He was out of line in asking to take him."

"Right? Thank you."

"I mean, now you're by yourself… at the zoo."

"That was my thought exactly. Like now what do I do? Do I look at the rest of the animals by myself or just go home? Either way I'm pissed. What a jerk. Not to mention a waste of money that I don't even have right now."

Jack looked at Michael. "You could walk around with us if you want."

I laughed. "I'm sure! The last thing I want to do is impose on your day together!" I laughed again.

Jack shrugged his shoulders. "Maybe you could get Michael to do a couple animal poses."

I looked at Michael. He was dipping French fries in ketchup. "Do you like pretending to be animals, Michael?"

He looked up at me and shrugged.

"How old are you?"

He looked at his hand and slowly counted out three fingers and held them up to me.

"Well, that's a fun age."

He stopped looking at me and went back to dipping his French fries in ketchup.

I looked at Jack and said, "Is Sam still over at that table, or did they leave?"

"No, they're gone," he said. "Left right after they walked over there."

I looked over my shoulder to see the empty table. "Okay, good." If I got up and walked away while they were still there, it would blow the whole *Jack and Michael were with us* cover. Of course, I was pretty sure Evan would blow that cover when Sam asked him who Jack was. But maybe he wouldn't ask. I mean, that was doubtful, but there was hope.

I started gathering up Evan's and my garbage. "I'll let you two enjoy your lunches. It was very," I paused, "interesting meeting you, Jack. And you too, Michael."

"You really don't have to go," Jack said.

"I know. Thank you." I stood to leave.

Jack stood too.

I paused for a second and looked at him. "Bye, Jack." I nodded my head a few times then said, "You've very kind."

He reached out and shook my hand. "Kelly," but then he didn't add anything.

I smiled at Michael and walked away. I wanted to turn around and see if Jack was watching me, but that would have been way too obvious. Why would he be? He was just a man I randomly met at the zoo because we'd arrived about the same time he had.

I kept walking. I could only hope that he was watching me for an ego stroke or something. I walked a couple more steps and turned around.

He wasn't watching me. He was talking to Michael.

That was probably for the best.

The Pharmacy Intern

On my way home from the zoo I had some time to kill and remembered that I had some prescriptions to pick up, so I swung by the grocery store to get them. I didn't feel like getting out of my car, so I went through the pharmacy drive thru. I hoped my favorite employee would wait on me. Josh was a pharmacy intern, and he was probably in his early 20s. He was adorable, but he was way too young for me—way too young. For some reason, he seemed to have taken a liking to me. Maybe it was the fact that I picked up a prescription every week (only a slight exaggeration as I was trying to work out some meds with my doctor that would curb my daily migraines—nothing worked), but he somehow remembered my name. I mean, maybe he knew the names of all his customers? But his one co-worker seemed a bit shocked (and then as a result he seemed embarrassed) the time when he turned and got my order from the drawer before I even reached the counter. So I don't think he knew everybody by name. It was a stroke to my ego—maybe the boost I needed after the whole zoo thing with Sam and his "date."

I pulled up to the window. Sure enough, there he was. "Hi, Kelly, are you picking up for you today?"

"Yes, how are you?" I said.

"No complaints," he said and turned to get my prescription.

The fantasy of this younger man died every time he asked to verify my birthday, and I had to give him the year. I always cringed a little and hoped he wouldn't mentally be like, "Wow, she's old!" Comparatively, that is. But this time he said, "What's your birthday? I should know this by now," as if he were my boyfriend or something. God, I loved when Josh waited on me! And it was just what I needed at that moment.

But then I got home and sat on the couch, and tears welled up in my eyes. "No," I squeezed them shut. I didn't want to cry. I was sick of allowing Sam to still have the ability to crush me. But at the same time I was still so angry. I paid money (money that I didn't even have) to be at the zoo with my son. I was the one who had made plans to spend the day with him. Clearly, Sam was capable of making plans. He had made them and had taken time off work to spend the day at the zoo with someone else and her kids. I was angry for Evan for having to have a dad who didn't include him—only tacked him on as an afterthought because Sam had gotten caught. I was angry that Evan had to grow up doing things with one parent or the other but not both together as a family. He was only five. He deserved to have a family and not just be living with his crazy mom who couldn't get her shit together.

I made a fist and hit the seat of the couch beside me. I hit it again and again and again until there was no stopping my tears. I brought my hands up to cover my face. "No," I whispered between sobs. "No. No, this is not my life."

Eventually, I stopped crying and got up and walked to my office. I stopped at the door. It was like there was an imaginary wall that was keeping me out. So I walked to my bedroom and cleaned. Dusted, swept. I walked back to the office but then walked past it to Evan's room. I cleaned his room too. The book may not get to be written, but at least I was going to have the cleanest house on the street.

After finishing up in Evan's room, I went downstairs to make dinner. But I just sat at the table with my plate in front of me for a few minutes. No wonder I was so skinny. I never felt like eating anymore. *I hate you, Sam.* I got up and threw the food down the garbage disposal.

The Drop Off

About 8:00 p.m. the doorbell rang. I opened it to see Sam with Evan who was holding an ice cream cone that was dripping all over the place. "Hey, Mom," Evan said as he headed toward the living room.

"Go right to the kitchen with that drippy thing and eat it at the table!" I said. "How were the rest of the animals?"

Evan was too focused on licking to answer.

I looked at Sam, "Are you coming in?"

He stepped inside and shut the door. "Should we talk?" he said.

"About?" I said.

"Are you okay?"

I looked at him not completely sure what kind of reassurance he wanted or needed. "It's your life, Samson," I said quietly so Evan wouldn't hear me. "I have no say anymore. Live it the way you want to as long as it's considerate of Evan and his feelings."

He raised his eyebrows. "And you do the same, right?"

"I'm not sure what you're getting at, but of course. I always consider Evan."

"So Jack seems nice," he said.

I laughed. "Yes, Jack did seem nice; didn't he?" I raised my eyebrows and shrugged my shoulders.

"Okay, Evan, I'm leaving," Sam called toward the kitchen.

"Bye, Dad," Evan called back.

"See you tomorrow night, Bud," Sam called to him. He opened the front door and looked at me. We stood there looking at each other for a couple seconds. I felt like I lived the whole relationship again in those seconds, and then Sam broke the stare and turned to the door.

"Good night, Kelly," he said quietly.

He didn't hug me and that felt good and bad at the same time.

He shut the door.

I shook my head and put my hand on the door. I made a fist and then pressed and lightly hammered it against the door. It was starting to feel like such a foreign concept—the fact that Sam and I had ever been in love. Had we been in love? I had thought so, but then how could we have gotten here. I took a deep breath through my nose and slowly let it out.

I pulled my phone out of my pocket and texted Dana, *Porch date in an hour?* She gave it a thumbs up. Then I walked into the kitchen to find my messy boy.

I got Evan bathed and tucked in. Then I grabbed the monitor in case Evan needed me and went out to the porch to wait for Dana. As I sat on the glider, I could hear her and Pepper. "Pepper," I said as they came up on the porch.

Dana let go of her leash, and Pepper ran over to me. She started to lick my face. "Manners, Pepper," Dana said and laughed as she sat down beside me. She grabbed Pepper's leash and patted the floor beside the glider. "Come on, Peps. Lie down." Once Pepper was lying down, Dana took a knotted rope and gave it to Pepper to chew.

"She's legit the best-behaved dog I know."

"I wish," Dana said. She patted Pepper and scratched her behind the ear, and then she leaned back into the glider and we started to slowly move forward and back. Dana looked at me, "So what's up?"

I rubbed my forehead for a few seconds. "I don't even know where to begin exactly. Do you want a glass of wine or something?"

"No, thanks," Dana said. "Lauren and I are recording in the morning." Dana was the host of a successful weekly podcast basically about nothing. They claimed that you won't learn anything but you'll laugh a lot. It started as a hobby with her and a friend, but a local celebrity happened upon it a few months in and shared the one episode, and it sort of took off from there and has become her full-time job.

"Ah, gotcha. So I'm having a bit of a meltdown, I guess."

She reached over and patted my leg for a few seconds. "That sucks. What happened?"

"So I took Evan to the zoo today and there was this guy and his kid there, and they kept watching us because Evan was being cute."

"Obviously."

"You know, just normal Evan stuff. And then we were eating lunch, and Sam ended up being there at another table."

"Wait. What? Kelly, you have the most bizarre life."

"I know! So, anyway, Evan got all excited to see his dad."

"Of course he did." Dana closed her eyes and shook her head.

"And I turn around and look, and Sam's at a table with a woman... and her kids! Seriously! He took the day off work to spend it with someone else's kids?!"

Dana's eyes and mouth opened wide. "Hold me back," she said slowly.

"I know. I was beyond upset with Sam at that moment. Do what you want to me, but mess with my kid?! I wanted to kill him."

"You should have. Seriously, you should have. I would have if I'd been there." She punched her fist into her hand a few times.

"The story gets better though, Day. That guy who had been watching us earlier walked over and asked if he and his son could sit with me because there weren't any other open tables, and they'd already bought their food."

"Do people even do that?" She stopped punching her hand and looked at me.

I laughed. "Right? So of course, I told him to sit because now I'm at the zoo with someone and his kid too. So Sam and I are on an even playing field, you know?"

She shot up in her seat. "Oh, my God! True!" She laughed.

"And I tell the guy that too. As Sam was walking over, I whispered something like, 'Pretend you know me.' Or something stupid like that."

She fell back into the glider and put her right hand on her chest. "You did not!" She laughed.

"I did. I have no shame anymore. So Sam came over and asked if he could have Evan... for the day."

"I hate that man. Cue the dark music." She shook her head a few times.

"You're not kidding. I was so mad. But what was I gonna do? Evan really wanted to see his dad. So he left with Sam, and I was left sitting with Jack and Michael—that's the dude and his son."

"Well, that's awkward."

"Yep. So, anyway, that's my life. Awkward."

"Oh, God! What is wrong with Sam? For real, what is wrong with him?"

I shrugged. "I dunno, Dana. When his friend died, he just sort of changed into this person that I don't really know anymore. And it makes me wonder if I was just ignoring this part of his personality or if it's truly something new." I shook my head.

"Yeah," she said quietly.

"I need to get over him. There's this stupid part of me that's been secretly holding onto this hope that he was going through a phase of some sort and that he'd come to his senses, and we'd get back together."

"Oh, man..."

"But, clearly, he's moving on." I shut my eyes and just felt the motion of the glider for a few seconds. "And I need to move on too."

"That's so hard, Kelly. I can't even imagine how I'd feel if Greg left me," she paused. "Like I can't even imagine having the person who you're supposed to be able to trust the most just..."

I started to cry.

She reached over and put her hand on my leg. "I'm sorry."

I closed my eyes and nodded my head. "I know."

"God, I hate him so much for you. I can only imagine how hurt you feel."

We sat there for a few minutes more, and I wiped my eyes. "Thanks for coming over. You need to get to bed though."

She nodded.

"You're the best," I said.

She shrugged and nodded. "Yeah, I'm pretty great, aren't I?"

I laughed and stood up. "Understatement of the year," I said while picking up the monitor.

Dana grabbed Pepper's leash, "Come on, Girl." Pepper, rope in mouth, jumped to her feet. "I'll take that, or you'll spit it out halfway between here and home." She grabbed the rope from Pepper's mouth.

"I'll talk to you tomorrow, Dana. Thanks again."

"Any time," she said.

I watched her and Pepper walk away. The further away they got, the smaller and smaller I felt.

Finally, I went inside and sat on the couch and cried.

FIVE

The Walk

After spending pretty much the whole night awake—again—I got out of bed and started a pot of coffee. While it was brewing, I looked at social media on my phone. I knew I should try to write for a bit before I got Evan up for school, but I wasn't feeling very creative at that moment and hoped that maybe something I saw while scrolling would spark, well, something.

But I got nothing.

A college friend was having a baby and posted a pregnancy update. Evan's preschool teacher had posted some photos of him playing at school. Lisa's mom was going to have an MRI later that day, and Lisa would be having lunch with her.

I poured myself a cup of coffee, yawned, and looked at the clock. I was a little relieved that it was a bit later than I had realized, so I could just skip the pretend writing session for the morning and get Evan up and ready for preschool. Kim and I had plans to walk at the mall after drop off. She thought we were just getting some exercise, but I was definitely aware of the fact that I was avoiding writing too.

Evan did not get out of bed easily either, so I had to rush him through his morning routine—which made it hell on me because it made him defiant and miserable.

I finally got us both out the door and to the school, and I met Kim in the parking lot by her car. The wind was blowing, and it felt kind of chilly. "I'm glad we're walking at the mall today," I said.

"Me too," she said and got into my car—well, got in after I threw two action figures, a hairbrush, and a box of tissues to the backseat and an empty bag of pretzels and a couple gum wrappers into the trash. I scooped up the coupons and handed them to Kim. My passenger seat didn't see a whole lot of action, so it tended to get junked up—I'm not even exactly sure how, but I blamed it on safety.

When I was driving, I would just dump pretty much everything in the passenger seat. And when I got home with Evan, sometimes it was hard enough to just get him out of the car and into the house without a huge fight, so I'd just leave whatever I'd put in the front seat for later—which usually meant weeks later. Of course, since Kim and I had taken to walking recently, I'd gotten to be a bit better about keeping things sort of clean in my car. She would disagree, but she was my family. My family shared the worst opinion of me. It had taken me 34 years to realize that—better late than never.

"How's the writing going?" she said after we'd left the parking lot.

I glanced over at her as I drove. She was sorting through coupons that I had handed her. People felt the need to clean and organize for me. I swear they thought I was helpless. Again with the *needing to take care of me* issue. I let out a little laugh.

"What?" she said as she was tossing a coupon in the trash.

"Nothing," I said and smiled. Then I remembered her question. "Writing isn't going so well. This timetable is really stressing me out. I don't know. I've come to some sort of mental block or something. I'm not sure what to do about it. It's like there's nothing left for me to say about these characters. They're done." I flicked my right hand at her like I was swatting at a fly.

"Kelly Ramsey... speechless?" She laughed—maybe a second too long. "Not possible. Can't you do some sort of mental relaxation game to put yourself into the character's mind or something? I dunno. I'm not a writer."

"I dunno, Kim. I'm seriously at a mental block." I pulled into the mall parking lot and found a spot. "And I feel like freaking out about it is making it so much worse. I can't figure it out. I can't get my mind off what's going on around me and into what's supposed to be going on in my book."

We got out of the car. "That sucks."

"Yeah, it sucks. But I don't think you really get it. If I don't finish this and get it published, I'm out of money, and I'm screwed." I waved my hands in front of my face. "Never mind. Let's talk about something else."

"So what do you want to talk about?" she said.

I wanted to talk about the zoo and Sam being there and the whole Jack situation—whatever that had been. But then I would have to admit to her that I was spending money that she hadn't budgeted for. "Anything, but you pick. I'm sick of making decisions."

"But you never make decisions." Me, again, through my family's eyes. "I'm teasing," she said and laughed. "I was being Mom."

"Good one," I said. "Okay, so listen. You're going to be, I dunno, frustrated with me or something, but I took Evan to the zoo yesterday."

She opened her mouth. "Kel-ly, was that in your budget?" She laughed.

"I knew that was going to be your reaction." I looked at her sideways. "We just needed a change of scenery. But, anyway... we were having a great time. Sat down to eat. And Sam was there."

"Oh, yuck," she said.

"Yeah," I said. "And," I took a breath, "he was actually sitting at a table with a woman and her kids."

She grabbed my arm and stopped walking for a second.

"Yeah, I'll let that sink in," I said while looking at her.

"He was at the zoo with a woman and her kids on a workday. Dude, take the day off to spend it with your own son at the zoo."

"Thank you," I said, and we started to walk again. "My thoughts exactly. But it gets even better though."

"No," she said.

"Yeah, So Sam came over and asked to take Evan for the rest of the day which left me alone at the zoo."

"Oh, my God. What an ass!"

"I mean, in Sam's defense, Evan probably had asked him."

"Stop defending him," she said and shook her head.

"I know. I need to. But, yeah, so Evan went with Sam."

"And you're left sitting at the table alone and sad."

I laughed. "Oh, wait! I forgot the funny part."

She laughed too. "Oh, good. I'm glad there's at least a funny part. What happened?"

"The lunch area was kind of crowded and this guy with his kid asked to sit with me because there weren't any tables left. So now from Sam's point of view, I was also at the zoo with someone and his kid."

She laughed. "Well, that is pretty funny."

"I even introduced the two of them when Sam came over."

"Oh, my God! Kelly!"

"I know. I have no shame," I said. "Best part was this dude totally played along." I laughed. "And then he invited me to spend the rest of the day with them."

She quickly looked at me. "Oh…"

"Of course I said no."

"Why of course?"

"I mean, Kim…"

"Maybe dating would be good for you. It's almost a year, right?"

"I'm not ready," I quickly said.

"I'm not talking *serious relationship* ready but maybe just putting yourself out there would kind of help you heal. Be part of the whole process."

"I'm not sure I wanna do all of that yet. And where would I meet anyone to date really?"

She shrugged. "I dunno. A dating app? Or, you know, the zoo or anywhere you are, really. You're always telling me stories about the people you meet when you're out and about. I don't think it would be that hard for you to happen upon a single guy."

I laughed. "What?" I said.

"You're friendly. And I hate to admit this since you're my little sister, but you're kind of magnetic." She looked over at me and tugged on my sleeve. "Plus, you're a head turner."

I laughed. "Stop!"

She laughed too. "So I dunno… I don't think it would be that hard if you mentally decided that you were open to it." She looked over her shoulder. "The guy that just passed us was totally checking you out."

"Whatever." I threw my hands toward her as if I were tossing away her idea.

"Just be open to it," she said.

"I'll think about it," I said but truly wasn't sure I could ever actually date anyone again. I mean, sure there were attractive men that I noticed—like the pharmacy intern Josh—and some of them were probably even appropriate ages for me to be attracted to them too. "I dunno," I said. I was quiet for a few seconds. "I'm not sure I can though."

She grabbed my arm and squeezed it really tight and pulled me close to her. "Yes, you can, Kel. You can. You truly have to at some point anyway. Sam leaving isn't the end of your romantic journey in this life. You deserve better than that." We walked a few more steps in silence.

I swallowed hard a few times and blinked back the new tears caused by her empathy.

"Trust me," she said.

I nodded my head and started counting my steps. We walked close like that without talking for a while longer until we saw a couple who we knew from our church, so we broke apart from her hold on me and said a brief hello.

Then we continued to walk and just chat about the kids and

nothing much. And, eventually, we sat down with some coffee. "Ouch! My knees are killing me!" Every time we walked lately my left knee, especially, acted up immediately afterward. "Am I getting old or something?"

"Must be," she raised her eyebrows and took a sip of her coffee.

"Aren't you supposed to say something like I don't look it or something supportive like that?"

"I'm your older sister. Any chance I get to knock you down a peg or two, I take."

"Okay, point well taken," I said and twisted my coffee cup on the table. "Are those bags under your eyes, by the way? I've been noticing them lately." I raised my eyebrows at her and then grabbed my coffee and started to walk away from the table as quickly as I could. But given my bad knee and her speed, she caught up with me pretty quickly.

I held my hands up in front of me and quickly said, "Before you hurt me in any way just remember who's driving you back to get your daughter!"

She halted her attack, pursed her lips, and looked up for a second. She let out a heavy breath. "You are so lucky I need that ride."

I laughed. "I remember. I used to live with you. You're ruthless. I was so happy the day that Dad married you off to Doug."

"Dad married me off to Doug?" We both laughed.

"He'd like to think so, anyway, when Mom's not reminding him of how strong and independent we are."

"Probably, huh? We're his little princesses," she said.

"Um, you were his princess," I corrected. "I was more the court jester or something."

We got into the car. "Yeah, no one quite knew what you were."

"Or how to handle me," I said while fastening my seatbelt.

"They still don't." Kim buckled her belt too. "Poor Mommy. She's always so worried about you. You know that's why she gives you such a hard time."

I started the car and looked at her. "Oh, instead of being supportive. Lovely. She needs to see Daddy for some therapy."

"They'd kill each other."

I backed out of the spot, and we rode the rest of the way in silence.

The Pickup

When Sam rang the doorbell Evan was in the bathroom. "Ev, Daddy's here."

"I'm pooping," Evan yelled.

Great. "Well, try to finish up as quickly as you can." I walked to the door, took a breath, and opened it.

Sam's eyes got wide when he saw me standing there. "Kelly," he said.

"Were you expecting someone else?" I joked. "Evan's in the bathroom. It might be a while."

Sam blew out his breath and stepped inside. "How are you?" He said as he hugged me.

I closed my eyes for a second, squeezed, and then released. "I'm okay," I said. That felt like a safe answer. I tilted my head in the direction of the living room. "You wanna sit down for a minute?"

He nodded. "Sure."

I walked over to the couch and sat. I pulled my feet up, squeezed my legs, and put my chin on my knees. "So..." I said slowly.

"I've been seeing someone," he said. "I don't think it's going anywhere. She's nice."

I had thought seeing him with another woman—another family—was bad enough, but I hadn't realized how each word coming out of his mouth would stab at me.

I nodded. "Good," I said quietly. "For how long? I guess it's not my business. I'm just wondering."

"I don't know," he said. He was quiet for a couple seconds. "You know how sometimes things start and you don't really realize you're in them until you're so far in them that you're already there." Then he added, "And you're like *how did I get here?*"

I wanted to cry but instead I chuckled and said, "Sounds healthy."

He closed his eyes and scratched his forehead. "How about you?"

"Me?" I said.

"And Jack, was it?" Sam said.

Then I full-out laughed. "Oh, that's not a thing."

Sam raised his eyebrows.

"He was just some random guy who needed a table to sit at, and I must have looked like a friendly enough face." I heard the toilet flush.

"Kelly," Sam laughed and shook his head. "You always did have a way of getting yourself into," he looked at me and smiled, "situations."

I smiled back at him and nodded. "Clearly, I still do."

"I miss that," he said as Evan ran down the steps and leaped into Sam's arms.

"Daddy!" Evan yelled, and Sam winced and pulled his ear away. Then he kissed the side of Evan's face as Evan held on tightly to Sam's neck.

"C'mere, Ev," I said.

"One second," he said because he was still squeezing his dad tightly.

"Go say good-bye to your mom, Buddy. Don't leave a lady waiting," he added.

And I tried to push away the memory of me waiting up for him to come home all night long on my last birthday.

Evan ran at me, and I hugged him. "You are the sweetest boy, and I love you so much, Little Man," I said while sort of cradling him in my arms.

"I know, Mommy. You tell me that all the time."

"Because it's true." I pulled back and looked into his eyes for a second before kissing his forehead. "Have fun with your dad. I'll see you in a little bit." I looked over at Sam who was looking at his phone. "Bye, Sam."

He looked up at me and nodded.

The Shopping Trip

I grabbed my purse and headed out to my car. There was no sense of me sitting in front of the computer and pretending I was going to write after just finding out that Sam had been in a relationship for so long before even realizing he was in a relationship. *How long is that?*

Also, maybe when I was out, I would see something that would inspire a scene for my novel or a character or something. It was sort of like I was doing research, and that couldn't hurt, right? I didn't have to stay out long. I thought of what Kim had said earlier about putting myself out there, and I guess I sort of wanted to test that magnet theory. Plus, maybe I could find a rug for my dining room. I needed something to make the place feel a bit cozier. And maybe that would help motivate me to get fully unpacked and settled into my new-ish home. And maybe a new rug would inspire a color for those white walls too. Not that I had time to paint.

I thought about Sam and the conversation one more time, shuddered at the memory, and then started the car. I headed to Gabes. Everything there was really inexpensive, so I couldn't do too much damage to my limited budget. Kim would be so proud, but I probably wouldn't mention it to her—just in case she wasn't. But maybe I would mention that I went out to put her theory to the test.

Walking back toward Gabes' rug section, I found the most adorable pair of earrings that would look fabulous with a million outfits that I already owned, so it wasn't like I would be spending any extra money to get something to coordinate with them. And they were about 75 percent less than what I would pay in the department stores (I knew this because that was what it said on the tag), so really if I passed on them, I would be throwing money away. Wasn't that how it worked? I put them in my shopping cart and smiled, thought of Kim, and reached for them to put them back on the rack. But I really wanted them, so I tossed them back in the cart. What Kim didn't know wouldn't hurt her—or, more importantly, me. And it was her idea for me to get out there, and there are limited activities that are totally free. So I figured I could find a way to make my shopping spree her fault—at least for this evening.

Beyond the jewelry I found the belts and scarves. There was this great silk scarf that would look awesome with the one jacket that I already had, and since it was only $7.99, what the heck? I put it in my cart too. "You need to stop," I said quietly. "Oh, screw it and enjoy yourself," I added because the shopping trip was starting to feel like the perfect pick-me-up after the zoo thing yesterday and then this evening's exchange with Sam.

I scanned the ceiling looking at all the different departments. "Shoes." How could I not take at least a quick look there? So I pushed my cart toward the sign, and on my route found an adorable pink t-shirt with red lettering. "Isn't life great?" it read. *Ironic, but true.* I checked the tag. Size M. "Perfect," I said and felt that maybe it was somehow intentionally placed there for me to see it, so I put it in my cart without even checking the price.

"Now, on to the shoes," I said and noticed a couple of teenaged girls looking at me and whispering. I rolled my eyes and started singing as I pushed my cart away from them, "The sun'll come out tomorrow." I figured if they were going to talk and giggle about someone mumbling under her breath to herself that they deserved a real show. "Bet your bottom dollar that tomorrow, there'll be sun..."

As I got a little further away, I heard them burst out laughing. I was glad I could add some amusement to someone's evening, and in all truth amusing them probably amused me ten times more. It was a sick pleasure of mine to be the center of attention—yes, I am that pathetic.

Anyway, I was finally to the shoe department, but there was nothing that I really liked in my size—I supposed that was a good thing. "Tomorrow, tomorrow, I love ya, tomorrow." I tossed a pair of shoes back into the clearance bin. "Damn it, song. Get out of my head!"

I looked around to find the rugs and wandered over toward them. I didn't really see a lot of single men out shopping on a Wednesday evening, so I figured that this whole *meeting people in the community* thing was probably going to be harder than Kim had predicted. The sibling rivalry in me sort of loved to be able to prove her wrong. I mean, I liked the idea of men falling all over me wherever I went (especially after the past couple days), but the reality gave me an *I told ya so* to rub in my sister's face, so...

The rugs were all hanging from these huge pants hanger type of things that were sticking out of the wall, and you turned them like book pages. There were some pretty ones that weren't my style. And there was another one that I was really drawn to even though it wasn't what I had been picturing for the dining room. It was a dark tan and had these beautiful deep pink and purple flowers all over it with green for the stems. I kept going back to that one and decided to get it for my bedroom. I didn't really need one for the bedroom, but it was so beautiful.

I looked around to figure out who was going to help me get this rug off the big pants hook thing that was about three feet above my head. There weren't any other customers in the rug department at that moment, but I was afraid to walk away and find a salesperson to help me for fear that another customer would come over and take my rug. I was getting to be more and more attached to it by the moment, and if I lost it at that point after losing Sam, my ability to write, and the prospect of meeting any single men that evening, I wasn't sure I could have handled the loss of that random rug too—as odd as that sounded.

So I started to gently tug on it. I pulled a little on the right side, and then I pulled a little on the left side. And I kept going back and forth between the two sides. I was hoping that a salesperson would wander over and notice my struggle, but no one ever did. Anyway, when I realized that the big hook wasn't going to pull off the wall, I started to tug a bit harder. The rug finally pulled loose and fell right on top of me. It was a lot heavier than I had thought it was going to be, but I managed to crawl out from under it, fold it up, and put it in my cart—well, sort of hanging out over the sides of my cart.

Now the trick was getting down an aisle without knocking over any displays on my way to the checkout through a department that had been empty when I needed help and now seemed to be bustling with shoppers. I had no clue where they'd all come from. I would start down one aisle and would have to back up (not turn around because I couldn't with a rug hanging off both sides of my cart) and try another way. Most people were so rude and wouldn't step out of my way—even when I said "excuse me" as they saw me coming down an aisle with a huge rug hanging over my cart.

I finally got to the checkout line, and it was about 50 miles long—no kidding. I really couldn't even see the cashier. Okay, I guess I could see her, but I couldn't distinguish her eye color.

I started scanning through the magazines to pass the time, meditating, deep breathing, anything really so that I wouldn't seriously go insane before it was my turn to pay.

"Kelly Carter?" I had been mentally relaxing on a warm Caribbean beach, so I wasn't especially excited to hear my name. And when I turned to find out who had uttered it, I was even less thrilled. Or rather on a scale from one to 10 with 10 being thrilled and one being not at all excited, I was around minus 50.

It was a woman named Liz, the mother of my high school friend Charity who I had intentionally lost touch with a few years after college. She was one of those friends where if you called her and opened with "How's it going?," she went into a three-hour, one-sided monologue on how it was going for her without even asking how I was. When I called to tell her that I was engaged to Sam, the same thing happened. I opened with "How's it going?" and two hours later when I had to get off the phone to leave for my mother's birthday party, I figured I didn't have time to tell her my news, so I saved it for another day. And I actually just never called her back.

That was my wake-up call with her when I realized that I was her friend, but she wasn't mine.

Anyway, there stood Liz, Charity, and two cute kids. "Hey there," I said.

"Kelly, what have you been up to?" Liz asked me. You know Charity wouldn't have because I'm sure the thought to ask someone how they were wouldn't have crossed Charity's mind.

I pointed to my shopping cart. "The usual, buying a rug," I laughed. "Pretty much how I roll." I pointed to their cart. "Who are these guys?" I smiled at them. They really were very adorable, and I was always a sucker for a cute little boy.

"This is Jacob. He's almost three. And this is Elliot. He just turned one," Liz said.

"They're adorable, Charity," I said and smiled at her.

She'd been staring me down since her mom approached me and softened a little. "Thanks. They keep me busy. Don't you, boys?" She tickled them, and they giggled. "I hear you have a little boy too."

"Yep." I nodded my head. "Evan, he's five."

"Is he home with Daddy?" Liz asked.

"Well sort of. We're separated. They're out, I dunno, at dinner or something."

Charity's mouth dropped open.

"Oh," Liz said.

"It's okay really. It's better this way. I mean, I feel bad for Evan, but I'm much happier." It was a line of garbage that I'd taken to throwing around. I hated the idea of people pitying me, so I used it all the time as my guise. It was so much easier to just say that I was better off without Sam than to admit that his exit from my life had killed something inside of me. And nobody wants to hear that anyway. I mean, eventually I might get over Sam, but I wasn't convinced that I would ever get over the fact that my husband could leave me—actually had left me. I wasn't sure there would ever be a time when thinking about that didn't cause tears to immediately well up in my eyes. I blinked a couple times and then looked at my watch.

"Well, that's good," Charity said. She pulled a piece of paper and pen out of her purse and wrote something on it. "Here are my numbers. Give me a call sometime. We'll have to get together. It's been so long since I've talked to you."

"Thanks." I stuck the paper in my pocket. "It was nice running into you." I looked at the boys. "And so nice to meet you adorable little guys. Looks like I'm finally next. Thank God!" *For so many reasons.*

They walked away. Again, *thank God!*

Now I just had to wash these pants before taking out the phone number, and I could in good conscience say, *oops...* I wouldn't have called, anyway, because I didn't have that kind of time to waste by listening to the saga of Charity—especially with the timeline Kim had made for me.

The Helpful Person

Paying for the stuff was one thing. But I hadn't really thought much about getting the rug into my car. Fortunately, a helpful manager-type was standing in front of the store and offered to watch my shopping cart while I went and got my car so I didn't have to push it through the parking lot. As I walked away, I had a moment of, *hey, did I just get ripped off?* But he was actually legit. And he actually had folded the rug nicely for me while I was gone so that it was bottom side out and wouldn't get dirty in my trunk.

Wow! There really were some helpful people in the world! I had a renewed surge of affection for people in general. But why couldn't there be more people like him?

Oh, wait…

Maybe this was what Kim had meant about running into men in the community, so I took a more critical look at him while he lifted the rug into my trunk. He was tall, maybe 6'1" and had a thin but muscular build. He had thick wavy light brown hair that was cut short and brushed back in a messy, stylish way. He had small eyes, and I couldn't tell what color they were without staring, a narrow nose that turned up maybe just ever so slightly on the end, and a small mouth with full lips. I mean, he was a good-looking guy.

So I struck up a little conversation with him—even though as far as I could remember, I wasn't very good at doing stuff like that. I'm great on paper. In person and talking sometimes felt a little awkward. But Kim seemed to feel otherwise, so… Armed with her compliments, I was about to test that theory. "God, this weather is beautiful; don't you think?" I said as the wind picked up and practically blew a stray tree branch into our heads. I brushed the hair out of my face and laughed. "To clarify, I meant the temperature. The wind's being a real bitch."

He laughed and reached up and shut my trunk. "Yeah, the

temperature is nice, but you have to be good at dodgeball if you want to stand outside for any length of time." He was funny too!

I laughed—maybe a little too hard. "Well, thank you for your help. I had a heck of a time getting that thing down from the wall and over to the register by myself, so it's nice to get some help outside here."

"No problem," he smiled. He was even cuter when he smiled.

I smiled back at him for a couple seconds. "You're probably married or gay or something, so I'm going to get in my car now because I'm making an ass of myself." I threw up some jazz hands— yes, I actually did—and started walking around to the driver's side of my car. I really was an ass. I would have crawled under a rock if there'd been a big enough one nearby.

I glanced over at him as I opened my door. He was smirking at me and looked down at his shoes and stuck his hands in his pockets. He looked back up. "I'm Tom." He cleared his throat and shrugged. "Could I get your number?"

Nothing like throwing myself at a man who showed me the tiniest amount of kindness because Kim had called me magnetic. I truly felt pathetic at that moment! So I tried to play it cool and stayed on the driver's side. "Sure," I shouted over at him.

He nodded his head and pulled out his phone, and I gave him my number.

"I should probably get your name too," he smirked and raised his eyebrows.

Like I said, I tried to play it cool.

"I guess that would make sense since I know yours. It's Kelly, and it's nice meeting you, Tom."

"You too, Kelly." He smiled and typed it into his phone then he slipped the phone back in his pocket.

"Thanks again for your help." I jumped into my car and drove away.

I started laughing as soon as I pulled out of the parking lot. "What the hell was that about?" *New rug, new me?*

Anyway, I hoped that would inspire some creativity in me, so I headed home and unloaded the rug—the earrings, scarf, and t-shirt.

Yes, life was great! At least it felt pretty good at that moment. I couldn't remember the last time I had intentionally flirted with a man who hadn't been my husband. And, truthfully, it felt kind of, I dunno, fun.

The Rug

I spread the rug out in the living room to vacuum the wool out of it several times before taking it to my bedroom. That seemed like the responsible thing to do. Plus, it killed a bunch of time that I would have been sitting in front of the computer while pretending to be working.

Then I went up to my bedroom and tried to figure out how I was going to put the rug in there by myself. Those were the times when I especially missed Sam. When I needed to do something that seemed like it was a two-adult project, I hated him a little more each time. But since I didn't want to admit defeat and ask him to help me when he dropped Evan off, I was bound and determined to figure it out on my own.

I dragged the rug upstairs and started lifting little ends of furniture bit by bit and shoving it under. It took a really, really long time, but I finally got it situated. It looked okay, but somehow it just wasn't quite me. The rug itself was very pretty—which I liked. That was what I had fallen in love with—those gorgeous flowers. But I liked pretty with a bit of funk, so I decided that I needed to angle it. So, again, I started to lift and twist until I got just the right angle. I was fully exhausted by the time I was done and had decided that if I ever got it in my mind to buy another rug that I would need to slide underneath furniture, well, I just shouldn't because it was way more work than I wanted to be doing on my own. And for a woman who was used to being taken care of, this had been one hell of an independent evening!

I laid down on my bed and thought about giving that guy my number. What was his name? Tim? I thought about running into Charity and the look on her face when I told her I was separated. I hated that look. I stood up and changed out of my clothes, threw them in the hamper, and put on some yoga pants and a hoodie. I picked up the hamper and took it to the basement. I pulled out the pants I had been wearing—along with some similarly colored clothes, and threw them in the washing machine. I poured in some detergent and started the load.

"Oops," I said as I walked back up to the kitchen.

The Drop Off

I was sitting on the couch with my laptop when Evan and Sam came in. Evan headed right to the stairs without saying hello to me. "Did you have fun?" I called to him.

"I guess so," he shouted from halfway up the steps.

Sam stopped in the entryway to the living room. "As you can tell, he's mad." He nodded a few times.

"What happened?" I put my laptop on the table and turned toward him.

"He started with the whole 'when are you coming home' stuff." He shrugged. "He didn't like hearing me say 'I'm not.'" He paused. "And then I may have yelled a bit because he wouldn't let up."

"That's a common question here too." I put my face in my hands for a second and shook my head while rubbing my temples. "Poor Evan. He hates this, you know?" I looked up at Sam.

Sam nodded, "He'll get used to it."

"Sure, eventually. But he doesn't need to be yelled at about it now." I stood up and walked into the kitchen.

Sam followed me. "He wouldn't let up. It was the whole evening, practically. He pushed my buttons."

I stopped at the sink and turned around and leaned against the counter. "Have some empathy, Sam. His whole world—everything he knew—was ripped away from him pretty abruptly." I looked him right in his eyes and added, "Be the adult. The boy is allowed to be frustrated."

He stared at me from the entryway of the kitchen. "I wish you'd have a little empathy for me sometimes." He left the room, and I could hear him walking up the steps.

I shook my head and took a few deep breaths. I'd had the patience of a saint with Sam after Jason had died. There was no cause for him calling me unempathetic. I stood there for a few seconds feeling thankful that Sam had immaturely left the room before I had a chance to respond because I would not have been very empathetic in that moment. "You know what? Maybe this is a good thing."

I walked back to the living room and sat down on the couch. I could hear Sam reading Evan a story in Evan's room. It had sort of been our deal that on Sam's weeknight with Evan that Sam would put Evan to bed. Sam was Evan's father. And bedtime was his responsibility too—or at least we had thought that when we initially established that plan. At first Sam had claimed that he wanted to be a part of Evan's life and do those normal dad things. Well, normal dads do bedtime more than once a week half-heartedly at best. And since Sam had to do bedtime at our house, it was kind of awkward. And I was starting to get a little sick of having Sam in the house— especially after conversations like we just had in the kitchen. Plus, Sam never fully committed to the task. He would do the abridged version (not author-approved either) of Evan's regular bedtime where I'd read him a few books or a really long book, and then we'd lie and talk and have a prayer. And then I'd lie with him for a good bit and finally leave when he was either sleeping or just about to fall asleep.

Sam was in and out. So my guess was that he read a quick book and gave him a quick kiss good night. Then he'd whip down the steps and be out the door in a few seconds before Evan could call for more attention.

About 10 seconds after Sam had shut the front door, I heard Evan's feet hit the floor and then the small little footsteps in the hallway. "Daddy?"

"Daddy's gone, Ev. What do you need?"

"He's… gone?" He had paused between the two words.

I took a quick breath in my nose and put my face in my hands for a second. I swallowed hard. "Yep."

"Why?"

My heart broke. I took a deep breath. "He went home, Ev."

"Oh." He started to walk back to his room. Some nights he'd get there. Some nights he'd even get back to his bed. Then he'd turn around and come back to the steps. "Mommy?"

"Yep?"

"Can you lay with me for a few seconds?" he said quietly.

I wiped a tear that had started to fall. "Okay, Evan. I'll be right up." I waited for it every week.

I got in bed beside him. "Did you have fun tonight?" I said.

"Sort of," Evan said quietly.

"What do you mean, 'sort of'?" I said. I reached over and rubbed his head and brushed some hair away from his eyes.

"I don't like this, Mom," Evan said.

I didn't say anything.

Evan started to suck his thumb and then stopped. "I want Daddy to come home," he said.

I took a deep breath. "I know you do, Sweets." I leaned over and kissed his forehead. "You are the sweetest boy, and I love you so much, Little Man."

He closed his eyes and started to suck his thumb. "I love you, Mommy," he mumbled.

I laid with him and rubbed his back until he'd fallen asleep. Then I laid there for a while longer and wished that I could make all the hurt he felt go away. I knew I couldn't though, and that was the worst feeling.

After a while I got out of Evan's bed and wandered into my office. I sat in front of the computer and spun my chair around a few times. I looked at the computer and sort of snorted at it.

I went downstairs, shut off all the lights, locked the door, and went to bed.

I couldn't sleep, so after a couple hours I crept back down to the living room and my laptop. I kept thinking about the whole situation with Evan and Sam. I was so mad. Then I started thinking about Kim saying I needed to put myself out there, and I decided to create a profile on an online dating site. I mean, maybe I wouldn't ever meet up with anyone in person, but the action of doing it made me feel a little less angry at Sam for some reason.

I kind of half-assed my profile though because, as Kim pointed out, I wasn't ready for anything serious (would I ever be?), and I didn't give the whole process much thought. I figured if someone wanted to be with me, let them see the mess that was currently me. So what if the profile made absolutely no sense. I wasn't completely sure I actually wanted to attract anyone, anyway, so the act of just getting it up there—as messy as it was—was what I had needed at that moment.

I posted it, read through it, laughed at its absurdity, and went to bed.

SIX

The app

In the morning I got Evan some breakfast and settled with a building project and then downloaded the online dating app on my phone and logged in.

There were five new messages in my inbox. "Seriously?" I said. I probably had finished the thing at like three in the morning. I glanced at the time on my phone. It was just past eight. I shook my head a couple quick times. "What?" I said as I clicked on the inbox.

The first message was from an 18-year-old looking for a one-night stand with an older woman. "Okay, this makes more sense. Y'all are a bunch of pervs." He wanted to know if I had any interest in being that older woman. As gross as the idea was, I had to admit the kid had some balls. Not only, at 18, was he soliciting a stranger for a one-night stand, he was also calling a woman in her mid-thirties "older." That part alone could make reaching his nineteenth birthday iffy. I toyed with the idea of replying with something—maybe a lecture about how he could end up dead if he continued down that path or something along the lines of how women deserved to be respected for their intellects and that we weren't just sex objects, but I decided that he may get off on *older* ladies lecturing him. "Delete," I said and hit the button.

There were some others that were just kind of not too off the wall freaky. Just the one guy looked about 20 years older than he said he was. Another was married but wanted to meet up. "How's your wife feel about that one, Buddy?" But then I figured who was I to judge? Maybe she was open to it. She probably had a side piece too. Maybe he was just trying to keep up.

Then there was one really nice, normal sounding guy, Dan. But there had to be a catch—didn't there?

So I read his profile. He was 37, fairly handsome, quirky black rimmed glasses, floppy dark brown hair, seemed to be employed, positive outlook on life.

Where was the catch?

"Oh, okay," I nodded my head. Here it was, dead wife. From what he said, she had died seven years ago. "Mmm. That's sad."

I clicked back on my inbox and hit reply, *Dan, Thanks for the nice, normal message. It was refreshing to hear from someone who actually sounds like a decent human being. I didn't realize that there were any of you out there on this app—well maybe except for me. And that may even be stretching it a little bit. Since I'm on a tight schedule and my creativity is really suffering the brunt of it all, I'd better get back to work. But I just wanted to thank you for not making me want to barf when I read your message. Kelly*

I hit send then reached for my laptop. I actually felt fairly productive in that writing session. I mean, I wrote probably a half dozen pages, which was way more than I'd written in as long as I could remember actually. "Hmm," I said. Maybe flirting with strangers on dating apps was just what I needed to finish writing this book in time. I laughed. "If that's the case, God damn, I hope he replies!"

I stood up and went to find Evan.

"Evan, let's go to the park," I said when I found him in his room looking at books. He was at my side in less than a second. "Somebody's ready to go. You need to go to the bathroom and put shoes on though."

"But…"

"Nope. If you wanna go, do it, and we'll get there sooner."

He went into the bathroom.

I grabbed a couple things that I might need—phone, keys, water bottle, sunglasses—and Evan met me by the front door.

The park wasn't too crowded. There was only one little girl, Beth, playing when we got there. She seemed to always be there. Her grandma was sitting on one of the benches, and I waved to her as we walked over toward the playground, but I hung back on the other side because I didn't feel like talking with her today. She was a very chatty woman—very nice. But I wasn't in the mood to listen to her ramble on about all her kids and grandkids. She was one of those people who could just talk on and on about anything. I guess I could be one of those people too if the mood struck me, but I wasn't in the mood today. I pulled out my phone and called Kim.

"Hello."

"Hey, Kim, what are you up to?"

"I'm shopping."

"What for?"

"Toiletries and stuff. Need anything?"

"Actually," I paused, "If you're serious, I'm out of soap."

"How can you be out of soap?"

"What do you mean? How can I be out of soap? I ran out."

"So what are you doing?"

"I'm at the park with Evan." I bent over and touched my toes so it would seem like I was getting ready to run or something. It felt like a park thing to do.

"No, Kel, I mean, what are you doing about cleaning your body!"

"Oh," I laughed. "I'm glad you're so concerned about my hygiene. I've been using those travel soaps that you get at hotels, but I'm almost out of those too."

"So you're not really out of soap."

"I'm out of the big soap. Are you going to buy me some?" I stood up straight and twisted my torso around as I seemed to still be going along with my pre-workout stretching charade.

"Yes, I'll get you some soap. Any preference?"

"Something that won't dry my skin out."

"Got it."

"Thank you, My Dear," I said. "Beth and her grandma are here."

"Ah, is that the real reason you're calling me?"

"No. I wanted to chat with you, Kim."

"Sure you did, Kelly. Sure you did. You didn't want to hear about how constipated she's been again lately. I talked with her about it yesterday."

"You are so wrong! She's sweet. But, yeah, that's TMI today." I twisted around the other way.

"Yeah, for me too—even though I like her."

"I do too!"

"Hey, I'm almost done here except for the soap I have to go back and get, so I'm gonna get going. Go over and chat with Beth's grandma and enjoy your day."

"Thanks!" I hung up.

I sat down on one of the benches and for some reason Sam crept into my mind. I hated that at any given moment I could be feeling good, and then suddenly he would pop into my mind and bring my mood way down. I definitely needed to get over him if this was truly the end for us—which it seemed to be. I guess part of me was worried that I would move on and he would come to his senses and change his mind. If that happened, I'd miss out on having my family back. But he'd been gone for almost a year, and it seemed like he'd been dating for a while now, so… I dunno. I should probably stop worrying about him changing his mind after I move on and just move on already.

I closed my eyes for a couple seconds and tried some deep breathing. Then I remembered taking a self-hypnosis class in college, and you had to open your mouth slightly and breathe in through your nose for five counts and out through your mouth for five counts. Actually, I dropped the class after a week, so I never got too far into it. I could have had it all wrong. In my memory though you thought *I am* as you breathed in for five counts, held your breath for a count, and then thought *relaxed* as you breathed out for five counts.

I kept doing that. And it seemed to be working a little bit. I started to feel pretty good sitting there in the park in the sun. I was keeping my eye on Evan having a good time on the play set, and the sun felt good and warm, and I actually did start to feel really calm and relaxed.

Then I started thinking about the characters in my book and how I had planned on expanding what was a short story into a novel. I wasn't as confident anymore that it could even be done. I mean I guess it could be done. Anything could be done, but I wasn't confident that it could be done well. And who wants to write a crappy novel?

I hated doing something if it couldn't be done well.

I was almost to the point of saying forget that and starting something completely new, but starting anything new at that moment felt scary.

I always had a million book ideas running through my mind, but what if they were just that—ideas—and I couldn't make them work. At least I had 60-some pages of that potentially crappy one finished—not zero.

I knew I was a good writer. I did know that. But ever since Sam left, I was scared shitless that I was going to fail at this. I mean, I never thought my marriage would fail, and, well, it did. I've failed at real world careers.

Writing was the only thing that I really wanted to do with my life, and suddenly I couldn't figure it out, and I was stuck, and that… that was scary as hell!

I looked at Evan on the monkey bars. He was sitting at the very top and smiling at me. I waved at him and started breathing. *I am.*

Relaxed.

I am.

Relaxed.

I am.

Relaxed.

SEVEN

The Reply

I woke up around 3:30 a.m. feeling very wide awake and figured I might as well get to work on writing. What else was there to do at that hour? But first, being the true procrastinator, I laid there scrolling through my phone for a little bit. When I got to my dating app, I saw a new message from Dan.

Kelly, Thanks for your message. I'm glad I came across as a decent human being and that I don't make you want to barf. That's always a good sign.

This weather has been great lately. A bit windy, but very warm. So much nicer than those cold snowy days that we seemed to have so many of for so long. I think we're done with all that mess though until next winter. Hope you got to go outside and enjoy it.

Couple questions. What's your job like? And how do you like to spend your free time?

Hope to hear from you soon. Dan

No kidding, it had been windy! I clicked reply. I probably should have waited until a more respectable hour, so he didn't think I was a lunatic who checked the app 24/7, but, oh, well. I had the time to kill at that moment.

Hello, Dan… I meant that other messages make me barf. Younger men soliciting sex, etc.

Yes, this weather has been beautiful—if you like playing dodgeball. I almost got hit in the head with a flying tree branch outside of a store a couple days ago.

As for my job… I'm a fiction writer, so I sit in front of a computer and make up stories. So I'm not sure I ever have "free time." My time is always just time I should be writing and time that I'm procrastinating. I'm on a very tight deadline with this project that I'm working on now. It's a long story (not my project—it's supposed to be a novel), but it's given me the worst case of writer's block. Anyway, that's probably why I'm up in the middle of the night killing time. Hope you're enjoying a good night of sleep. Kelly

By the way, what do you do and how do you spend your free time?

Okay, I covered my butt on why I was a lunatic up in the middle of the night sort of. And, oh, yes, I totally did steal Tom's dodgeball line.

I got out of bed and went into my office, opened up my document, and worked until I finished half a chapter, so I guess flirting (or whatever you'd call it) with strangers on the Internet truly was sort of good for my creativity. And it felt great to accomplish something—no matter how small. At 8:00 a.m. I got Evan up and ready for school. After dropping him off, I came home, set my alarm on my phone, and immediately fell asleep. I woke feeling refreshed and hopeful—like the best-selling author that I dreamed of being, Kelly Carter Ramsey. *Make room on your bookshelves!*

After grabbing Evan at school and eating some lunch, I sat down at the computer to get back to work, but I picked up my phone and checked the dating app first. After all, maybe that had been the good luck that I needed—messaging Dan—to get me going on that chapter.

Sure enough there was a new message from him—thank

goodness because I wasn't sure if I would've been able to write at that point if there hadn't been a reply. "Thank you for your promptness, Danny-boy," I said as I opened it.

Kelly, Thanks for the message and the laugh! I work in a hospital. In my free time, I like to be outside pretty much doing anything since I spend long hours inside with work. I had the past couple of days off, which was great, and I got to spend a lot of time outside. Didn't have to dodge any low flying tree branches, just a few stray balls from my neighbor's kids but they weren't coming at me too quickly.

So aside from being funny and sitting and making things up, tell me a little bit more about yourself.

I'm 37. I was married for 2 years before my wife died 7 years ago. It was one of those accidents that shouldn't have happened. It was horrible, but I've had a good support system that has helped me heal. I just thought I should put that out there in case you read my profile and were wondering about that.

OK, your turn, Dan

"Oh, crap!" Why did he have to be a nice guy! I mean, of course I would want him to be a nice guy if I really wanted to date him. *Did I?*

I replied.

Dan, I'm so sorry to hear about your wife. That's horrible. I'm glad you had the support you needed to help you through it.

So you work in a hospital? Doing…?

As for me, I'm 34. I've been separated for about a year. I have a 5-year-old son who is absolutely adorable! When he's with his dad, I get to sleep odd hours and work and hang out with my friends. But when he's with me, I enjoy hanging out with him and doing the 5-year-old boy thing too.

Well, enjoy your day—working long hours at the hospital doing God knows what?—and I'll do the same (only not at the hospital)! Kelly

There. Now I'd be able to write. I was sure of it!

I started working on my next chapter. It wasn't going quite as smoothly as I'd hoped even with the message from Dan and the reply.

Could it be possible that messages from random men weren't actually the lucky charm I had thought they were?

Weird.

I got up and left my office.

The Invitation

I was walking downstairs when my phone started ringing—back in the office. I spent half of most days looking for, well, pretty much everything that isn't actually physically attached to my body. The phone rang again, and I ran back up the steps and into the office. The call was from a number I didn't recognize. I answered it. "Hello?"

"Is this Kelly?"

"Yes, it is," I said walking back downstairs.

"Hi, it's Tom."

Tom? Tom? Tom?

"Tom from Gabes."

Oh Tom! "Hey, Tom. I knew that. I was just noticing a spider crawling up the wall. Just a second." I paused to let him think I was killing something. "Got it." Then I immediately hoped he wasn't one of those people who always captured bugs and took them outside (like my dad) and would've been offended by my skit. "How are you?"

"I'm good," he said. "I wanted to make sure you got your rug home okay."

I laughed. "Yes! It looks great actually. It was kind of hard getting it situated by myself, but I managed. I'm capable." *What a laugh!* I decided to leave out the part about the whole process almost killing me. He didn't need to know I was such a wuss.

"So I'm not really in the habit of calling women who ask me if I'm married or gay, but I guess you're the exception to that rule."

"If there's a rule to be broken, count me in." *That makes no sense. Shut up, Kelly!*

He laughed. "Hey, I was wondering. Do you want to get a cup of coffee sometime or do you just want to come by the store and harass me about my sexuality and relationship status there and not, you know, on a date?"

I laughed. What did I want to do? I took a deep breath. "Since I don't think I need anything from Gabes any time soon, I'll opt for harassing you with the coffee option."

He laughed. "This weekend is kind of busy with a couple family things, but I'm off Monday evening. How's that work for you?"

Hmm, I'd have to figure out something for childcare, but that shouldn't be a problem. "Monday should work," I said.

"Let's meet at Joe's around seven?"

"Okay," I said.

"Okay," he echoed. "I'll see you Monday, Kelly."

The Freakout

We hung up. "What the hell just happened there?" I walked into the dining room and sat at the table. "Oh, my God. I just sch... Did I just sch... I just sch... I sch... Oh, my God! How did I do that?"

I dialed Kim's number. She answered after a few rings. "Hey. What's up?"

"I just scheduled a date for Monday," I said.

"Like for the dentist or something? You need me to watch Evan?"

"Kimmy, listen to me. I just scheduled a date for me and this guy to go out on Monday—this random guy I flirted with at Gabes!"

She laughed. "Aw, you did it, Lady! I'm so proud of you. Where are you going?"

I laughed. "Joe's for coffee."

"That's good. It's well lit. Lots of people," she paused. "Wait a minute. You were at Gabes? I hope you were returning something. What about your budget?"

Damn it! Next freakout call Dana. "Kimmy, can we not talk about the budget for, like, a second? You said I needed to get out there. Getting out there costs money. Also, I'm kind of losing my mind here. I have a first date with a man for the first time since I was 20. That's 14 years. So I need us to let go of the budget for a second and talk about the fact that I may actually kiss somebody!" *Do I really want to kiss somebody?* I shuddered a little and shook my head. Could I even bring myself to kiss someone who wasn't Sam? I mean odds were looking good that Sam and I would never kiss again. So I figured I'd probably end up kissing someone else eventually. *But could I now?*

"All right, we can let it go for now, but I'm not letting you off the hook on this one. We need to find some *putting yourself out there* activities that don't involve money!"

Get off it, Grandma! I screamed in my head. "Okay," I added quietly.

"As for the date," Kim said. "It's exciting, Kel! Does he seem like a nice guy?"

"I think." *I mean, I've talked to him for about a grand total of three minutes, but he had helped me with that rug...*

"It's coffee. If it's horrible, get in, get out. Right?"

"Okay," I said and put my head on the table.

"Just go in with a light, fun attitude. That should be pretty easy for you. Just pretend like it's a scene from one of your books. Shouldn't be too hard. It's been 14 years, but you're young, and you can do this. You have to do this. It's going to happen sooner or later. And you might as well practice with a couple of people that you're not really sure you like, right?"

I thought about that for a couple of seconds. "You're right. Thanks," I sat up and propped my head on my hands and looked at the pile of junk mail on the table. "So back to your original question. Yes, I do need you to watch Evan if you're able at like 6:30?"

She laughed. "Of course I'm able. Now can we talk about the budget?"

"Nope. I have to work. Six months, remember? Gotta go." I hung up the phone, grabbed the pile of junk mail, sorted through it quickly as I walked up to my office, and threw it all into the trash.

I sat in front of the computer. But I was too nervous to write. My God! I was going on a date—worse yet, a first date—with a man I hardly knew other than the fact that he helped me put a rug into my trunk, and he was cute. Since I hadn't met him on the dating app, I couldn't even read his profile or stare at his photos. And I didn't even know his last name to google him or check his social media. I thought about calling Gabes to ask what his name was, but then I realized that he might be the person to answer the phone, and that would have been all sorts of awkward! Plus, they probably had some sort of confidentiality thing where they didn't give out employee's last names to random women who called asking for them. "How did I even date before the Internet?"

God, then I really started thinking about the fact that beyond being cute what did I know about him? *Nothing!* What if we didn't have anything to talk about?

But I could probably talk to anyone and could seriously hold up my end of the conversation as long as he could hold up his end. My God! What if he couldn't hold up his end of the conversation?

And why was I so freaked out? It was just coffee. No big deal. If I didn't like him, I could be out of there in less than an hour.

I took a few deep breaths, spun the chair around a few times, and opened the file for my book to start working on it. But I had nothing.

Nothing!

Scheduling this date with Tom had completely zapped me dry! Flirt with someone over the Internet, and I was filled with creativity.

Talk to someone in person, and I was a hot mess. And the worst part was the fact that I had to walk around like a crazy zombie woman all weekend while obsessing over it all. And why was I obsessing over it all? He was just a man. A man who worked at Gabes, no less! Not that working at Gabes was a bad thing—for all I knew he could have had a PhD or something. Damn, if only I could google him! Or at least see his level of education in his profile.

I took a deep breath in and slowly blew it out.

I am.

Relaxed.

I spun the chair around a few more times.

I wasn't going to let myself give him a second thought for the rest of the day. I'd never get anything done if I did!

And through some magical powers that I didn't even know I possessed, I somehow pushed him right out of my brain, but I still couldn't write.

After getting Evan tucked into bed, I decided to play dress-up and figure out what I would wear on my first first date in 14 years. "What do people even wear on dates for coffee these days?" I giggled at the idea of googling that. Then I shrugged, pulled my phone out of my pocket, and actually did google that. Then I went to my room in search of *graphic t-shirts, jeans, booties, and chunky sweaters.* Who knew?

I kept going back and forth between amusement that I was actually prepping for a first date and fear that I actually had to go on it. I couldn't leave my wardrobe selection for Sunday night—or worse—Monday. That could be a disaster.

I opened my closet. It seemed the one thing I had fully unpacked was my clothes. There were way too many because of spending too much time comfort shopping over the last several months. Also, organizational skills were lacking. My clothes hung in no particular order—a winter sweater was wedged in between a sundress and zip hoodie—and were packed in so tightly that I could've pulled out several hangers and none of the articles of clothing would have dropped. I knew this for a fact because the first few hangers I grabbed came out empty.

I laughed and started pushing and digging and pushing some more. I ended up pulling out everything that I owned that would be good for Joe's and coffee. Considering my recent Google search, I had eventually narrowed it down to, well, two choices. Jeans and an orange t-shirt that said "Sunkist" with an off-white chunky cardigan or jeans and a white camisole with a short-sleeve white eyelet shirt over it and a tan jacket.

I wasn't thrilled with either decision.

Not to mention the fact that once I sat on the floor and dug through my laundry baskets of shoes at the bottom of my closet, I really wasn't thrilled with my shoe options. And this was making the whole stress of the date stress me out about a hundred million times more—if that were even possible. I actually decided that I had to lie down—not just because I was being dramatic.

I wasn't feeling well.

There was just too much pressure.

I was ready to call Tom and cancel or even just not show up and pretend that I'd been in an accident on the way there or something. Fake my own death maybe? *Would it be wrong to take out an obit in the local paper to make it look legit?*

I was making myself sick over it.

Literally.

I ran to the bathroom and threw up.

Why did men have this power over women—or maybe it was just me? They could truly turn me—an intelligent, sometimes well-spoken woman—into an idiot, either stammering or tight lipped depending on the situation.

There totally must be some secret to the penis. It was like a magic wand or something. If only I could somehow borrow one and study it. That was probably part of the reason why they were attached. And, OH, MY GOD!, why was I seriously thinking about this!

I couldn't wait until Tuesday when, good or bad, the date would be done. Of course, there was always the possibility of me being dead from embarrassment by then. And I really didn't want Sam to rear Evan, so I hoped that this date went well enough that I survived.

At least it was only coffee. How bad could coffee be? *Seriously? How bad?*

I ran to the bathroom and threw up again. Maybe I had the flu?

EIGHT

The Pre-Date Prep

Eventually, the weekend ended, and I got to Monday.

I dropped Evan at preschool, and then Kim came back to my house to help me finalize my outfit. Since the only thing that seemed to keep my attention lately was men, I said, "You know I don't think dating app dude has replied to my last message."

"Hmm. When was the last time you heard from him?" she said as she pulled a pair of earrings out of my jewelry box and held them up to her earlobes.

"I think it was, like, Friday maybe," I said. I finished pulling on my jeans skirt and Sunkist t-shirt and sat down beside her. I took the earrings and put them on. "You like?"

She nodded her head. "They look pretty. He must be super busy or maybe not interested. Either way, there are other men." She pulled out a necklace. "That whole process of meeting someone online must be kind of weird; isn't it?"

I took the necklace and unfastened it. "I'll let you know if I ever actually meet someone. But it's definitely," I clipped the necklace together and looked at myself in the mirror, "different." I stood up and twirled. "Well, I guess I have my outfit then."

She clapped her hands. "Yay," she grabbed my hands. "Look at you all pretty and going on a date. I feel like we're kids again."

"Aww. A do over would be nice."

She grabbed my skirt and pulled it straight. "Nah. You don't want a do over. You might not have Evan. And I adore that boy!"

I turned back to the mirror. "Yeah, you're right," I rolled my eyes, "as always."

"You know it." She stood up and looked at her watch. "Get out of that, so we can go get the kiddos."

The Date

I pulled up outside of Joe's. Well sort of outside of Joe's. I didn't want to park too close. I mean, if Tom had a good memory, he knew what my car looked like from *the great carpet caper*. I didn't want him to watch me get out of my car and adjust myself a million times before walking toward the restaurant. So I parked several rows back and walked slowly toward Joe's.

As I got closer, I thought, *It's not too late to turn back.* Then, *It's getting slightly harder to turn back.* Finally, *Reaching point of no return.* I opened the door and looked around. *Okay, this is about where I've committed myself.*

Tom was standing to the left of the entrance. "Hi, Kelly," he said.

"Hi, there," I reached my hand out to shake his. He really did have a great smile—not to mention a nice firm handshake. I tried to relax a little bit, but it was hard to do. I wished he wasn't so cute. Why was he so cute? I made a mental note to do myself a favor and only flirt with unattractive men from that point on. I laughed.

"What's so funny?" He asked.

"Oh, I was just thinking about something stupid I did earlier."

"You have to share." He pointed in the direction of the hostess stand.

Shit, Kelly! "You wish."

"No, you have to share." He nodded his head sincerely.

"Two?" The hostess said.

"Yep, just us two chickens," I said. *My God, Kelly, what the hell is wrong with you!* I looked over at Tom and laughed. "I guess you're not exactly a chicken but more a cock—I mean... because you'd be the male bird. Isn't that what the male chicken is called?" *Good Lord, Kelly, shut up!*

Tom laughed. "You're twisted. Aren't you?"

"I am." I swallowed. "A little bit." I nodded my head.

We followed the hostess to the table and sat down and ordered two cups of coffee while I made a mental note to let him take control of the conversation from that point on. Obviously, I didn't have a clue as to what the hell I was doing.

We looked at each other. *Damn!* He was really so cute!

Silence.

"So," I said. "You're thinking one cup of coffee couldn't last too long with this crazy lady, and you're outta here." So much for me letting him lead the conversation. He was just making it difficult for me with those long pauses.

He shifted in his seat and looked down at the table then smiled at me. "Do you think I'd tell you that if I were?"

"Depends on whether you care at all about hurting my feelings." I shrugged my shoulders.

103

Our coffee came, and it couldn't have been better timing. I almost grabbed the waitress' hand when I thanked her and said, *no seriously, thank you*. But of course I didn't.

Tom looked at his coffee for a second and smiled. "We could always try talking about something else. Do you buy rugs often?" He ripped open a sugar packet and dumped its contents into his coffee.

"No. Work at Gabes long?" I picked up my cup and blew on the coffee.

He rolled his eyes and picked up his spoon and started stirring. "Too long. Started in high school in the stockroom. Worked summers through college. After graduation I was looking for a real job and a manager's position opened up so I took it, and, after a while, I stopped looking for a real job." He smiled. "How about you? Where do you work?"

"I'm a writer." I took a sip of my coffee. "So I work at home. Right now I'm working on a book, and I'm having the worst case of writer's block, and I have this deadline that's driving me insane." I nodded my head quickly a couple times. "It's too much pressure. I was avoiding writing the other evening when I was out shopping."

"I'm impressed. What kind of book?" Tom opened a creamer and poured it into his cup.

"It's fiction. It's about these friends who grew up together and then grew apart and just stuff about their lives. I know. I'm not making it sound too exciting, but I don't think you're my target audience. I mean, it probably would appeal more to women. So that's why I won't want to bore you with more details." Well, that and there weren't too many more details unless I could figure out how to expand the project.

"No, that sounds great. That's really impressive." He seemed sincere.

"Thanks." I nodded.

He started stirring his coffee again. "So what do you do for fun?" Tom put his spoon on his saucer and took a sip of his coffee.

Is that all men cared about—what someone did for a living and for fun? Those were the same two questions Dan had asked me. I shrugged. "Play with my five-year-old mostly. I guess."

Tom's eyes got a size bigger, and he took another sip of his coffee.

"And shop. Hey, how old are you anyway?"

He laughed a little and set his cup on the saucer. "I'm 25."

I took a sip of coffee and tried to act like the nine-year age difference was no huge deal. "So what do you do for fun? I'm guessing you don't hang with your five-year-old?" I smirked at him.

The waitress came over and poured more coffee in our cups. We thanked her, and she walked away.

Then Tom looked back at me. "I don't have any kids yet," Tom said. "I go out with friends. Watch movies. Run." He started stirring his coffee again.

There was about 30 seconds of silence as we each took drinks of our coffee.

I took a breath and broke the silence. "So how uncomfortable are you right now?" I raised my eyebrows and set my cup down.

He looked me in the eyes and smiled. "Kelly, I'm not as uncomfortable as you're imagining I am."

"Aren't you the least bit curious about my age?"

"Well I'm guessing you're a little older than I am. The five-year old kid threw me for a second, but I assume you're in your twenties somewhere. And does it really matter?" He drank more coffee.

Okay, with me flattery will get you everywhere, and I think at that moment I fell madly in love with him. So that's a slight exaggeration. *But seriously...* The man said I looked like I was in my twenties. He could have followed that statement up with a swift punch to my stomach, and I still would've gone out with him again if he asked. "Not really," I said. "I mean I guess there's a point where it gets creepy."

"I don't think we're at that point," Tom said.

Oh, we're close to it. I took a sip of my coffee so he couldn't tell I was about to laugh. "So do you get hit on a lot while helping people load their cars?"

Mid-sip Tom almost spit his coffee. After swallowing he said, "Usually only by people my grandma's age. Yours was a unique situation. Very flattering." Again with that killer smile which was followed by more awkward silence.

I finished my coffee and set the cup down. "I should probably get going, Tom. Got that five-year-old to pick up and get to bed." I laughed. "But this has been fun though." I nodded at him.

He looked at his watch and nodded his head. "All right." He motioned to the waitress. "Can I have the check please?" He looked back at me. "Well..." He said.

"Well, what?"

"You wanna do this again? Maybe without calling me a cock next time?" He smirked. He really was so handsome!

I swallowed and cleared my throat. *He's nine years younger than you, Kelly.* But then I heard Kim reminding me to put myself out there and see what happens. "Um, yes. I do. Do you?"

He nodded. "Yes." The waitress handed him the check. "Thanks." He looked at it. "Plus, you're a really cheap date!"

I laughed, we stood up and walked to the cash register, and he paid.

He opened the door for me, and we stepped outside. "Let's take a walk," Tom said.

"What?" I said.

"It's a beautiful evening, and I'd love to spend a little more time with you. I know you have to put your kid to bed, but do you have time for a quick walk?"

"Umm," I said and pulled out my phone to look at the time. It wasn't even eight yet, and Evan was truly a night owl. "Sure," I said. "Which way?"

"There's a trail behind Joe's," Tom said.

"A trail?" I said and squinted my eyes at Tom.

"Yep, you've never been on it?" he said.

"No, should I be scared that you have?" I said as I followed Tom around the building.

He turned around and laughed. "Why? I run on it all the time," he said.

"I feel like I'm walking myself into an episode of some unsolved murder mystery show or something." He stopped, and I poked him in the back then stepped around beside him.

"See, a trail," he said and gestured with his hand.

"Well I'll be damned," I said.

Tom laughed. "Which way do you wanna walk?"

I looked both ways and then pointed to the right. "This way."

He took my hand in his, and I looked at them. He shrugged his shoulders and smiled at me. "Do you mind?" he said.

I squeezed his hand and patted it with my other hand. "Not at all. I would consider myself to be a hand holder, I guess," I said.

"I am too," he said and squeezed my hand. "Well, obviously."

I laughed. We walked a few steps. "God, it is beautiful tonight," I said.

"It is," he said.

I looked up at him. "People seriously don't hit on you that often at work? You've got quite a face."

He laughed. Then he put his hand up over his eyes for a couple seconds. "You're going to make me blush, Kelly," he said. "So tell me a little bit about your kid."

"Evan? Well like I said he's five," I paused. "He's in preschool. He's super funny. Likes to hang out naked. And he's always up for an adventure." I laughed. "Is it just me, or does that sound like a cheesy online dating profile?"

"I was going to say that there are so many jokes forming in my head right now, and I know I should just keep them to myself."

"That's probably the best choice," I said.

"Maybe I'll share them on the third date," he said and laughed. "I'm totally kidding by the way," he added.

I laughed. "It's okay. My maturity level is about the same as an eighth-grade boy's when it comes to stuff like that. So really not many jokes strike me as inappropriate."

"Good to know," Tom said. "Got anything else to add about your son?"

"Hmm," I thought for a second. "Nope. I don't think so."

"Well, we've covered the weather and the fact that I run… on this trail," Tom said.

"How often do you run?" I said.

"Almost every day. My mom's a runner, and I started running with her when I was a kid. Did the whole cross country and track thing in high school."

"Marathons?" I said.

"No, I'm only half crazy. I've done several half marathons. My mom'll run the full marathon, but I don't wanna put in that much effort. I just like to run enough to clear my head. It's also extremely peaceful to be up and running early in the morning."

"You lost me at early."

He laughed. "I look at it this way. When I was in high school, I had to get up at 5:30 to get to school on time. So I just stuck with that routine in college even though I took later classes. It's just when my body is used to waking up."

"I haven't intentionally woken up at 5:30 in a long time."

"So what's your thing? How do you clear your head?" He said.

I thought for a couple seconds. "Sadly—and this is going to make me sound super pathetic—I clean my house. That's been my escape lately. That and I walk. I'll take really long walks and count my steps."

"Whatever works. Cleaning is definitely not my relaxer though."

We came to the end of the trail at a street. "Well, that's the world's shortest trail," I said. "I could maybe wrap my mind around running if I only had to go that far."

He laughed. "I let you pick, and you picked the short way. The other way goes on for miles. It's all about the choices we make." Tom squeezed my hand.

We'd stopped walking, and I looked up at him. Was he that wise or just making conversation? He smiled at me and shrugged.

We looked at each other for several minutes before we turned around and started walking back.

We took several steps in silence before I said, "So tell me about the last person you were in love with." Then I laughed. Where had that come from? Well Sam had just flashed through my head after Tom's observation about the choices we make, so I assumed that was where. I looked up at Tom.

"Uhh," he said. He looked at me and smiled. "Are you serious?"

"Sure. Why not? I mean, unless you're still dating. In which case, I should let go of your hand and go home."

He squeezed my hand and laughed. "Well, her name's Victoria. We were together for over two years—not quite three." He paused. "What else do you wanna know?"

"Whatever you wanna tell me," I said.

"Probably none of this, really," he laughed again and tilted his head back. "We broke up about a year ago." He looked at me and shrugged. Then added, "It just wasn't the right fit."

"Fair enough," I said and wished I hadn't brought up the subject.

I could feel him looking at me from my peripheral vision.

"What about you?" He laughed. "Fair is fair."

I didn't really want to talk about Sam because truthfully the answer may not be that he was the last person that I had been in love with—on some level the feelings were still there. "Hmm, I guess that's true. Why did I think asking you that was a good idea again?"

"I have no clue," he laughed and shook his head. "A lot of weirdness comes out of that mouth of yours."

I laughed and then took a deep breath. "To be honest I've probably only ever been in love with my husband. We started dating when I was fairly young, and I've always been a little guarded with my emotions, so before him they were just crushes probably." I pressed my lips together.

Tom nodded.

"We separated almost a year ago. I wasn't a good fit for him at the time, I guess." I glanced up at Tom. "His name was Sam—still is," I laughed. "And that's all I have to say about that."

We walked a few more steps.

"How do you feel about cotton candy?" I said.

"You are all over the place; aren't you?" Tom said. "Is this *normal Kelly* or did you get drunk before the date?"

I laughed. "I'm totally sober. I was just trying to think of something a little lighter," I said.

"Cotton candy is light. It's sweet and sticky and addictive. In a nutshell, I love it," he laughed. "If I see someone selling it, I'm in line! I don't care that I'm not four years old."

I reached over and grabbed his arm. "Well that's passion right there! Considering you seem to take good care of yourself, I was expecting a different reaction."

He laughed again. "You find cotton candy offensive?"

"No, I love it! I'm just not as, um, fit as you are. I'm not up running on this trail every morning at 5:30."

"Now you know why I need to," he shrugged. "Cotton candy addiction."

His deadpan delivery was hilarious—and endearing—and kind of reminded me of my dad a little bit. I laughed and looked up at him. "You're very amusing; you know that?"

He shrugged then laughed.

We were almost back to where we got on the trail. "Should we call it a night?" I said and leaned into him. "Did you get enough time with me?"

"Well, considering your line of questioning, the next question would be something, uh, deeper, so, yep, I'm good. Time to go home." He squeezed my hand.

We got off the trail, and he walked me to my car. I hugged him goodbye. I mean it was just a cup of coffee and a walk. That seemed appropriate. Plus, being totally honest, I was scared to death to kiss him. "Thanks for the coffee. I'll see you later," I got into my car.

"Yep," Tom shut the door for me and stood there as I backed out and drove away.

I survived! I'd gone on my first first date in 14 years and had survived it. I felt a little numb though, and a little disappointed that I was at this place in my life where my husband had left me and I was starting to move on. I mean, I didn't think things with Tom were going to be a great love connection, but he had a very sweet, endearing side to him.

The date had its awkward moments, yes. But he could be fun to hang out with again. And he sure was beautiful to look at. Would he be super freaked out when he found out I wasn't "in my twenties?" That it was actually mid-thirties? I guessed time would tell. But aside from me actually telling him, how would he even find out? And even if he did. What would it really matter? I wasn't really ready to be in love with someone new, so this was going to be low key, if anything.

The Phone call

I needed to get out of my head so I called Dana.

"Hello," she answered after a couple rings.

"Dana…"

"Hey, Kelly. What's up?"

"Dana," I said. If she were with me, I would have grabbed her shoulders and shaken her.

"Kelly. What?"

"Are you busy this very second?"

She laughed. "Well Greg and I are watching TV, but clearly whatever it is you have to say 'this very second' is important so go ahead."

"Are you sure?" I said. "I know how much Gregory likes his *Dana TV time*." It was sort of their thing.

She laughed. "He'll survive for a few seconds. Greg, go get a snack or something. Fire away, Kelly," she said.

"Okay, I'll make it quick," I said. "I went out with Tom tonight."

"Which one's Tom? The dating app guy or the rug guy? No, wait! He's the zoo guy!"

I laughed. "No, he's the rug guy."

"Oh, yeah, yeah, yeah. How'd it go?"

"Well, I'm not sure. I think ultimately it went okay, but..."

"Hmm. Elaborate," she said to me. "Pepper, sit," she told her dog.

"Dana," I giggled.

"What?" She laughed.

"I called him a cock."

"You didn't!" She screamed with laughter. Pepper started barking.

"I did, but it was calling him a cock as opposed to a chicken so it's not that bad. Right?"

She stopped laughing. "Wait. What?"

"I said, 'Just us chickens' to the hostess."

"Why?!"

"I don't know! I say shit... And then I said to Tom. 'Well you're more a cock than a chicken.'"

"Oh, Kelly Ramsey, you need a chaperone." She laughed.

"Maybe you can join us next time."

"Sure. Let me know when."

"Anyway, guess how old he is?" I said.

"Why would this be an issue? I'm thinking maybe I'll be scared?"

"You'll be impressed. Try. Come on," I said.

"Okay, I'll play your reindeer games. Let's try 28."

"Eeeernt. Younger."

"Holy hell! Where'd you meet him again? Evan's preschool?"

"Shut up! Not that young. He's 25."

She was quiet for a second. "Nice," she said slowly.

"And he wants to see me again. Well, at least he did before we took a walk, and I asked him to tell me about the last person he was in love with."

"Oh, my God! Kelly, why? Just why?"

I laughed. "Truly I think it was because Sam popped into my head for a second or something. I dunno, Dana," I said.

"Oh, no, no, no, no, no," she said. "No, no, no, not good."

"I know. I may not be ready to date. I mean, Kim wants me to put myself out there, but…"

"You're not a hundred percent ready," Dana finished. "Yeah, I get that. But truly it doesn't hurt as long as it feels fun, right?"

"I mean, if fun is putting my foot in my mouth and calling people names and asking them awkward questions and stuff, then, yes, I had great fun!"

She laughed. "And I guess you didn't offend him too much by calling him a cock because he wants to see you again."

"Right. He liked it. Called me twisted."

"Which you are," she said. "I'm glad he noticed."

"And that's why you and I love each other's company so much, Dana. You're twisted too."

"Too true, Kelly. Too true. So are you going to see him again? I mean, unless you scared him away with the conversation about exes."

"Umm. I said I would."

"Yeah?"

"Yeah. I mean, that's what I said when he asked. We'll see what I say if he actually calls me back." I laughed. "He's sweet though. Plus, when he smiles…" I shook my head. "Damn, he's cute! You know?"

"I mean I've been married for about five years now, but I think I remember." Pepper started barking. "Hey, quiet! So what's going on with the dating app guy?"

"I don't know. I need to check my messages. Nothing really. I haven't called him anything offensive yet, so I guess that's a plus."

"Just give it time," she said. Then, "Pepper! God, Kel, I need to take this dog out."

"Okay, I'll talk to you later."

"Keep me posted. I'm living vicariously through you."

"You poor thing! Hey, Dana, one more thing."

"Yeah?"

"Take a bag."

We both laughed and hung up.

Did I really want to go out with Tom again? I shrugged and drove the last couple of minutes in silence.

The Dating App Guy

After reading books to Evan, I laid in bed beside him and pulled out my phone. I clicked on the dating app. There were the normal perverted messages. One guy asked me if I liked to walk in fields with my shoes off. What was that about? I was a city girl. The answer was definitely *No!* Of course I wouldn't give him the sick pleasure of a response so I deleted that message. Another guy liked my lips. They reminded him of an ex-girlfriend's. *Was that even a compliment?* I think it was meant as one, but, seriously, was mentioning an ex a good way to open a dialogue? Of course I had done it earlier with Tom so really was I any better? I deleted the message.

Way down at the bottom of the list, there was a message from Dan.

Kelly, I work in one of the offices part of the time. It's not too bad. Most days I enjoy it. Sometimes the hours get long and tiring. But that's just the nature of the job.

I'm sure your son keeps you busy. My neighbors have what seem to me to be a house full of children, and they seem to be running around constantly from one activity or another. I think there may only be 2 kids but the noise level makes it seem like much more sometimes.

I have a couple nieces who I used to like to spoil when they were little, but now that they're teenagers, they pretty much only want my money and not my time. So it's not as fun for me anymore.

Here are a couple more questions for you. What's your favorite snack food? What's your favorite vacation spot? Dan

Hmm. He worked long hours in an office at the hospital. Rather he worked in the office, *part of the time?* What was that about? That could be anything from a janitor to IT computer geek-type. *Why all the mystery?*

I hit reply.

Dan, what's with all this mystery surrounding your job? Why won't you just come out and tell me what it is exactly that you do, in fact, do in the hospital? Is it that gross?

I deleted it and started over.

Dan, nice to hear from you. I'll start with your questions, but you have to answer too. My favorite snack is potato chips. I love them—maybe too much. My favorite vacation spot is any beach. I'm a sucker for a sunburn and a bathing suit full of sand riding up my butt.

My son's in preschool, so he's not too busy yet. We don't do a lot of rushing around, except for just normal stuff. I haven't signed him up for any extra activities. He hasn't asked to do anything yet, and I'm not encouraging it. Maybe I'm a bit selfish. Don't know.

That sucks for you that your nieces have ditched you for their own social lives. Too bad they don't want their uncle hanging around, but you have to admit that there just reaches an age where hanging out with your older uncle just isn't cool. I'm sure that even Superman's nieces felt the same way eventually. Did he have nieces? Well, they would have if he did.

So let me know your favorite snack and where you like to vacation too. Glad to hear you're enjoying your office work at the hospital. Kelly

Weird.

He worked in the office—part of the time? What for like 15 minutes a day taking out the trash? Yeah, I was pretty convinced that he was a janitor. If he had a job that paid well, why would he be using this free dating app?

Dan's vague answers were driving me insane. I should probably just stop messaging him, but I was sort of intrigued. I needed to know what his actual job was because he seemed so intent on keeping the information to himself.

Again, men and their penises. I wished I could get my hands on one for just a few minutes and figure that thing out.

I got ready for bed and walked into my bedroom. I looked out my window and could see the moon, and I wondered what Sam was doing—and truly who he was with at that moment, if anyone. I stood there for a while just sort of thinking and not thinking at the same time. I really wished that the mind-erasing thing from the movie *Eternal Sunshine of the Spotless Mind* was an option for me. Moving on would be so much easier if I just didn't have to remember any of it. Like that stupid time capsule that I knew was still in my purse. I could practically picture the envelope tucked in between my wallet and my makeup bag. It was pretty much all I could think of since finding it. I couldn't bring myself to finish reading it because currently that part of Sam—the part where he loved me and wrote and hid sweet love notes for me—was captured in that envelope. But when I opened it back up and finished reading the letter, that part would be gone—released back out to the world, back to him, back to wherever it would go. It would no longer be here, within my reach.

I looked at the moon for a couple more seconds then turned and looked at my bed.

NINE

The Nudist

I wasn't exactly sure why Evan hadn't woken me up, but I slept in the next morning which felt really odd. Most mornings Evan was pretty creative about how he woke me too. I've been woken to a toy trumpet concert. Once he performed a puppet show at the foot of my bed. Perhaps my favorite time was when he just woke me up by saying, "Hey, Momma, I have something to show you," and then when I was aware enough to realize what he was doing, he flashed me. Yes, he flashed me. My son had on a plaid blazer that my mother had given him to play dress-up in and nothing else underneath. That kid was a hoot, and I was determined to enjoy his creative mind and help him cultivate it as long as I could.

But this morning, instead of waking me, I found him watching TV naked—no big shock, right, for my nudist. I just shook my head and walked by. He barely acknowledged me as he was laser focused on his shows.

In the kitchen I could tell that he had eaten a bowl of cereal—or at least attempted to—because there was clearly a huge milky, mushy mess. I also found some really wet pajamas which explained why he was watching TV naked. I stood there looking at the mess for about a minute, and then Evan walked into the kitchen. "Hey, Mom."

"So what happened here?" I pointed to the table and floor.

He looked at the table, looked at himself, and smiled at me.

I smiled back at him. "Yeah," I nodded my head. "Did you forget that you were naked?"

"Kind of." He put his hand over his mouth. I would hope in a few more years his reaction would be to instead cover another part of his body when he realized that he was naked in front of someone, but for now the mouth cover up was pretty cute.

I laughed and shook my head. "What happened?"

"See that car?" He pointed to the table.

I looked. "Yes."

"I was reaching to get it. And I couldn't get to it, and when I went too far, I got all wet everywhere, so I took everything off because it felt gross."

I squinted my eyes and did one big nod. "Makes sense. But you," I pushed into his tummy like the dough boy and he laughed, "have to help me clean it up, and then you have to wash yourself with a wet washcloth and put some clean clothes on."

He stood there shaking his head and making faces.

"What? What's the head shaking for, Ev?"

"I'm not doing any of those things. I'm comfortable like this, and my shows are on." He started to walk back to the living room.

"Uh uh. Stop!" He kept going. "Evan, one, two…"

He stopped. "Okay." He came back in and got a towel from the drawer. He stood there and looked at the table for a couple seconds and then threw the towel over his shoulder. "I don't even know how to clean it, Mom," he said.

"Just wipe it up, Ev. Then we'll wet the towel and clean it up so it's not sticky."

He squinted his eyes.

"You can do it. It's easy. Almost as easy as making the mess—just a little less fun."

He pulled a chair out, was about to climb up onto it, and then pointed and said, "I better wipe this up first." I glanced at the chair and noticed milk on the seat.

I tousled his hair. "You better check all the chairs, okay?"

"Aren't you helping?" he said.

"I mean, I am but mostly helping you learn how to clean up a mess you've made," I said.

He blew his breath out and started to wipe the seat. "Not fair."

"Yes, fair," I said and grabbed a few more towels from the drawer.

After the mess was cleaned, Evan was dressed, and my coffee was made, I sat down in my office to get started working. I mean, I was supposed to be writing a book that seemed to be taking a back burner to everything else going on in my life.

Anyway, before getting started, I opened the dating app to see if Dan had replied to my message.

He had.

Kelly, you have a very unique perspective on the world. I'm not sure if Superman had nieces, but I guess you're right. I don't think they would have wanted to hang out with him as they got older. Do you think their friends might have wanted to hang out with him though?

My favorite snack food is chocolate chip cookies. I eat them by the dozen. My favorite vacation spot is Cancun.

Do you have any siblings? Are you close with them? What's your favorite color? Just wondering. Dan

I hit reply, *Dan, I've been told that I'm twisted. Thanks for using the term unique instead. That's a bit gentler—perhaps kinder. I agree that Superman's nieces' friends would have insisted on hanging out with him, but apparently you're NO Superman. Sorry, I couldn't resist!!*

I have 1 sister. She's 2 years older, and we get along famously. How about you?

My favorite color is red. Again, how about you?

Eagerly awaiting your response. Kelly

I hit send and opened my book. Maybe I was just completely on the wrong track with my novel, but I just seemed to have nothing extra to add these days. The characters had been there, done that, and they didn't want to do it again. They were bored with it—and truly so was I! The characters were old. They were tired. And they just wanted to stay in bed and sleep. Everything seemed to be pretty much resolved, and I only had about 60 pages. That didn't quite constitute a novel. My agent would laugh in my face (well, in my ear as we communicated either via phone or email) if I presented her those 60 pages as the finished project. And, really, nothing was finished about the project, but it truly felt done.

I sat there scratching my chin for a few minutes, and then I opened a new document and tapped my fingers lightly on the keyboard while hoping that some brilliant idea for a new story would pop into my brain, and I'd just be able to start typing away.

Nothing came to me.

I closed my eyes—partly because I was sick of staring at that bright white screen (it was almost blinding) and partly to stop the tears that were about to fall if I didn't.

It was too late for the second part though, and I wiped my cheeks.

I got up, went outside, and sat on the front porch. There were a million things going on in my brain, but nothing could come out on paper.

That just sucked so badly.

"Why you outside, Momma?" Evan cracked the screen door.

"I just needed some air, Honey. Do you wanna come out?"

"No. I'm watching my shows. I was just checking on you."

"Okay," I smiled. That made it all better—for the moment anyway. Nothing was really better, but I had Evan, and he was the sweetest boy and that made me cry even more. How did I get to be so lucky to be his mom, and how could I secretly wish that Sam and I had never met so that I would stop feeling this hurt? Wishing that was wishing away my sweet boy. I shook my head. I didn't want that for sure.

I sat there for a few more minutes and went back inside.

There was another reply from Dan already. My God, he was fast today!

Kelly, I have a younger brother who I get along very well with. And my favorite color is green. I'm headed to work, so this is short. Have a good day. Dan

Yes, that was short! Did it even warrant a reply?

I wasn't sure, but I was in a mood, so I hit reply anyway. *Dan, how are you today? I hope you had a great day at work. I'm having a horribly shitty day here trying to write, and I can't think of a damn thing to say. Not to you though, obviously—just for my book.*

My day began by walking into a wall on my way from my shower to my bedroom. I still haven't checked to make sure my eye isn't black and blue. I'll have to do that before I leave the house. And then when I got downstairs, I found my son sitting naked watching cartoons because he had made a horrible mess by spilling cereal and milk all over his clothes and pretty much the whole kitchen! Anyway, that's all cleaned up now, but, my God! What a way to start the day!

Last night I called some guy a cock by accident because I was correcting the gender when I had originally called him a chicken. Why was I calling a man a chicken you wonder? Well, don't ask. It's a stupid story. Basically, I've just been having one thing like that after the next happen to me lately. And if you think that's just dumb luck. Nope! That's my life, Dan. That's pretty much how it goes with me! It's one thing like that after the next ALL. THE. TIME. So feel free to never reply to me again if you want to steer clear of a certain level of dysfunction that you may not be accustomed to in your normal suburban life. I mean, don't get me wrong, I live in the suburbs too. But for some reason I just can't seem to get the hang of it like most people. Kelly

I laughed and hit send.

That felt good. That felt so good! And for a couple minutes I toyed with the idea of using the dating app to make a connection with someone to get the opportunity to send over-the-top messages to and keep track of how many men I could completely scare away. Maybe I would turn that idea into my next book.

TEN

The Dumpster

I hated how I felt myself turn into a drill sergeant every time I had to get Evan up and ready for preschool. He, who normally would wake me on his off days, was Mr. Slowpoke on a school day.

He didn't want to get dressed, eat breakfast, brush his teeth, or go to the bathroom. Some mornings things ran smoothly. And some mornings it felt like a nightmare. This morning wasn't too bad. It could have been better, but we both got out of the house without killing each other. I guess that was a good enough way to start our hump day. And I even remembered to take my huge bag of paper to recycle at his school so that was even better. It had been sitting in my basement just waiting to be tripped over for at least a week.

Kim, of course, had Meri there already. I could only assume they'd been at least 10 minutes early too. "Hey, Ev, how are you this morning?" She asked him as we walked past her on our way down to the classroom.

"Evan, say good morning to Aunt Kim." I nudged his shoulder.

"I'm too grumpy," he mumbled through clenched teeth.

"He's a lovely boy in the mornings when we have to leave the house," I said and smiled at her.

"I can tell," Kim said. "I love you, Evan. Your day will brighten. Just wait."

"I love you too," again through clenched teeth, but I was happy that he at least said it.

Downstairs—just outside his classroom door—we had a routine where he gave me two hugs and two kisses. It was pretty dramatic as most kids got dropped off at the upstairs door and walked to the classroom independently, but that was my Evan. I chalked it up to the separation between Sam and me and Evan's whole anxiety with a parent leaving him places at that point in his life—which gave me another thing to be pissed at Sam about.

Anyway, after all that drama, I cleared off my front seat. Kim got in, and we drove to the paper recycling dumpster in the back of the parking lot. The bag of paper was under her feet, so Kim offered to dump it for me. I gladly let her since I wasn't sure I could have pulled it out from under her feet. Since she would've had to get out of the car anyway, she might as well just take the few extra steps to the dumpster.

"They must have just made a pickup," she called to me.

"It's empty, huh?" Some days it was almost overflowing.

She jumped back in the car and handed me my empty plastic bag and we headed to the mall to walk.

"So what was wrong with Evan today?" she said.

"He had to go to school."

"Still not liking it? Meri loves school."

"You're so lucky to have the perfect child," I said.

"I know."

"How'd you do that?"

"Not sure," Kim said and cracked the window.

"You didn't marry Sam for starters."

She snorted. "That helped."

"You liked that one, huh?"

She laughed. "Your deadpan delivery while cutting right to the reality of it. Yeah, that was pretty funny."

I laughed. "Glad my tragedy can bring a giggle to others."

"Yep, that's the part that sucks about it though, right?"

"Mmhmm."

We drove the rest of the way in silence. I pulled into a parking spot. Then we headed into the mall for our walk.

"So, how's your budget? Are you sticking to our spending plan?" My family was priceless. But I guess all families were, right? They were always all up in your business.

"Yes, I think I am. You had allocated funds for a weekend in Vegas, right? Because Lisa called this morning and said that she and her sisters were doing a girls' weekend and asked me to join them. I told her to totally count me in."

Of course, Kim pretty much ignored me. So I had to build on my fantasy. "What? Do you wanna join us? Are you mad or something? Let me call her and see if she can get another ticket." I pulled my phone out of my pocket and dialed Lisa's number. I got her voicemail. "Hey, Lees. It's Kelly. I was calling to see if you haven't bought the tickets yet," Kim was hitting my arm and telling me to shut up. "Wait, this is fun," I said to Kim. "Lisa, if you haven't bought the tickets yet, get one for Kim too. I am so excited! Vegas'll be a blast! Talk to you later." I put my phone in my pocket and started to laugh.

She hit me on the arm. "You are such a dork," she said.

"I know. But it's fun. She'll just think I'm day drinking again. It's no big deal. I can see a text coming from her later in all caps," I held my hands out in front for emphasis. "'WHAT THE FU—'"

"Yeah, probably," Kim interrupted. "So what's wrong with your leg? Why are you limping?" Kim asked me.

"Am I limping?" I looked down at my legs.

"Yeah, I keep noticing it more and more each time we walk. At first, I thought I was imagining things, but you're really limping now."

"Oh, God." I was hoping I'd been imagining it too. "It really hurts, and I keep telling myself it doesn't because I really don't wanna go to the doctor."

"Don't you love your doctor?"

"I mean," I shrugged, "as much as you can love someone who inflicts pain on you. I go in, and we have a playful conversation because I'm nervous. It makes for a funny story that I share with you. But I'd hardly consider that to be loving him. I don't send him a Christmas card or anything like that."

"Well, you need to call him today. In fact I'm going to stand beside you after walking to make sure you do because you're limping like an old lady, and it's getting kind of embarrassing for me."

"Once again someone from my family crushes my self-image. At least this time it wasn't Mom."

"Ah, I'm sorry. I didn't mean to." She patted my arm.

"Okay, new topic. I had a few new ideas for books since I'm getting nowhere fast with my current project. What did you do with those papers that I gave you to hold when I cleaned off my front seat for you?"

"I threw them in the paper dumpster, Kel."

"No. You threw the bag of paper in the dumpster, but I gave you a few pieces of paper to hold onto when you got into the car."

"I threw everything into the dumpster."

I stopped walking.

Kim walked a couple steps, stopped, and turned to look back at me.

"Are you kidding me, Kim? It's not funny if you're joking."

"No," she said barely above a whisper.

I turned and ran back toward the exit. "We have to get them."

She started to run beside me. "What are we doing?" she said.

"We have to get them," I kept running out of the mall and toward my car. I grabbed my keys out of my pocket and jumped into the car.

"Okay, so what is it?" She asked as we drove back to the school.

"It's just ideas that I wrote down on paper, Kim. It's original thought—not backed up or saved anywhere but there. And I've been having so much trouble with this stupid thing. And what if someone dumps something in there or takes them or what if they make a pickup."

"They just did, Kelly. They won't make another for..."

"But what if they do?" I yelled. "It'll all be gone. And I'll never finish this book."

"Okay, we'll get there," she whispered.

"I'm sorry," I said.

"I know. I am too," she said.

We got to the dumpster, and I jumped out of the car. I ran around to the back opening where Kim had dumped the bag in. I saw a bunch of Evan's papers so, fortunately, it looked like no one had really dumped much in after Kim had. That was a relief.

I was scanning the papers, trying to see if I could see my handwriting, and hoping that Kim had dumped the bag first and thrown my papers on top. That would be key. I wouldn't have to dig around.

Kim was saying something to me, but I was too focused on my search to pay attention to her words. And then there they were—my papers shining up at me like a beacon of light!

I felt like I could just lean in headfirst, grab them, and then hoist myself back out so that was what I did—well, the first two parts anyway.

"Do you want me to get you a chair?" I finally made out her words as I dove for my papers. I had my hand on them. I was holding them! *Yes!*

But since my upper body weighed more than my legs and I was dangling in the dumpster headfirst, I couldn't push myself back out. And, my God, the pressure was killing my stomach. "No, I've got them. Just pull my legs out!"

"So you got everything?" she asked.

"Yes, grab my legs and get me out of this thing!"

She did. Thank God she was strong.

"Okay, let's go to your house to schedule an appointment with your PCP."

"Will you ever just let me just have fun for, like, an extra couple of seconds?" I said.

"No. I won't." She paused. "Not ever."

I laughed. "I know, but I had to at least ask."

The Question and Answer

Back at my house after scheduling my appointment with my PCP for—lucky me!—later that very same day because of a cancellation, I sat on the couch and checked my dating app while Kim made us some coffee. I was really curious to see if Dan would reply—and how he would reply if he had. And, yep, there it was.

Kelly, I'm sorry to hear about the bad day. And I hope you're not mad at me for laughing out loud at your expense. Your message was really funny! Your book must be hilarious.

How's the eye? And should I even ask how today is going?

If it helps, my day didn't go so well either. Although I can't say that I walked into any walls or had to clean up anyone else's spills or called anyone a cock—that's classic by the way! Again, I laughed out loud reading that. You must be a very fun person to hang out with.

Speaking of which, any interest in getting together at some point? Dan

"Oh, my God! You've got to be kidding me!" I practically shouted at my phone.

"What?" Kim walked in and handed me a coffee mug.

"Show a person your true dysfunction, and they want to go out with you. Read this."

I handed her my phone as she sat on the couch beside me.

"Aww, he sounds sweet," she said.

"I know," I paused. "But look at his picture. I'm not that attracted to him."

"Where?"

"Click on his name, and it takes you to his profile."

"He's not bad. I mean, he's okay. But, yeah, I see what you're saying. You're not swooning over him or anything. I like his glasses though."

"Yeah, those are pretty great glasses. I can't tell whether he's a nerd or just stylish though," I paused and sipped my coffee. "Tom's really cute."

"Kelly, Tom's 25. Can you even compare them?" She leaned her head back on the couch.

"If it's two men that I'm possibly dating at the same time, then, yes, I can." I bopped the tip of her nose with my pointer finger.

"I guess you have a point." She read his profile. "He sounds really nice. Really grounded."

"Of course, you'd like him. He's the older of two."

"That's what you need, Kel, a male me. Keep you in line." She tugged on my arm as she said the last sentence.

"Who says I'm out of line? Aside from Mom."

"Ruling her out," she tossed the phone at me, "no one."

"That's right. I am the line."

"What does that even mean?" She drank some coffee.

"I dunno. It just sounded funny in my head." I blew on my coffee. "Not so much once I vocalized it."

"I'd love to jump in your head, Kelly, for like three minutes. I think that's all I could handle before being terrified."

"Thanks. But seriously, Kim, same with you. I would be totally freaked out in that mind of yours. I picture your brain being a very quiet place."

"What?"

"No, I didn't mean that as an insult. I just meant that you're so organized. You don't have to have thoughts shooting around constantly about what you need to do and stuff so you can just kind of have quiet time up there. Whereas my brain is constantly firing thoughts like, 'Did I turn the oven off?' 'I forgot Evan's permission slip!' 'Would that fit with my character's personality?' 'Wait! Did I zip my pants?' 'Blah, blah, blah.' Never mind."

"Yeah, let's talk about something else."

We made small talk for about an hour and then went and picked up the kids at school.

After lunch I took Evan to the park so he'd be super good and tired out, and I could reply to Dan's message in peace. Sadly I had taken to tiring my kid out so that I could write messages in peace instead of writing fiction.

The park was nice—quiet. Even Beth and her grandma weren't there for a change. Evan ran to the monkey bars, and I sat on a bench. "Ouch," I winced as my knees bent to sit.

So... I needed to figure it out. Was I interested in getting together with Dan? I supposed I could take a few days to think about it before replying, or I could just ignore his question and see if he asked me again.

I mean, he definitely was a more age-appropriate suitor than Tom was. And I guessed the only way I could tell if there was going to be any connection was to actually meet... in person. I figured I might as well just get it over with. As much as the messaging had been amusing—or maybe just distracting—me, I just had a feeling it wasn't going to be much more than that. It wasn't that he was bad looking. He sort of had nice features, but he just kind of had a geeky look about him. I couldn't see myself being extremely attracted to him in person, and being attracted to a person you're dating is important, in my opinion.

Of course, thinking about attraction made me think about Sam because, yes, I was attracted to him. However, his actions since he left and the way I felt he should be (but wasn't) treating Evan definitely made him less attractive to me so that was at least good. I let out a deep breath. Why did it always have to come back to Sam— to check in with how I was emotionally disconnecting to him before I was moving forward with my life? I was hoping there would come a day when I could make a decision without him popping into my head.

Evan played for a while longer, and then we walked home. I got him settled with a show he liked, and I sat down on the couch. I opened Dan's message and hit reply.

Dan, my eye is fine. No bruises. My day today is just about normal for me. That means the only wacky thing I've done so far is dive head-first into a paper recycling dumpster to retrieve some important papers that my sister accidently threw in with my bag of paper to be recycled. I could have killed her. But at least I got back what I needed.

As for my book, it's not a comedy so I hope it's not too hilarious or I'm not doing my job well. Perhaps I should try writing something funny. Maybe I wouldn't have writer's block. It's been pretty bad lately.

I would enjoy getting together at some point. Let me know how you want to go about doing that. Kelly

PS I hope your bad day got better.

I hit send and got Evan ready to leave. I needed to take him to my mom's so I could go to my doctor's appointment.

The Doctors

"Grandma!" Evan ran and jumped into her arms as I walked up her sidewalk behind him.

"There's my boy!" She gave him a big squeeze and set him down.

"I'm glad you were off today, Mom. Thanks."

She opened the front door, and we all went inside. "I know. What would you have done otherwise?"

I pulled the door shut behind me. "I could have taken him to Kim's or taken him with me. You weren't the last resort."

Evan sat on the floor to take his shoes off.

"Well, this worked out," she said. "I haven't gotten to play with him in a while." She was a doctor and still worked a lot of hours—even though she was trying to cut back and retire in a few years.

"So you're going to see Steven?" She sat on a bench and watched Evan working on his shoes.

"Yes, Dr. Oliver." I nodded my head.

She laughed. "I don't know why you insist on calling him that."

"Because he's my doctor, Mom." I laughed. She really wanted me to get all casual with him, but I refused to do it—mostly because it pissed her off. "How would you feel about your patients calling you Grace? Never mind. I know the answer." She had always told all her patients to call her Grace, and some of them had. But Dr. Oliver had never asked me to call him Steven. "Okay, I'm leaving, Ev. I'll be back soon." I squatted down beside him and kissed him on the forehead.

"Bye, Momma," he said and looked up from untying his shoes.

"You know you don't actually have to unlace them all the way," I said.

He smiled and nodded. "I know that." He giggled.

I raised my eyebrows and nodded at him. "Okay, good. Bye, Evan. Be good." I stood up. "Bye, Mom."

"Goodbye, Kelly. We'll be fine." I loved the way my mom said my name. It always took me right back to childhood. She hung on to the first syllable maybe half a second longer than was normal and then placed about equal emphasis on the second syllable or something. She was the only one who said it that way.

"I know you will. I'm not worried, Mom." I opened the front door.

"You look worried."

"What? I don't look worried. Well maybe I look a little worried. I don't like going to see a doctor. That's why. It has nothing to do with you and Evan spending time together—although it probably should. So, yeah, now I'm extra worried. Thanks, Mom," I said and smiled at her.

She laughed. "Kelly, your own mom is a doctor. You would think you'd be more comfortable around them."

"Yes, you would think." I laughed as I walked out the door and shut it behind me. "Perhaps had you not been so critical of me, Mom," I said under my breath as I walked to my car and then smiled.

I checked in with the receptionist and updated all my information. I'd forgotten to bring a book, so I tried to find a magazine that I liked. There was nothing that I was in the mood to read. For some reason celebrity gossip didn't do it for me these days.

I tried my deep breathing technique. *I am. Relaxed. I am. Relaxed. I am. Relaxed. No, I'm not. This is ridiculous. I'm in the waiting room of the freakin' doctor's office. How can I be relaxed!*

I closed my eyes and started to try to focus on the music that was piped into the waiting room. I started kind of swaying my shoulders and bopping my head around a bit. I probably looked ridiculous, but I really didn't care because there weren't that many people waiting. Plus, it was helping some. "Kelly," the nurse said.

I stood up and followed her.

"Nice dance," she said.

I smirked. "Thanks."

She weighed me, took my temperature, blood pressure, and asked me a bunch of intake questions. The usual being, "Do you smoke?" "No." "Do you drink?" "Socially." "Drugs?" "No." "Are you pregnant?" "You're funny. No." She laughed. "How old are you?" "34."

She looked up at me. "Are you serious?" she said.

"Why? Do I look older?" I said.

"I thought you were going to say about 21."

"Are you serious?" I laughed.

"Yes, you must get that all the time."

"Not really." I thought for a second. "Well, people offer me student discounts sometimes, but I always just assume they're kidding."

"No, you seriously look like you're 21." She stood up.

"Thanks. You made my day!" She walked out of the room. "You need glasses, but you made my day," I mumbled and laughed.

Dr. Oliver walked in a few minutes later and shook my hand. "Hello, Kelly. How's your mom? Tell her I said hello."

"She's good and I will."

"What can I do for you today?" he said.

"Well, basically my left knee kills me when I walk on it too much."

"Kills you?"

"Yes, I think that's the technical term so I could be using it incorrectly."

"Okay, let me look at it, and we'll see if there is anything I can do for you."

He pulled out the leg rest and pushed around on my left knee and then my right knee—I assumed to compare and contrast the two.

"There is definitely something weird going on with this one." He wiggled it around a little bit. "Does it hurt when I do this?"

"Like hell!"

"Sorry about that. It feels like there's some fluid on it, and I think you need to see a specialist because they would know more about what's going on there than I would. I can recommend someone."

"That would be great."

"Anything else I can help you with today."

"Umm, can you help me with my writer's block? I'm under this tight deadline, and it's putting an extreme amount of pressure on me. Couple that with the fact that Sam left... you know?"

"Hmm." He crossed his arms and leaned back on the counter behind him. "Have you considered seeing a therapist?"

"I was sort of kidding."

"Well, all jokes aside, it may help to alleviate some of the stress and help with the writer's block. Would you like a referral for that as well?"

"I guess it couldn't hurt, right?"

"It may help," he said and smiled.

"Okay."

"When you check out, they'll get you the numbers for those two referrals. Give me a call if you need anything else, Kelly."

"I will. Thanks." He smiled at me and walked out. Aww, Kim was right. I did love my doctor. Why did I have to love every man who was nice to me?

I checked out, got the referral numbers, and went to get Evan.

"So what did Steven have to say?" my mom said.

"He asked about you and said hello, and he referred me out."

"He's sweet. I figured he would though. To whom?"

"I don't know. Some group. I have the number."

"Kelly, don't you care at all?"

I looked over at her to see if she was possibly serious or if it was just one of her normal over-the-top reactions. She was busy relacing and tying Evan's shoes and paying little attention to me and our conversation. "Not really, Mom. Slice and dice me. Poke me with needles. Whatever they need to do. Dr. Oliver made the referral, and I trust him implicitly."

Now she looked up at me to see where I was with the conversation. I had my eyebrows raised and was smiling at her. "Oh, Kelly, I'll never quite understand you."

"I know, Mom." I walked over and hugged her. "Can we keep it that way, please, and just agree to see things differently?"

"You know I'd love to, but I probably can't."

I held onto her shoulders for a second. "At least you're honest, Mom. I'll give you that."

"Grandma, can I take this home?" Evan walked over to us carrying a few toys.

"Are you going to bring them back? You know Grandpa likes to play with them."

He laughed. "You're funny. I'll bring them back next time."

"Okay then. Go ahead and take them. Hug your grandma goodbye. I love you so much, Evan."

"I love you so much too, Grandma." He gave her a bunch of kisses and a little piece of my heart melted. I swear when he was not driving me nuts, that boy was the most loving child ever created. How could Sam willingly walk away and miss out on seeing him every day? I mean, I know he wasn't leaving Evan, but maybe he was on some level since he wasn't trying to spend more time with him. Once a week for a short visit and every other weekend wouldn't have been enough for me. Wouldn't he have done everything in his power to make it work out with me to be a part of this?

Our marriage wasn't even that bad. We hardly ever fought, and we enjoyed each other's company and were happy quite often. Sam used to say, "Who has more fun than we do?!" The answer was, "Nobody!" But he'd left that. He left me and he left our family. I just couldn't imagine not being around Evan daily. I guess kids weren't for everyone…

"Are you okay, Kelly?" my mom said which pulled me away from my thoughts.

I looked at her and then nodded, and Evan and I headed home.

In the car my phone rang. It was Tom. "I actually forgot about you," I whispered, turned the radio on, and answered the phone. "Hello."

"Kelly," he said.

"Hey, Tom, how are you?"

"I'm good. I was just calling to say hello for a couple minutes."

"Oh, hello. I'm just driving back from picking up my son at my mom's—which is delightful for me since she's super critical of everything I do."

"Parents can be like that. It comes with the job."

"And here I had thought my mother was just a bitch. I had better apologize the next time I see her."

He laughed. "Oh, Kelly, Kelly, Kelly."

"Yes, Tom, Tom, Tom. Hey, do you play the drums?"

"Why do you ask?"

"When I said Tom-tom it made me think of it. I added the third

Tom just because you had with my name, but I could easily have stopped with the second and been thoroughly satisfied."

Again, he laughed. "I don't play the drums."

"Oh, bummer. That would have been classic."

"Kelly, you're so weird."

"Really? I'm weird?"

"Yeah," he paused. "I like it though. It's charming in a strange way."

I felt my cheeks warm. "So I'm almost home. I better get off the phone."

"Well, I've enjoyed this conversation, Weirdo."

"Yeah, me too, but honestly I couldn't even tell you what we talked about, Tom. Was I not paying attention, or did we just talk about pretty much nothing?"

"I don't know. Hey, do you want to get together again?"

Did I? Something inside me quickly thought *yes!* "I'd like that."

"Great. I'll call you sometime this weekend, and we can set something up."

"Sounds good. Bye." I hung up.

I glanced around and noticed that Evan had drifted off. I wondered why he had been so quiet. Normally, when I was on the phone, he hounded me. I opened the windows a bit and turned off the car.

I dialed Dana's number. "Hello?"

"Dana."

"Kelly."

"Guess what?"

"What?"

"Tom just called, and he asked me out again."

"Wait, Kelly, which one's Tom? The young guy, right?"

"Yes, but, oh yeah, the dating app hospital-janitor guy also asked me if I wanted to get together sometime, and for some reason—I think because his last message was really sweet—I said I did."

"Oh, yeah? Wait. Hospital janitor? I don't think you told me that part."

"Oh, well, that's just a theory I've been tossing around in my mind because of this vague answer he gave me when I asked him what kind of work he did in the hospital. But, yeah, he asked me out. I had sent him this rant about what a horribly dysfunctional person I am and how I call people cocks and walk into walls and some other stuff. I forget. But he just wrote back that he was having a bad day too and that he hoped I wasn't offended that he had laughed out loud at my message. Maybe he was just waiting for me to get real with him or something. I wish he would get real with me though instead of all the mystery about his job. 'I work in an office—when I'm not cleaning the bathroom.'"

She laughed. "Why are you stuck on the janitor thing? Maybe he's a doctor. Maybe he works in an office when he's not making rounds."

"If he were a doctor, he would say that." I reached over to the passenger floor and found a plastic bag that I started to gather up trash in.

"Or would he? Maybe he's a shy doctor. And he doesn't want people to ask him for medical advice."

"You're funny, Dana. And I hope he's not a doctor. I lived with a doctor for enough years. Let's just say that I've had enough of doctors."

"So you think janitor? What about hospital administrator or president?"

"Hmm. I hadn't thought of that."

"Think outside the box there, Kel."

I thought about it for a couple seconds. "No, I still think janitor. I kind of like the idea of him trying to seduce women on dating apps by telling them that he works in offices part of the time—but it's just cleaning and taking out the trash. To me... that's really funny."

"But I don't think someone who actually does that would put it that way. Do you?"

"I don't know. I'm twisted. You can't go by how I think, Dana. You know that. Anyway, I called to talk about Tom, not Dan."

"Yeah, the 20-year-old?"

"Twenty-five-year-old."

"Holy hell, that just blows my mind. Do you know what I was doing at 25?"

"I don't want to know what you were doing at 25, Dana." I used a sock of Evan's that I found to dust the dashboard.

"You really don't. So when are you going out?"

"I don't know. He's calling me this weekend to make plans."

"For this weekend?"

I stopped dusting. "I'm thinking no. Wouldn't that be too soon? Is that how people do it? God, I am too old for this guy if that's the case."

"I think you might be—even if it's not the case."

"Shut up! Oh, wait, this is priceless! The nurse at my PCP today said she thought I looked like I was 21. No lie… 21. No wonder Tom likes me."

"Really?" She laughed really loudly.

"Don't act so shocked!"

"No, I mean, you look young, but 21?"

"That's how I felt. I think she was exaggerating." I sat back in my seat and stopped fidgeting.

"How are you dressed?"

I looked down. Printed t-shirt, hoodie, khaki mini skirt, canvas sneakers. "Normal stuff I wear."

"You do dress young."

"Are you saying I dress inappropriately young?" I put my right hand on the steering wheel.

She laughed. "I might have just accidentally said that," she laughed some more. "But it looks good on you. You're lanky. You can pull it off," she paused. "So maybe now that I'm rethinking it all maybe I do agree with that nurse. Maybe you do look 21-ish. Even though I had never thought about it just because I sort of knew about how old you were. Maybe had I met you and you weren't with Evan. Was Evan with you?"

"No."

"See! That changes things," Dana said.

"You think?"

"Yeah, you see someone without kids, and they automatically look younger."

"You mean like my grandma?"

"No, Smart Ass, I mean like you!"

We both started laughing. "God, Dana, this conversation has degenerated into a good bit of nothing, so I'm going to wake Evan and go inside. I've been sitting in my driveway for a good five minutes now chatting about how young or old I do or don't look. If you want to walk on over and actually look at me in this outfit, that would be fine. Otherwise, I think we've pretty much killed this topic."

"Yeah, I think I'll just stay here and work for a bit. I mean, I'm sure you look cute as usual, but I've got some stuff to finish up before Greg gets home. But you know what? Send me a selfie if you really want me to see."

"I'll get right on that." I laughed. "I'll talk to you later. Thanks for the giggles." I waved to my next-door neighbor who was getting in her car.

"Yeah, you too." We hung up.

I twisted around to look at Evan. He was still sleeping and had slumped over to the right. I got out of the car and managed to scoop him into my arms. I wasn't going to be able to carry him like this for much longer. He definitely was not my baby anymore.

I kissed him on the nose, carried him inside, and put him on the couch. I was shocked that he barely woke up. My mom must have really worn him out—that and playing at the park earlier didn't hurt either.

I called Kim. Doug answered.

"Oh, hello, Doug," I said. "Where's my sister? And why are you answering her phone?"

He laughed. "She was washing her hands. She's right here."

"Can I speak to her? Hey, how are you, by the way?"

"Hey, by the way, thanks for asking," he laughed. "I'm good, Kelly. Meredith, please would you sit down in your chair?"

"Listen to how calm you are, Doug."

"Hold on. Here's Kim."

"What's up, Kelly?"

"I saw the doctor. I just figured you'd want the report." I walked into the kitchen.

"And…"

"Nothing much. He just referred me to two specialists."

"Two?"

"Yes, one for my knee because he thinks it looks funky. And one for my head because he thinks it will help to talk out my writer's block."

"Ahh, therapy. Great idea! I wish I'd thought of that. You should see if Dad knows him."

"I'd like to keep Dad out of it." I started filling a pot with water to boil macaroni noodles.

"Why?"

"I don't need Dad all in my business—getting all nosy and asking too many questions. Don't you remember growing up? 'So how does that make you feel?' 'Don't keep it all bottled up.' 'Blah, blah, blah.'"

"You and I did not have the same childhood experience."

"Dad never psychoanalyzed you?"

"I don't think so," Kim said.

"Well, then no, we didn't." I turned on a burner. "Anyway, Mom wasn't too bad today."

"Well, that's good, at least. Right?"

"Yep. Oh, wait. On the way home Tom called and asked me to go out again."

"How 'bout that!"

I could hear Doug asking Meri to use her fork. "It sounds like you guys are having dinner. I'll let you go."

"Okay. Thanks for the update."

Sam took Evan for a quick dinner. They were back home in about an hour. "He's super wound up today," Sam said as Evan bolted past me when he came in the front door.

"He took a nap too late and for too long," I said and shrugged.

"He's going to be hell to get to bed tonight," Sam said. "Good luck with that," he added as he headed toward the door.

So it looked like Sam wasn't even going to try. "You think?" I said to his back as he was opening the door.

Sam paused for a second with the door opened a couple inches. He turned and looked at me. "I'm not sure if you're acting more like a baby or a bitch."

His comment took me off guard for a second. He had a lot of nerve to talk to me like that—especially when he wasn't even asking if it was okay with me if he left early and didn't even try to put Evan to bed this evening. "Well, since babies don't usually put their own kids to bed, I would definitely go with bitch."

He raised his eyebrows and tilted his head a little. "What are you implying, Kelly?"

I felt my body start to shake, "Just leave, Sam. Get out of here." I didn't want this fight or whatever it was to escalate loud enough for Evan to hear it.

Sam stared at me for a couple seconds longer and then walked out and slammed the door.

I took a few deep breaths and sat on the couch. I stayed there until I stopped shaking and calmed down enough that I could interact with Evan without taking out my frustrations with his dad on him.

Evan ended up staying up until almost midnight—playing with toys in his room. Coming into my room. Telling me he was hungry and thirsty. Telling me he was scared. He had to go to the bathroom. He even came in and said he wanted to take another bath to relax. Now that was classic.

Finally, he wore me down, and I told him to crawl into bed with me. He ran back into his room for his favorite blanket, and then he crawled into bed and tucked himself in under the covers. He was asleep in a couple minutes and was sucking his thumb so loudly that I could hardly hear myself think. I appreciated the distraction because I'd been thinking about Sam and how disappointed I was in him.

Evan's thumb started to slip out of his mouth as his mouth opened in a deeper sleep, and just as it was about to fall out, he started sucking very vigorously and pulled it right back in. He rubbed the hand he wasn't sucking on the hand he was. He was a really passionate thumb sucker, and that made me love him even more. I had really loved sucking my thumb as a child too, so I had a soft spot in my heart for thumb suckers. I leaned over and kissed his hands and then his nose. "You are the sweetest boy, and I love you so much, Little Man," I said quietly.

I eventually fell asleep too.

ELEVEN

The Cup of Coffee

I dropped Evan at Kim's and decided to write at a coffee shop. I sat down with my coffee, opened my laptop, opened the document, and just sort of looked at the screen for a while. I started to wonder if anyone was wondering why I was just looking at my screen instead of typing and that made me start to feel self-conscious. I mean, why would anyone be looking at me? They wouldn't be, right? But thinking about it made me feel paranoid so I took a sip of coffee, put my hands on the keys, and started to type. *Once upon a time there was a writer who couldn't write. I guess couldn't isn't the correct word. She could write. She was damn good at it. But she just couldn't find the right words. My God, Kelly, you are pathetic for sitting here pretending that you're working.*

I shut my laptop with a flourish and picked up my coffee. Since I made eye contact with someone sitting across from me on one of the sofas, I rolled my eyes and said, "People drive me nuts." I don't know why I said that other than to pull off the whole typing madly and then shutting my laptop quickly skit I had just performed. It just sort of went with the character. Why was I playing a character?

"I know what you mean," she said and looked back at her magazine.

I put my laptop in my bag. "Honestly, I have no clue what I'm talking about." I picked up my coffee and stood up. "Enjoy your coffee," I said in her direction and walked out. I stood just outside

FLIRTING WITH A NEW LIFE

the door for a couple seconds and thought, *Could something interesting please happen to me?*

I decided to go to the library to write for a bit—what better place, right? I would be surrounded by books—that had been published. Maybe some creativity from them would rub off on me. I started to walk to my car.

"Kelly," I heard someone shout my name and turned to look.

Tom was running toward me.

That was fast.

"Hey, I thought that was you," he said.

"Hey, there. What are you up to?" I said. He stopped beside me and gave me a quick hug. "Oh, hi," I added.

"You look really pretty," he said.

I shook my head and laughed a little then reached up and touched my glasses. I hadn't expected a compliment like that when I'd put no effort into my appearance, and my mind went totally blank. It was like one of those scenes in a movie where the person clearly is trying to say something but no words come. So I just stood there with my mouth open until he saved me by saying, "What are you doing?"

Happy to have the subject changed from my looks, I snapped back to reality. "Um, I was trying to write. I didn't give it much effort and gave up. It was a pretty pathetic attempt, actually." I patted my bag with the laptop in it. "So I came out here hoping something interesting would happen that might inspire something."

He held out his hands and smiled (God, that smile), "And here I am."

"Don't flatter yourself." I patted him on the stomach. *Nice!* "Where were you headed?"

"I'm off today, so I was getting some coffee and taking it to my mom's house." He blushed a little and shrugged. "I do that when I get a day off sometimes."

"My God, you're sweet; aren't you? I hope to God my son wants to do that for me someday." I adjusted the strap of my bag on my shoulder. "Well, this was a pleasant surprise, Tom." I smiled at him. "I better let you go and get that coffee, and I'm gonna go to the…"

"Are you free tonight?" he said.

Again, I was rendered silent. On some level I was free—but I had Evan, and Tom should have asked me sooner if he wanted to see me tonight.

"That's rude. I'm sorry. I shouldn't have put you on the spot like that. It's just I work tomorrow—and pretty much all weekend, and I should have thought of it sooner."

"I, uh, already have plans for tonight anyway," I said and shook my head.

He looked at his feet and then back at me. "Fair enough. How about next week? I think I work all daylight. What works for you?"

I laughed and shrugged. "I mean, Wednesday is probably good," I said. "6:30ish?"

"Good. Yes, yes. Save it for me." He reached over and squeezed my hand, smiled at me, and then started jogging toward the coffee shop. "I'll call you Tuesday evening to confirm."

I nodded and waved my hand at him. I guess that would have to be something interesting enough for the moment.

The Library

I wasn't sure why I hadn't thought about working at the library sooner. It really seemed like it could be a really great place to work without too many distractions, and the drive was only about ten minutes from my house too.

I pulled into the parking lot and grabbed my bag. At least at the library I wouldn't feel like everyone was staring at me when I was looking at my computer.

I stood near the entrance and looked for a quiet spot. Normally, I'd have Evan with me, and he pretty much called all our library shots and led me right to the children's room. That didn't seem like the best location for a person without a child to sit alone.

I walked through the main floor for a bit and just kind of looked around. There were several people sitting at the computers. There were a few of those spaces open, but I didn't need a computer because I had my laptop. I walked around that area for a little bit though. There were some tables near the computers, but I felt like that area had the potential to be too distracting for me. I distracted extremely easily, and there were way too many people to look at. "Can I help you find something?" I looked to where the voice had come from and saw a woman pushing in a chair and picking up some scratch paper. She was smiling at me, so I assumed she was the person who had said that.

"I'm just looking for a quiet place to work." I pointed to the table that I was standing beside. "Do you have any other tables tucked away somewhere?"

"Sure, follow me." She led me into another room where there were several rows of tables and some with private cubicles around them. "This is our quiet study area. Do you think this would work for you?" She spoke in a much more quiet tone in this room.

"This looks perfect, thanks," I said and matched her hushed tone.

"My name's Julie. If you need any help, just let me know."

"Thank you. I'm Kelly."

She smiled at me and walked away.

I walked over to one of the empty tables, sat down, and looked around. There were about five other people in the quiet study area. They all seemed really focused on what they were doing. It was kind of inspiring on some level. I hoped that maybe some of their focus would rub off on me. I looked around some more and noticed the view out the window beside me. It was lovely. It looked out onto what looked like a community garden area. It was too soon for gardening, but I could tell that there were individual beds that were sectioned off with two by fours.

Someone wandered over to a standing computer and looked something up. He wrote something down onto a slip of paper and then headed into the bookshelf area. I kind of zoned out on that person for a little while before snapping back into the reality of why I was at the library and pulled my laptop out of my bag. I was here to write—not people watch. *Focus, Kelly.*

I highlighted what I had written at the coffee shop, shook my head, and deleted it. But nothing else was really coming to me. I started to re-read my book from the very beginning (for the 100 millionth time). It amused me that one of my main characters was named Julie. *Well, I guess we now know what happened to Julie after the book ends… She becomes a librarian.* It took so little to amuse me, but then I started to think that librarian Julie pretty much actually did fit the description of my character Julie with about 10 years added onto her.

Okay, so Julie becomes a librarian. How? Since I knew nothing about becoming a librarian, I pulled out my library card, logged into the Wi-Fi, and googled "how to become a librarian." I read about that for a while. I had no clue that you needed a master's degree to be a librarian. Maybe that wasn't my Julie's best career choice. I didn't see her going back to school any time soon. Since I was essentially creating her, I could make her do whatever I wanted her to do. So why not make her go back to school? Did I have the energy—or the knowledge—for all of that though?

I looked around at the people sitting near me again. The one man had a bunch of crumpled papers and tissues all around his table and on the floor, and I noticed he wasn't wearing his shoes—or his socks. *Gross!* The next person I focused on was a woman who maybe was a student or something. She seemed to be writing something, and I figured she was working on a paper. Maybe she was writing a book like me though. Well, I mean, she was actually writing, so she wasn't exactly like me. The man at the table closest to me was reading newspapers. He was older, and his hands shook as he turned the pages. He had Velcro sneakers on his feet. Julie walked back into the bookshelves with an older woman, but I couldn't see where they went. I thought it would be creepy if I followed them, so I stayed put. After about a minute Julie walked out alone. A few minutes later the woman walked out with a stack of books. I tried to notice what their subject was but couldn't so instead I noticed a man picking his nose and wiping his fingers on the table. *Are you kidding me?* I was pretty sure I didn't want my character Julie to have to deal with this stuff. I was kind of grossed out and, to be honest, was way more distracted here than I ever had been at home.

I read through a little bit more of my story, and then after a while I packed up my laptop. I started to walk back toward the entrance and noticed a desk that I hadn't really seen before even though I had walked right past it. Julie was sitting there typing something. "Thanks again," I said to her.

"You're welcome. Have a good day." She seemed really friendly, so I stopped at her desk.

"This is an interesting crowd," I said.

She giggled a little bit, and I felt like she knew what I meant.

"I never knew you needed a master's degree to be a librarian," I said.

"Nobody knows that," she gestured with her hand, "well, except for librarians. Everyone's always shocked. Are you thinking about becoming a librarian?"

"I was doing research for a book I'm writing."

"A book about librarians?" she said and squinted her eyes.

I felt my cheeks get warm as I realized how stupid this was going to sound. "Not really. I have writer's block, and one of my main characters is named Julie. So I started to think about what would happen if I turned her into, well, you."

"Oh," she said and laughed again.

"That sounded creepier than it was meant to sound." I thought about the guy with no shoes and the one wiping boogers on the table, and I figured she must be thinking that I fit right in with this odd crowd. "Hey, have a good day."

"Thanks. If you have any questions about being a librarian, let me know." I could hear that she had started typing again as I was walking away.

The Boop

After I picked up Evan at Kim's, we did a whole bunch of nothing—especially since I had blown all my fun money Kim had allotted me pretty much for the month on a half-day zoo trip and a new rug. It was totally unfair. When Sam had Evan, it was like he was on a mini vacation. They would go bowling, to the movies, out to dinner. All these fun things that I couldn't afford to do with him. The most fun activity that I could do with Evan was walk over to the park or drive over to the mall and people watch.

I wondered what it felt like to get to be the fun parent. I pictured Evan and me bowling, him getting a strike or a spare and running over to give me a hug. It must have been awesome to be the fun parent.

I looked at Evan who was sitting on the couch beside me with a bowl of pretzels and was watching his shows. I put my finger on his chest. "You got something there." He looked down and, "boop," I got his nose.

He laughed and blew some mushy pretzels out of his mouth at which I laughed.

"Let me try that," he said.

So we sat there doing that back and forth to each other for about five minutes. See. I could be a fun parent too. Who needed money?

I wondered how Sam could willingly miss out on all this quality family time. Maybe these thoughts were a bit sarcastic. After all, he had left early last night—probably in time to head out with his friends. And Evan hadn't heard from him since. Did Sam even remember that he had a son today? Did he even care?

It made me feel so mad. And it made me even angrier with myself that I allowed Sam's actions to rattle me so much. But I mostly just wished that he would take more responsibility when it came to Evan. There was more to rearing a child than the financial stuff. I mean, thank God he was good about the financial stuff. But Evan needed his time too. Evan needed his phone calls. Evan needed his visits—not abbreviated versions of them either. Evan needed his dad not to cancel on him when his dad was expected. The look on Evan's face when I had to tell him that his dad had left early or had canceled all together always broke my heart and made me hate Sam a little more each time. Evan deserved better.

After I put Evan to bed, I opened my dating app and then opened a message from Dan. *Kelly, how do we go about meeting? Well, I guess there's the normal way where we pick a location and then we show up at a certain time. Would that work for you? Do you want to know anything else about me first? Or do you want to save it for face-to-face conversation? Dan*

I hit reply, *Dan, Okay, pick a location. I'm pretty open, but I book up fast so you may want to get on my calendar ASAP. As for wanting to know more about you? Hmm. I guess I'm wondering when you're at work, do you sit at a desk? Kelly*

I got him on the desk question! No janitor would sit down in the office, right?

I opened my book and started to work on it a bit—or rather I tried to. All I really could focus on was how Dan was going to answer that question. I almost wished that I hadn't asked. It would have been better to just wait until we meet and decide from there—bring it up in the "face-to-face conversation." Face-to-face... That felt a little scary. Did I want to see that face in person? Did I want to go from dating one man that I wasn't sure I even wanted to date to dating two men I wasn't sure I wanted to date. And that whole situation with Sam calling me a bitch or a baby was really pissing me off too. I needed to call that therapist and that specialist first thing in the morning.

But getting back to Dan, how could you tell if someone was a janitor from just sitting across a table from him? I wasn't sure it was possible in normal, street clothes. I mean I'd be shocked if he came right from "the office" in his work jumpsuit—complete with a badge that read, "Dan Lastname, Janitor." Work uniforms typically weren't first date attire—at least they weren't when I recently googled it. They especially weren't if you wanted a second date. And as much as I really, really wanted to know, I couldn't picture myself coming right out and asking what his job was with him being so secretive about it all. Why was he being so secretive about it all?

I saved the three sentences that I had written in the two hours that I'd stared at the computer since sending my message to Dan and went to bed. Maybe if I got up early and worked, my brain would feel fresher.

TWELVE

The Scheduling

I actually did wake up early. Or maybe I never really slept much. But I was in the living room with my laptop by 6:45 a.m. I was even showered, dressed, and ready for the day. As I sat down, Lisa texted me to ask when I wanted to come over that weekend. I replied that I would get back to her as soon as I knew my schedule.

I had an email from Evan's teacher with several adorable photos of him playing at preschool with his friends. I stared at the pictures for a few minutes and thought about how much I loved him, and then I opened three emails from my mother reminding me to call the specialist about my knee. I'm not lying. There were three! As I finished reading the third, I got a text from Kim telling me that Mom had called and asked her to help remind me to make an appointment. "They don't trust me at all."

I replied to Kim, *Consider it done!* I ignored the emails from my mother, but she knew I would. She harassed me. I ignored her. It was the way we interacted.

Then I opened the dating app. And there was a message from Dan. *Kelly, Are you free on Sunday for brunch at Tucker's at 10:30 a.m.? If that doesn't work, I can try to figure something else out. I want to get on your schedule before you're booked! I hear that happens quickly. Dan*

"Oh, my," I whispered.

I googled Tucker's. It was a new restaurant on Carson Street, so I hit reply. *Dan, Sunday should work out great for me. I'll see you at 10:30 a.m. at Tucker's (on E. Carson St., right?). I'm looking forward to meeting you in person. Kelly*

"Looks like I'm meeting the janitor. Yikes." I put my face in my hands and took a few breaths. I stared at my laptop for about 45 minutes and then got Evan up and off to school. At least he had been in a fairly good mood.

Driving home I started to question my whole date with Dan. I mean, part of me was excited and part of me was scared to death. He was a widower. For some reason that was really freaky to me. How can you even get over something like that? Not that the relationship would end up going anywhere, but if it did, could I ever get past the thought that I was only with him because his wife had died. Like does he still have pictures of her around the house? I mean, why wouldn't he? But how will his next wife feel about that? Is it weird for your husband to look at a picture of the deceased wife on his nightstand before turning out the lights at bedtime?

And the fact that I had distorted his whole job situation out of proportion in my twisted brain was just... I don't know. I was afraid I might ask him for advice on cleaning products. "Oh, my God! Do I even really want to meet this guy?" And was I actually ready to be dating—even casually? Even though it had been almost a year since Sam had left, on some level going out with someone else made me feel like I was cheating on Sam. I knew I wasn't, but that whole "until death parts us" vow... It messed with my mind sometimes. I needed to call that therapy referral. I pulled into the driveway and got the numbers for the referrals out of my purse. I figured if I made the calls right there in the car, I wouldn't have time to chicken out and procrastinate and push the calls back.

I called the number for the specialist first. I expected to have to wait a while to see a specialist, but because of a cancellation right before I called, I got an appointment for Monday morning. I questioned for a moment whether my mother had had a hand in that, but I knew that likely wasn't possible. The call to the therapist went to voicemail, "Hi, this is Kelly Ramsey. I, um, I guess I wanted to schedule an appointment if you're taking new patients." I left my number and hung up.

I texted Kim. *My appointment's on Monday. Yes, 3 days from now. Please tell Mom.*

I went inside and sat down in my office. But as my butt hit the chair, I felt my heart start to race. This writer's block was becoming ridiculous. There was no way I was going to finish the book in six months—closer to five months really.

I decided that I needed to just write, and it didn't really matter a whole lot what I wrote. I just needed to sit down and get words on paper. I could edit out the garbage later. Since I assumed most of it would be garbage, I'd have a lot of editing to do. But I just needed some quantity to work with. Maybe I could turn the quantity into quality in the editing process.

In theory it sounded good. But I couldn't get started with the typing part. As usual, I started reading and read what I had written up to that point.

It was okay.

I had once thought it was good.

But now, eh, it was getting demoted to okay. Maybe I was just getting bored with each read through. And since there wasn't much writing going on and only 60 or so pages, there were a lot of read throughs.

I went into my room and looked in the mirror. "What the hell is wrong with you?" I said.

I stared at myself for a while and picked up a brush. I turned on the hair straightener and played with my hair for a while. I tried a new eye shadow and added some blush and lipstick. Then I picked up the phone and called Dana. She'd know what to say.

"Yell-ow."

I laughed. "Why does that always work?"

"What's up," she said.

"Same old same old. I can't write, but I need to."

"Then give up," she said.

I laughed because that wasn't what I'd expected her to say.

"Give up and get a job," she added.

I let out my breath. "I wish I could." I sat on my bed.

"Why can't you?"

Why couldn't I? "Because I'd never forgive myself," I said.

"So hang up the phone and write something."

I looked in the mirror and hardly recognized myself. It was a smaller (albeit more made up) version of who I used to be. "Okay, I will," I said quietly.

"Call me when you've written something you're proud of."

We said good-bye. I hoped I'd be able to call her again at some point before I died. I got up off the bed, went into the bathroom to wash my face, and then walked back into my office.

I picked Evan up at school and brought him home for lunch. "How much longer do I have to do this school thing?" he asked as we walked through the front door.

"What?" I said.

"How much longer do I have to keep going to school again, and again, and again?" He flopped on the couch.

"Cramping your style a little, is it?"

He nodded.

"What would you rather be doing?"

"Watching my shows."

"You don't want to end up living with me all your life." I walked into the kitchen.

"Yes, I do!" He followed me.

"So grilled cheese or peanut butter and jelly?"

"That depends," he sat down, put his elbows on the table, and rested his chin in his hands.

I sat across from him and mirrored him. "On what?"

He was trying not to smile. "Is there tomato soup?"

"Yes. Does that mean you want peanut butter?"

"Mom!" He sat back in his chair and wrinkled his nose. "That would be disgusting!"

"I'm onto you," I stood up and got a can of tomato soup from the cupboard and a can opener from the drawer. I put them in front of him. "Here. See if you can figure that out."

I got out the cheese, bread, butter, and a pot and pan and started fixing the sandwiches. "How're you coming with that can of soup?"

"Voila," he said and handed me the opened can.

"Good job, Ev." I handed him the pot. "Make yourself useful."

For some reason that cracked him up. "Make yourself useful," he chimed and laughed as he dumped the soup in the pot.

My phone rang.

I handed him a spoon. "Here. Stir this." I fished my phone from my purse. It was Lisa. "Hello."

"Kelly, my long-lost friend!"

"Hey, there. How've you been?"

"Oh, just dandy. You know how it goes. Keeping my girls happy. Keeping my man happy," she paused. "It's exhausting."

"Must be."

"Did you get your schedule figured out? Are you coming over this weekend or what?"

I had momentarily forgotten about our loose plans. "Um, how about tomorrow?" I flipped the sandwiches and gave Evan the thumbs up on his soup stirring skills.

"Evan's with Sam?"

I glanced at Evan. "Yeah."

"Bummer. Okay, well, you wanna come around five, and we can have dinner and some time to hang with the girls before they go to bed?"

"Sounds good. I'll see you then."

"Later," she said, and we hung up.

"This smells so good!" Evan squealed.

"You're a good cook." I kissed him on the top of the head. "I think it's ready. Have a seat."

I put the food in front of him and sat down.

"Voila," he said again.

I laughed. "Let's eat, so that I can get some work done on my book."

"Aren't you done with that yet?" He dipped his sandwich into his soup and took a bite.

I rolled my eyes. "I so wish, Evan."

"Me too," he said.

"Maybe after lunch I'll finish it."

"Good!"

If only it was that easy.

The Call Back

After lunch, getting Evan settled with a craft, and getting me settled in my office, I heard my phone ring—oddly enough it wasn't anywhere near me.

Then I heard Evan's voice say, "Hello."

I stood up. "Evan?"

I heard his muffled voice.

"Oh, good lord." I went to find him.

He was sitting on the couch with his legs crossed, and he was scratching his head with the opposite hand he was holding the phone.

"Evan, who are you talking to?"

He looked up at me and smiled. "Oh, hi, Mommy."

"Who is that?" I sat beside him.

"Some lady." He leaned his head on my shoulder. "She's nice."

I kissed him on the top of his head and took the phone, "Hi, this is Kelly."

"Hi, Kelly, this is Brynn Allen."

The name didn't ring a bell.

"I'm returning your call," she continued. "You left me a message this morning about coming in for an appointment."

Oh, the therapist. "Hi, sorry about my son. I didn't realize he had my phone."

"No worries at all. He's a sweetheart. I am taking new patients. When would you like to come in?"

"What about next Wednesday morning? My son has school from nine to 11:30 a.m."

She paused for a second, and I assumed she was looking at her schedule. "I have a 10 o'clock open. Would that work?"

"That would be perfect." I walked to the kitchen and jotted it on the wall calendar.

"Do you know where my office is?"

"Yes, my doctor gave me your information. I'll see you next Wednesday at 10 a.m."

"Great! Wait in the reception area, and I'll come out for you. Thank you, Kelly." We hung up.

I looked out the window into the backyard for a while and then started to make a cup of tea. "Maybe this will help." I put the teabag in my mug. "God, I hope so."

After drinking my tea, I sat in my office for a while. Mostly I alternated between spinning on my desk chair and looking out the window at the street. Sometimes I got caught up in the idea that there were people—families—living in all these houses around me just doing their own thing in their own houses while Evan and I were just doing our thing in our house. And then I would start to mentally zoom out above the house and street and the town and even further. And I'd think about how tiny we all were in the grand scheme of things.

I'd start to think about all the people I was connected with. Then I'd place them in their houses on my mental map. And I'd always end up thinking about how somewhere—in another house in another town not too far away—a man lived without me, a man who used to live with me in my house. "Shit," I said quietly. "I don't wanna have to see that man this evening."

I still couldn't believe he had called me a bitch. He definitely was not the same man who had married me. How could someone change so drastically? I thought people didn't really change all that much. Had he always been this mean, and I just hadn't noticed? I shook my head and shrugged.

Eventually, I took Evan for a walk. He was always up for doing something—if he wasn't too into his shows at that moment. We ended up at Dana's house. Evan could hear Pepper barking, "Do you think we should say hello to her?" he asked me.

I knew he meant Pepper and not Dana and that sort of made me giggle. "Do you want to say hello to her?"

He nodded.

"Okay, go ring the bell."

He ran ahead to ring the doorbell, and I bent over to pick up her newspaper.

Dana opened the door and was holding Pepper back by the collar. "Hey, Ramseys," she said. "This is a nice surprise."

"Peppy!" Evan squealed. He loved that dog.

I laughed a little. "I hope we're not interrupting too much."

"Just work. I can take a short break." She opened the door for us, and we went inside.

Evan rolled around on the living room floor with Pepper while Dana and I went into the kitchen. "I scheduled an appointment with the therapist and the knee specialist for next week."

"Oh, that's good," she handed me a glass of lemonade.

"Oh, and I'm meeting Dan on Sunday." I sat at her table.

"The janitor?" She took a drink.

"Yep. I figured what the hell. We probably have a lot in common since all I do is clean my house instead of writing these days."

"You're so bad. He's probably not a janitor, you know." She leaned against the counter.

"Nah, I'm pretty convinced he is. That and I'm going out with Tom on Wednesday night. How the hell did I suddenly get to be so popular?"

"I have no clue! You make my life look pretty boring. That's for sure."

"I'd trade you in a second—well, if I could bring Evan with me."

"You got a crush on Greg now too?"

"May-be," I said slowly.

"Maybe you can squeeze him in for Saturday night if that's still open. I'd like some time to myself." She winked at me.

Evan walked into the kitchen with Pepper by his side. "You have lemonade, Dana?"

"Always," she said and got him a glass.

He sat at the table, and Dana handed him a glass and grabbed Pepper so that she would leave Evan alone to drink it.

"When you're finished with that, we need to let Dana get back to work," I said.

"You probably need to get back to work too, Kelly," she said.

I closed my eyes. "Don't remind me. Technically, I shouldn't be talking to you yet, but Evan wanted to see Pepper."

"Blame the kid." She tousled Evan's hair. "You're always welcome here, kiddo! Pepper and I love to see you—Greg too, but he's never home."

"Are you talking to your friend today, Dana?" Evan said to her.

She laughed. "No, not today. I'm listening to the recording of when we did talk though." She winked at him.

He nodded at her and smiled. "I like to listen to you talk! Mommy plays it for me sometimes when we're folding clothes."

She laughed.

"It's true," I said. "We love to do chores with Dana and Lauren."

Dana shook her head, "I still don't completely understand how so many people find our stories fascinating, but, hey, I'm glad they do."

"Oh, my God! You two are a hoot! Even Evan gets a big kick out of the stories."

He nodded his head and got off the chair to play with Pepper again, "I do!"

"My famous friend!" I winked at her.

"My famous friend," she said back at me.

I crossed my fingers and held them up at her.

We left about 10 minutes later and went home. Evan put on his shows, and I went up to my office. I actually did write—a little bit. More than usual anyway, so that was a step in the right direction.

Then I got Evan's weekend bag packed and waited for Sam to arrive while I tried to make some dinner—which was pretty slim pickings. I desperately needed to get some groceries.

Sam was running late, so Evan was sitting and waiting on his suitcase by the front door. Finally, I heard a car pull up and saw Sam walking toward the door. "He's here, Ev," I said.

Evan squealed and jumped to his feet. He opened the door, "Daddy!"

"Hey, Bud, is that your bag?" he said and grabbed it. "Say goodbye to your mother, and I'll be in the car waiting for you."

Oh, okay, that's how we're going to play it now. The man who called me a baby or a bitch couldn't even come in to say hello.

Evan ran over toward me and said, "Bye, Momma!"

I scooped him into my arms as he tried to dash away, "Wait a second, Kiddo!" I kissed him several times on the cheeks and neck. "You're not getting away from me that easily!" I kissed him some more and he giggled. "I need to get all my weekend kisses in before you leave." I winked at him.

"Okay, Mommy, I gotta go."

I let go of him. "Okay, Sweetheart. I'll see you on Sunday."

"Not if I see you first!" He said loudly and ran to the door.

"I love you," I said as he slammed the door.

A second later the door opened, and Evan popped his head back in. "I love you too!" He smiled and gave me a thumbs up, and then he shut the door.

The Grocery Store

I grabbed my purse and walked out to the car. We needed groceries and I figured Friday evening would be less crowded than Saturday morning. I hated the grocery store almost as much as I hated Sam at that moment. That thought made me laugh as I buckled my seatbelt.

The whole situation graduated from bad to worse when I realized they had changed the whole store layout again, and all the food had been rearranged. This would not be a quick trip anymore. I had to go down every aisle and look for the things that I normally could easily find. There used to be a nice organic foods section in the front of the store, but they had since moved that a couple of changes ago. I still wasn't able to find some of the things I used to pick up there. I had given up the idea of ever eating another veggie dog. "God, I hate this place," I said as I was doubling back to look for bread for the second time. "You're killing me!"

"That seems a bit harsh," I heard someone say.

I hadn't realized that I was talking so loudly. If I were being totally honest, I hadn't realized that I was talking out loud at all. *Whoops!* I turned my head in the direction of the voice.

A man who looked to be my age, give or take 10 years (since I could be a horrible judge of age), was smiling at me. "Please tell me that you know where the bread is," I said.

"I just got some one aisle back." He tilted his head in the direction he meant.

"You're a lifesaver." I pushed my shopping cart in the direction of his head tilt. "Thank you. I hope to repay the favor at some point." I started to walk away. "I know where toilet paper is. Let me know if you need some!" I called back to him.

I heard him laughing as I walked down the next aisle.

"Bread! Amazing. See. It pays to talk out loud to yourself."

I finally made my way to the cash registers and scanned the lines for my favorite cashier. "Bingo!" I saw him and pulled into his line.

That boy was absolutely adorable. He was so fast and friendly, and he had fantastic customer service skills. I knew he was going to be something big at some point. I hoped he was in college and that this was just his part-time job, but I really didn't know for sure. His line moved quicker than any other line—again, he was fast. He scanned the food like he was always 20 minutes late for the next place he was going. But at the same time, you didn't feel rushed— more like he cared enough about your time to get you out as quickly as possible after being lost in the chaos of the ever-changing store for the past hour. I loved that kid!

And since I picked his aisle each time, he'd gotten to know me too.

"Hi, Kelly, how are you?" He greeted me when it was my turn. I kept telling him my name each time until he finally started using it.

"Hi, Jonathan. You're a breath of fresh air at the end of this maze. Why do they keep changing the store layout?"

"You're not the first person who's complained about that." Despite our conversation, he never slowed his pace as he scanned my food.

"Well, when you get used to your bread being in a certain spot and you can't find it, it sorta makes you feel a little crabby!"

"I'm sorry. I'll let my manager know," he paused as he finished up my order. "A hundred fourteen thirty-three."

He handed me the receipt and smiled genuinely, "Have a wonderful day, Kelly."

"You too, Jonathan."

God, I loved that kid!

In the parking lot I heard, "You look a lot less annoyed." It was the same guy from earlier.

I smiled. "Fresh air," I said, but really it was the whole Jonathan checkout experience. Again, customer service was key.

THIRTEEN

The Visit with Lisa

Saturday I got out of bed and cleaned my house. There wasn't really anything that needed to be cleaned. But I gave the house a quick once over just to kill some time. Then I showered and made some cookies that I was going to take to Lisa's later.

Around 3:30 I got a text from Tom, *Why don't you come and buy a rug or something? Work is way more exciting when pretty strangers flirt with me.*

I replied, *Can't. I'm headed out soon. And since I'm no longer a stranger, it would lose some of the excitement, but hang in there. Maybe you'll get lucky and someone else will need some assistance with her purchases.*

I went up to my office and opened my document. There was about an hour to work until I needed to leave. I re-read the end. Why had I thought I could turn this short story into something more? I think I had an idea about where I wanted to go with it when I applied for the grant. But now I was so distracted, and I truly couldn't remember what that idea had been or if I already unsuccessfully tried it out.

Maybe I needed to pick a character I'd mentioned earlier but hadn't gone into any details about and give that person a story. Maybe that would work. So I spent the next 45 minutes skimming for a minor character I liked enough to focus the majority of the rest of the novel on.

Was this stupid?

I saved and closed my document and left for Lisa's.

On the drive there I decided to call Kim. "I'm headed to Lisa's for dinner. How are you guys?"

"We're good. Just hanging out. Meri's twirling—you know she loves a good twirl."

"Full skirt, must twirl. I know the feeling, Girl!"

"Exactly," Kim laughed. "Oh, wait! Mom's thrilled that you scheduled with the specialist. She called me three times yesterday to see if I knew any more details."

I laughed. "By the way, I love that she calls you all day long. Actually, she sent me, like, three emails yesterday. Can we please sit down with her and teach her how to text?" I laughed. "And why am I the email daughter, and you're the phone daughter?"

"Duh, because you don't answer your phone when she calls."

"Well, that's true I guess."

"Yeah, she gave up calling you. She told me that a while ago—probably on the phone when she and I were actually talking."

"Okay, so let's teach her how to text."

"You try," Kim said.

"Okay, so I have another first date tomorrow."

"Wow, Kelly, look at you!"

"Yeah, you're getting me out there whether I wanna be out there or not. I'm still deciding. But here I am… out there!"

"Is this the guy from the dating app or did you happen upon another stranger in your travels?"

I laughed. "Yeah, it's the hospital janitor guy."

"So where are you meeting? And what time, so I can check on

you if you don't turn up later."

"Because every man on dating apps is a serial killer? Great, you didn't tell me that," I laughed. "You watch too much true crime."

"I know. But Keith Morrison can make any story six million times more intriguing."

I laughed. "We're meeting at Turner's. I think he said 10:30. We're having brunch."

"Well, I can't wait to hear how that goes."

"Yeah, me too. I dunno. I'm not super excited about it so it makes it sort of chill on my part—which is good. I stressed myself out too much about my first date with Tom. Oh, and by the way, I'm seeing him again on Wednesday for dinner."

"Wow, you're really leaning into this dating thing."

"You told me to!"

"I know. I'm teasing. It's all good. No matter what happens, it's practice and it's giving you something to focus on other than Sam being a jerk."

"You know me so well. Because truly that's all I obsess about anymore. Even on the first date with Tom, Sam actually popped into my head, and I asked Tom about the last person he was in love with."

"Kelly!"

"I know! It was a bad move."

"You think? Alright, Lady, Doug is needing my assistance assembling his new plant stand."

"Oh, God! Another plant stand? That man loves his foliage!"

"Yes, and yes! Hey, check in with me after the date tomorrow, okay?"

"Yes, Ma'am! Later, Kim."

A couple minutes later I pulled into Lisa's driveway, grabbed the cookies from the backseat, and headed to the door. "Mommy, Kelly's here," Olivia's voice called from the front door.

"Let her in," Lisa called back.

Olivia opened the door for me. "Hey, Olivia! How are you?"

She smiled at me and nodded.

"You're so helpful. Look at you being the greeter." I bent over and kissed her on the cheek. "I made you and your sisters some cookies."

I handed her the plate. "Thank you. They look so good," she said and carried them to the kitchen. I followed her.

"Mommy, Kelly made some cookies for me and Julia and Jenn."

Lisa was standing by the stove. She turned and smiled at Olivia. "Oh, wow! Put them on the table. Did you thank her?"

Olivia nodded big.

"Good. Did you want to go back outside and play with the girls and Daddy for a little bit before we eat?" Lisa asked her.

She did a little twirl so that her dress spun out around her and headed for the back door.

"Stinkin' cute!" I whispered.

"She's been so excited for you to get here that she stood by the door watching for about 20 minutes." Lisa took a casserole out of the oven and walked into the dining room with it. "She was hoping that Evan would come too."

"I know. I need to bring him. All he and I do is sit around and watch TV when it's my weekend with him. Coming here would be way more entertaining for him."

"Next week then," Lisa said as she finished setting the table.

"That could work," I said. "Oh, wait a minute. I'm going to my friend Holly's wedding on Saturday."

"Aw, I remember Holly. She's getting married?"

I nodded.

"That's sweet. Congratulations to her."

I rolled my eyes.

"What?" Lisa said. "Is she marrying an asshole or something?" Lisa handed me a dish to carry to the table.

"No, Bill's great. I'm just," I paused. "I'm just not sure I'm ready to go to a wedding." I set the dish on the dining room table and looked at Lisa. "Is that weird?"

She rubbed my arm for a couple seconds and shook her head. "No," she said and hugged me. She held on really tight for several seconds. "I can't even imagine what you've been going through, Kelly. If Phil left me… I just don't know if I could survive that."

I closed my eyes and didn't say anything. I had always thought the same thing about Sam, and somehow I was surviving it. You figure it out when you don't really have a choice.

She let go of the hug and smiled at me. She took a deep breath and walked to the back door. "Come on in," she called to her family. "Time to wash your hands for dinner."

Olivia came skipping in the door and over to the sink. She was followed by Phil, who was carrying Jennifer, and Julia, who was carrying a few cups. Phil walked over toward me. "Kelly," he said and hugged me and kissed my cheek. I kissed Jennifer while she was still in his arms.

"How are you two?" I said and tickled Jenn on the neck.

She pushed my hand away and giggled. She reached out her arms toward me. "Hud," she said.

"Absolutely!" I took her into my arms and squeezed her while walking her to the sink so she could wash her hands. "Let's get you all cleaned up so we can eat." I leaned over toward Julia who was drying her hands. "How've you been, Jules?"

She rolled her eyes and flipped her hair behind her shoulder. "Exhausted!" She sighed deeply.

I almost burst out laughing as I held Jennifer over the sink and turned on the water. "How so?"

She did a big gesture with her hands. "These kids! They're exhausting!"

"Ah, I see. You're helping mom and dad with them?"

"Yes," she paused. "Too much."

"Sounds like you either need a raise or a break!" I pulled the towel from the rack so Jennifer could dry her hands. She threw the towel at Julia and laughed.

"See what I mean?" Julia said.

I rubbed her shoulder. "I understand. Let's eat."

We walked to the dining room.

The meal was fantastic. Lisa's food always was! Baked macaroni and cheese, steamed spinach, a pear and walnut salad, homemade rolls, and apple crisp for dessert.

Afterward the girls went outside to play while Lisa and I watched them from the back porch. Phil stayed inside to clean the dishes.

Lisa and I got caught up on life.

"So it sounds like you've been super busy since the last time I saw you. Maybe call and catch me up next time instead of keeping it all for when you visit." She laughed.

"Okay, yes. I've been a little distracted and out of touch. I get it."

"Here's my two cents for what they're worth." She raised her eyebrows. "You don't seem all that excited about the date tomorrow. And you seem lukewarm about the second date on Wednesday." She paused and took a sip of her wine. "I think you're dating the wrong men."

"I mean," I shrugged. "I think you're onto something. Kimmy calls them practice dates for the right man."

"Okay, so I agree with that on some level. But when the right man comes along, I don't think you'll need the practice. It'll just all naturally fall into place."

"Hmm."

"I mean, I hate to bring up an asshole, but remember when you started to date Sam?"

I thought about that for a few seconds and then blinked my eyes a few times. I squeezed them tight for a couple seconds and then nodded. "Yeah, I see what you're saying. Everything just kind of fit."

"Yep, like a puzzle. These two guys are from the wrong box." She shifted in her seat. "I mean, go out with them again to be sure. Whatever. It's already scheduled. I get it. The one guy is gorgeous. The other guy's mysterious. But I don't think you'll be calling me with any love stories next week."

I didn't say anything, but I knew she was right.

I left before the girls went to bed. I had an early morning, and I wanted to make sure I was rested and ready.

FOURTEEN

The Second First Date

So Dan and I met for brunch at what turned out to be this really nice restaurant. I was shocked at the location. By that point, I'd convinced myself that Dan had to be a janitor. Why else wouldn't he tell me what he did? I was pretty sure a janitor couldn't afford this place, so I was feeling confused as I looked for a parking spot.

After I found a spot, I looked at my outfit—black canvas China doll shoes, a jean skirt, my *Isn't life great?* T-shirt, and a black zip hoodie in case I was chilly (pretty much the same outfit recycled from my first date with Tom only a little more casual with the sweatshirt hoodie instead of sweater because it was brunch—but this place was way fancier than Anthony's). *Lovely.*

"This'll sure impress him!" But it was too late to go home and change, so I got out of the car, adjusted myself, and walked toward the restaurant.

Dan was standing inside the entrance waiting for me. At least I assumed it was Dan because he was smiling at me, and there was something in his eyes that was familiar from his photo. But, my God, he was gorgeous!

He was taller than I was expecting him to be—at least as tall as Tom and maybe even a little taller than that. His dark brown hair was styled back and to the left. He had big brown eyes that had been hidden in his photos by those glasses, full lips on a large mouth, and a large nose that didn't seem too large because all his features were big. He had a very pronounced jawline and nice cheekbones. If I were a cartoon, my eyes would have popped right out of my head and hit him in the face, and my heart would have burst out of my chest and started beating like a drum—for real! He was that good looking.

The upper hand that I had anticipated having—given his occupation as janitor and his looks as being so-so from the photos plus me being only lukewarm on the whole idea of dating him—had totally vanished. He was wearing a navy button-down shirt, khaki pants, and loafers. And they weren't just loafers. They were the kind that looked like they had cost him a small fortune. Casual but nice enough for this place. God, I felt like such an oaf! He smiled at me, "Kelly?"

"Yeah," my voice cracked and was barely above a whisper.

He reached his hand out to me.

"Nice to meet you." His voice was deep and melodic.

I put my hand in his. "I'm so underdressed. I've never been here. I didn't realize."

He shrugged his shoulders. "You look cute, Kelly. Don't worry about it. It's brunch." He pointed to my chest. "Yes. It is."

It took me a few seconds to realize that he was responding to *Isn't Life Great?* I didn't laugh. I think I just stared at him—I hoped it was with my mouth shut, but truly who knows.

"As for this place," he said, "it just opened. I read about it in the paper last week and figured we could give it a try and see if it's any good to recommend to our friends. Wanna be a guinea pig with me?" He winked, and I felt a little bit better.

I nodded my head. "Sure."

He went to the hostess and put his name in. I was curious to hear what it was—since we hadn't exchanged last names yet. But he only said Dan.

We got our table right away since we were one of the first parties in the restaurant, but no one came to take our order for a good 10 minutes. So we sat and sipped on our water and tried to chat. I was so nervous—again, his stunning good looks had really thrown me for a loop, and I felt very much like a schoolgirl. Back to the whole *penis having the ultimate power over me* thing. My mom, the feminist, would've been so disappointed in me.

Finally a waitress came over and asked us what we wanted to eat. Of course, it would have been helpful if I'd been looking at the menu. We started by telling her that we wanted some coffee, and we immediately knew that there was going to be a problem. I think "Can I take your order?" may have been the only English that she knew.

"Coffee?" she said—as if she wasn't quite sure what we meant.

"Yes, two coffees," Dan said and pointed to the word in the menu. Thank goodness he was on top of this. "Kelly?"

"Um, I'll have," I quickly scanned the menu. "Pancakes and hash browns."

Dan found what I wanted and pointed to it on the menu, so the waitress could see. She was nodding and writing. "And I'll have the same."

She squinted her eyes at him.

"Two orders of the same thing." He held up two fingers and

pointed to it again. "Pancakes and hash browns. Bring two of the same." He was so patient with her. It was really rather sweet to watch him explain our order.

She nodded, took our menus, and walked away.

We looked at each other and burst out laughing when she was out of earshot. "Oh. My. God," Dan said. "Perhaps I should apologize to you, Kelly, for suggesting this place."

I wanted to tell him that I should actually thank him because it was giving me material for a future book, but I was being way too shy, so I kept that comment to myself and only said, "No. It's fine."

A couple minutes later what seemed to be the manager came out with our coffee. "Hi, I'm Jason. How are you?"

"We're great. Thanks," Dan answered for us.

"I just wanted to verify your orders to make sure that everything goes through."

Dan looked at me for a second and then looked at Jason. "We both ordered pancakes and hash browns, and you brought the coffee, so we're good. Thanks."

"Excellent. Thank you. We'll get that right out to you."

Dan nodded.

As Jason was walking away, I noticed something out the window. It seemed like a bunch of what looked like the wait staff—perhaps all the wait staff—were leaving out some side exit. "Hey, Dan. Look over there." I motioned toward the window.

He looked. "You've got to be kidding me," he said and looked back at me. He raised his eyebrows. "Well, this is going to be interesting. Do you mind seeing how this plays out? I'm intrigued."

"No, not at all." People at the other tables started noticing the wait staff leaving too. "What!" "I'm out of here too!" "This is ridiculous!" Several tables cleared out, and I started to hear Keith Morrison's voice narrating in my mind, *They thought this was a normal Sunday brunch. Oh, they were wrong…*

"Well, that gives us a better shot at actually getting something to eat," Dan laughed.

"The coffee's good," I said after taking a sip.

"Yes. Yes, it is good. In fact, this is the best damn cup of coffee I've ever had!" He smiled widely and nodded his head. Leaning back in his chair, he crossed his arms on his chest.

Oh, my God! How could he photograph so poorly and look so good in person! I just sort of awkwardly stared at him while trying to find some words.

About a minute later a woman with gray hair tied up in a red scarf who looked to be Jason's grandmother—perhaps called out of bed—stopped at our table. She placed some French toast in front of me and a Belgium waffle in front of Dan. "Thank you," we both said.

"Enjoy. Need more coffee?" She asked.

"Only when you get a chance," I said. "I'm sure you're busy." I pictured her in the kitchen all by herself. She reminded me of my grandma. She winked at me and waddled back away from our table.

"Would you rather have this?" Dan asked.

"I'm good if you are," I said.

"So since we're the only table with food, and who knows when these vultures at the other tables may dive bomb us," he picked up his fork and leaned toward his plate, "we better eat fast and get the hell out of here."

"Agreed," I said.

We ate hunched over our plates, and I force-fed myself two pieces of French toast even though at that moment I really wasn't hungry. It was more a matter of principle and an adventure. Upon finishing, Dan pulled $40 out of his wallet and threw it on the table. "That should cover it."

We got up and walked out.

"Well, that's one place I won't be recommending to my friends," Dan said. "You?"

"Yeah, I'm with you on that one," I said. "Thanks, Dan. That was a very amusing experience."

Dan looked left and then right. "Where are you parked? I'll walk you to your car."

I looked around and shrugged. I hoped that I would see my car and could casually say, *right there*, like a normal person would, but today my car was playing hide 'n seek with me so instead I said, "I'm sure it's here somewhere."

Dan raised his eyebrows. "Are you sure?"

Okay. He knows I'm crazy.

"Sometimes I forget where I park it. Wait! There it is." I pointed across the street and then pressed my lock button to prove it was mine, and the horn beeped.

Dan laughed.

"I know. It's stupid. It's just not something I think of when I get out of the car, and then I have to search for it. You'd think I'd learn."

We crossed the street, and he held out his hand to me. "Well, it was nice meeting you, Kelly. This has been an experience."

"Yes, it has." I shook his hand. "It was nice meeting you too, Dan."

"Well, I'm a block that way." He gestured with his hand.

"Okay."

He smiled at me and walked off in the other direction, and I got in my car.

I pulled my phone out of my purse and called Kim.

"Kelly, you're alive?"

"Ha ha," I said. "Yes, I'm alive but dying from embarrassment."

"Oh, no! What happened?"

"Oh, my God! Kimmy!" I put my forehead on the steering wheel.

"What?"

"I don't know what just happened to me." I smacked my hand on the steering wheel several times. "I was, like, the most awkward, boring person ever. I'm not even exaggerating. Every intelligent or funny thought totally left my brain as I sat across from this man," I paused, "this very attractive, well-dressed man." I sat back up.

"Okay, wait. I need to break this down. My sister, the chatterbox, had some trouble with conversation while sitting across from a handsome man? I thought you said your date was with that dating app guy. Did you go out with Tom again?"

"No, that's Wednesday. This was Dan. And, my God, his pictures are such an undersell." I leaned my head back against the headrest and shook it a few times. "The man could model. Well, I guess he couldn't because he doesn't photograph well or whatever. But he may have been seriously the most gorgeous man I've ever laid my eyes upon in person. I'm not even exaggerating. And if I had been expecting that, I think I could have handled it better. But since I was expecting someone not extremely attractive and this vision showed up, I was a little gobsmacked."

Kim laughed. "Oh, Kelly, that's... Well, that's actually quite funny."

I laughed too. "It is, but I wish it hadn't happened to me!" I sat up straight and put my key in the ignition.

"I mean, I get that."

I took a couple deep breaths. "Okay, well, I was just checking in. I'm going to start my car now, pull my thoughts together, and figure out what I'm going to do the rest of the day."

"Okay, call me if you need me."

"I will."

~~~~~

I went home and went to bed. I was sick of dealing with it—with deadlines, with dating, with being separated nearing divorce. I set my alarm so I would be up well before Evan arrived home, but what I needed for the next several hours was to just not think about anything.

I hoped that I could sleep. I shut my eyes and laid there. I started with some deep breathing.

I am.

Relaxed.

I am.

Relaxed.

I wasn't, but eventually I fell asleep anyway.

I woke to the doorbell ringing and after a few seconds to my phone ringing too. I fumbled for it—it was Sam.

"We're here. Can you open the door?"

I pulled my phone away from my head. It was only 2:00. Sam normally brought Evan home at 5:00. My alarm was set for 3:00. "Wait. What?" I said. I laid my head back on the pillow.

"I said, 'Can you open the door?'"

"It's only 2:00, Sam. What's going on?"

"Kelly, goddammit, can you open the door? Evan has to pee."

I hit end and went down the stairs and opened the door. "Hey, Buddy," I said to Evan as he ran past me and up the stairs.

I turned my attention from the stairs back to Sam. "Am I missing something? What's going on?"

"I texted you. I needed to bring Evan back early. Dinner plans."

I swallowed. "I didn't see your texts." I put my hand up adding, "And what if I weren't even home? Don't you think you should ask me if it's okay before bringing our son home three hours early?"

"I did ask you… in the texts."

"Did I respond?"

Sam shrugged. "No, but…" He shook his head.

Evan ran back down the steps.

"Okay, Evan, I'll see you on Wednesday." Sam leaned down and gave him a hug. "Thanks for a good weekend."

"Bye, Daddy," Evan said. Then he grabbed my leg. "Hi, Momma."

I bent down and hugged him as I shut the door hard—sort of in Sam's face. Evan had his back to the door, or I wouldn't have done that. But it felt good to shut the door on Sam. *Dinner plans…* What an ass. "Hey, Kiddo," I said and kissed Evan on the cheek. "Guess where we have to go?"

"Where? I'm tired."

I tousled his hair. "I know, Buddy, but we have to get toilet paper."

His eyes opened a bit wider. "Can I play?"

"If we leave pretty much right now before they close the playspace."

"Then let's do it. I already peed."

I laughed. Evan knew I always made him pee before we left the house. "Let me go pee—and grab my purse too. Your daddy woke me up. I was napping when you got here."

"Silly Daddy," Evan said. "I'll wait here for you." He sat on the bottom step.

"Give me two minutes."

The Grocery Store… Again

So, yes, after bragging about knowing where the toilet paper was on Friday evening, I'd forgotten to get some, and we were down to a quarter roll.

My favorite attendant was at the playspace when I checked Evan in. We were both named Kelly, and she'd taken a liking to me because of our same names, I assumed. "Hi, Kelly! I haven't seen you for a while," she said as I was getting out my driver's license.

"I know. I've been shopping while Evan's at school mostly these days." I peeked in and saw a couple other kids playing. The one boy looked familiar, but at first I couldn't place him. Then I realized his nametag said "Michael," and it dawned on me that he was Michael from the zoo. My stomach flip-flopped at the thought of seeing Jack again. Why had my stomach flip-flopped? Was I really interested in Jack or was it just how the situation from the zoo had all gone down with him empathizing with me when Sam was being a jerk? Anyway, Michael could be at the store with someone else.

I got Evan all checked in and said good-bye to him and Kelly.

Since I only really needed toilet paper but knew Evan wanted to play, I got some coffee and sat down with it. I felt a little jumpy knowing there was the possibility of running into Jack. I calmed myself by thinking that the odds of that were slim to none. First of all, it was a huge store, and if Jack were the one who had brought Michael, he was probably over on the other side of the store by now anyway. But really instead of that thought being reassuring, it sort of bummed me out a little. If Jack were in the store, I kind of wanted to run into him. I guess I kind of wanted to see how he would react to me or see if he would even remember me.

I picked up my coffee and started walking up and down each aisle fairly quickly. I mean, I'd never catch up to him if I dilly-dallied.

In the toilet paper aisle, I grabbed a small package and was throwing it in my cart when I heard, "You found it." I jumped and turned.

The face smiling at me was familiar, but it definitely wasn't Jack's. "I thought that was you," he said.

"Oh, hey," I said, but I was frantically running faces and names through my head and trying to remember where I knew him from. Then it hit me. It was the guy who knows the bread aisle from Friday night. "Did you find the toilet paper okay the other day?"

He smiled again, "All good."

I wiped my brow dramatically and pointed at him, "Phew. I was prayin' for you." I turned to walk away because I still wanted to quickly keep going to see if I could catch up with Jack, and this conversation was slowing me down.

"Since we seem to be on the same shopping schedule, I hope I will." He seemed to be walking behind me. "Do you hang out anywhere else around town?"

I turned back and shook my head. "Not really. Just here and home. I'm pretty boring."

"Ah," he said. "Okay."

I kept walking.

"Do you want to hang out anywhere else?"

Do I? He was fairly attractive—seemed nice enough. But he would be one more distraction from writing—which I definitely didn't need, and at that moment the only man I possibly wanted to add to the mix of distracting men was Jack, not *Bread Guy*. I stopped and turned to face him. "I'm a hot mess. I'm gonna do you a favor and say no."

"You can't be that bad," he smiled. He was pretty cute. Blond hair, blue eyes, about average height. But I kept thinking that I wanted to catch up to Jack, and that felt telling.

"I really am." I nodded my head. "Seriously... You remember my meltdown because I couldn't find bread the other day?"

He laughed. "You have a point."

I pointed at him. "I sure do," I turned and started walking.

"Let me know if you need help finding anything else," he called to my back.

"Awesome," I said. Hoping he wouldn't keep following me, I started to walk quickly again. It didn't sound like he was, but I wasn't sure. I stopped in the next aisle and pretended I was looking at the pasta so I could glance over my shoulder.

He wasn't there. I shook my head and laughed a little. "Oh, good lord," I said quietly. Then I started to quickly walk again—possibly toward Jack.

I got all the way to the other side of the store. I hadn't seen Jack anywhere, but instead of feeling relieved, I started feeling really disappointed. Maybe I had just somehow missed him. Maybe he and I had switched aisles at the exact same time, and we just kept missing each other. Maybe my short conversation with *Bread Guy* had taken too long.

I doubled back walking back up and down the aisles. When I got halfway back, I sort of gave up. This was so stupid anyway. What would I have even said to him if we'd run into each other?

I headed toward the registers. Jonathan didn't seem to be at any of them today, so I went through the express aisle and paid for my toilet paper.

Michael was gone by the time I picked up Evan. I almost wanted to ask Kelly if it had been a man or woman who had picked up Michael, but I figured telling me would break some sort of confidentiality. It also would make her wonder why I was asking. Maybe she was friendly with Michael's mom too like she was with me. And that would just make things awkward.

So I left it a mystery instead, and Evan and I went home.

FIFTEEN

The Message

I got Evan up and to school without too much struggle for a Monday morning and then headed to my appointment with the orthopedic specialist. I got checked in and scanned the waiting area which was totally packed. I squeezed in between two semi-friendly looking people. One person looked like she was about 16, had a knee brace on and crutches beside her chair, and the other person was a man maybe mid-thirties and had a cast on his arm. "Tough break, huh?" I said to him as I sat down, but he didn't even smile at me. *Geez, tough crowd!* I felt thoroughly out of place, so I pulled out my phone and clicked on the dating app to pass the time while I waited.

Kelly, I have to be honest. You seem like a very nice person, but I just don't see any connection between the two of us. Am I wrong? Dan

Ouch. That hurt. That really, really hurt. I slunk back into my chair and stared at the message for a few minutes. If I could have physically kicked myself in the head a good 10 times, I would have. Seriously. I really would have.

I mean he wasn't wrong. But reading the rejection so bluntly stated… It stung. Part of it stung because it took me right back to Sam leaving me—my last male rejection. But it also stung because I'd turned into such a fool yesterday. Why was it that I could normally hold up my end of the conversation with anyone about anything but then yesterday I clammed up and was the most pathetic creature alive in front of this really great guy—possibly janitor guy, but still?

And he was totally right. We probably weren't going to end up being a great love connection, anyway. But with one awkward date and one short message, he took away the chance to find out for sure. I took a deep breath and wished I weren't in this packed waiting room when I had opened this.

Whatever. I shifted in my seat. At least I looked cute. I was wearing this dorky orange t-shirt that said "Student of the Year" on it, a full black eyelet skirt, and my black canvas China doll shoes. My hair was in two low pigtails. I quickly scanned the room to see if I were drawing the attention of any other men who were noticing how cute I was. Dan and Sam didn't have to have the final say in the matter, but no one here seemed to be noticing my cute-ness though.

I distracted myself from Dan's rejection by imagining myself asking people "What are you in for?" like we were in prison or something. But the people around me didn't seem all too friendly all of the sudden with that *tough break* miss on the friendly-looking guy to my left. Plus, the Dan rejection was making me feel a lot less, well, engaging at that moment.

I really wished I had remembered to bring a book. I should always just have a book with me.

Then I started to imagine myself passing the time by starting a sing-along in the waiting room. That thought made me giggle—more like snort a little—and the guy to my left shook his head and let out a sharp breath.

"You have no sense of humor. Do you?" I asked him.

"Ma'am, you are annoying," he said.

I smiled at him—mostly because I knew it would be even more annoying for him. Worse than calling me annoying, he had just called me ma'am. I didn't like that at all and wanted to punish him for it.

He stared at me for a couple seconds and then looked down.

Oh, yeah, I thought. Outstaring him was a minor victory, but I'd take it.

The nurse opened the door and said, "Zane."

He got up and walked toward her. *Zane*—what an interesting name wasted on such a grumpy man though.

"You know what his problem was? Other than being a huge stick in the mud," I whispered to the girl with the crutches.

She laughed. "No," she whispered back to me and giggled a little bit.

I put my hand to her ear and whispered. "Small," I paused, "hands."

She let out a high-pitched chortle and quickly covered her mouth with her hand then looked at me and smiled.

I shrugged and rolled my eyes.

The man sitting across from us smirked and shook his head from side to side. "I don't even want to know what information you corrupted her with."

"Are you eavesdropping on our conversation?" I smirked at him.

He raised his eyebrows. "Kind of."

Of course, since the waiting room was pretty packed and I was pretty loud, I was pretty sure everyone was. "Well… what are you in for?" He was pretty cute, and I could flirt with him for a while. Why not? I needed an ego boost after the whole lack of connection comment from Dan.

"I'm 'in for' chauffeuring her. I'm her father." He nodded toward the girl sitting to my right. "How about you?"

"Bum knee." I pointed to it. "Whenever I walk, well, it hurts."

The nurse opened the door and we all looked at her expectantly. "Stephanie."

"Daddy, wait here," the girl to my right said.

"Are you sure?" he said.

I watched her nod as she hobbled past me on her crutches. "Good luck," I said quietly.

We went back to saying nothing. And then, eventually, the nurse called me back. She asked me a couple questions about my knee. Then she took me for a couple x-rays and brought me back to the exam room and told me that Dr. Peterson would be with me in a few minutes.

"Thanks." Since I didn't have a book, I just sat there and looked around the room.

It seemed like it took Dr. Peterson ages to get back to me. I could feel crow's feet starting to form around my eyes a little—it felt that long, and I started to do the *I am. Relaxed.* breathing exercise to try to stay calm. I hated seeing doctors—especially specialists.

Finally, I could hear some movement outside my door. There was a knock, and the door opened.

Dr. Peterson walked in holding my chart, "Well, normally, I introduce myself, and..."

"Yeah, this is a bit awkward." I wanted to crawl under the table and hide.

Dr. Peterson was actually Dan.

I shrugged my shoulders. "This is a nice office you work in," I said.

He looked at the ceiling briefly. He was wearing his glasses from the picture. "Yeah, I work here mostly." He tilted his head from side to side a couple times. "Sometimes I work down in the OR."

I laughed and nodded. "Right."

He looked down at the clipboard in his left hand. "So, uh, your knee is hurting you? Let's look at the x-rays." He turned his back to me and put them up on the x-ray board.

I put my face in my hands in my lap and shook my head.

"Kelly, are you with me?" he said.

"Yep, right here." I jumped up beside him and did the bump into his hip.

He looked at me sideways and actually laughed a little. Then he directed his focus at the x-ray and said, "This looks good." He was pointing and saying things like that.

"I don't really follow you, Dan. It's okay if I call you that, right? It'd be kind of weird at this point to switch it up to Dr. Peterson."

He nodded. "Absolutely." Calling a doctor by his first name—my mom would be so proud!

"Why didn't you just tell me you were a doctor? What's the big deal?"

He shrugged. "I dunno. I get a lot of weird responses to that. Or I've had people think I'm loaded as a result and only see dollar signs." He adjusted his glasses. "I'm not, by the way."

"Hmm." I didn't say anything for a couple seconds then pointed to the x-ray. "Anyway, don't expect me to understand a word you're saying, okay? It looks like you know your medical stuff, but," I paused and shrugged, "I write books."

"So don't even point stuff out and show off?" He laughed.

"It's lost on me, Dan. You're basically speaking a foreign language. I know it's my knee and my health and I should pay attention, but I zone out."

"Point well taken." He turned toward me and gestured to the exam table. "Let me get you on the bed then."

"I thought you didn't want to see me anymore," I smirked then lightly punched him on the arm with the side of my fist.

He closed his eyes and shook his head. "You're not going to make this easy on me. Are you?"

"Why should I?" I turned my body to face his. "You undersold your photo, and that just wasn't fair." I said, walked to the exam table, and jumped up on it.

"What?" I could tell by the look on his face that he really didn't get how good looking he was, and that made him about a million times more gorgeous than he had been yesterday.

"Take a good look at that picture you have posted and then look in the mirror. There is a huge difference. I mean, you're really rather... gorgeous."

His cheeks turned pink, and I remembered that he hadn't felt any connection.

I waved my hands. "I'm sorry. Never mind. It doesn't matter. Which way do you want me?"

He was quiet for a couple seconds. Finally, he said, "Left knee?"

"Correct."

He pointed and said, "Legs that way first."

I laid down, and he started lifting my right knee and twisting it and asking if it hurt when he did this or that and taking notes. It was pretty sexy to watch him work—this janitor turned doctor in a lab coat who was touching my legs.

"So where are you taking classes?" he said.

"What do you mean?"

He looked at my chest and raised his eyebrows.

"Oh," *student of the year*, "don't tell anyone, but it's a fake."

He winked at me. "Patient confidentiality." He smiled.

"Cool," I said and rolled my eyes.

"Swing your legs down and lie the other way for me, please."

"Sure." I did.

He started doing all the same stuff now with my left knee.

"Ouch, Dan!"

"Hurts here?" He pressed again.

"Yep. Just as much that second time!"

"Should I do it a third time?" He smiled and raised his eyebrows.

I shook my head and started to giggle.

He laughed too.

For a couple seconds we both just laughed really hard. Neither one of us could compose ourselves, and I felt like we were in middle school or something. Then he closed his eyes, took a deep breath, and went back into doctor mode. "This one seems like there's a lot of fluid too." He kept playing around and twisting my knee. "Hear that?" There was a distinct clicking.

"Yes, I feel it too."

"Does that hurt?"

"No, not really."

"Okay, you can sit up for me. I'm going to send you for an MRI and have you come back in so we can look at that together."

"So what you're saying is you do wanna see me again?" I winked at him. "You're so darn confusing, Dan. You men and your penises."

He held his hand out and helped me jump off the table. "Kelly, I wish you would've let your humor shine a little when we were at Turner's yesterday."

I let out half a laugh. "So I'll see you after the MRI here at your office."

"Carla will schedule your MRI for you. She's right outside the door here." He nodded and smirked a little. "It was nice to see you, Kelly. And a little awkward." He smiled at me and left the room.

My God, he was really very handsome.

I took a deep breath and blew it out. "Boy, that was weird," I said quietly.

I scheduled the MRI appointment and my next appointment with Dan. The MRI could be done on Wednesday afternoon, and I could see Dan again next Monday.

I walked out to the parking lot and got into the car and started it, but I just sat there and tapped my thumbs on the steering wheel. Finally, I put my car in drive. "And life goes on," I whispered and went to pick Evan up at preschool.

Outside Evan's school, my phone started ringing. "Hello?"

"Hi, Kelly. It's Tom. How are you?"

"Hey, Tom. I've been better, but I've been a lot worse so I can't complain. How about you?"

"I'm good. What's wrong?" He actually sounded like he cared— or maybe I was reading too much into it.

"I've been having trouble with my knee, and I just came back from the specialist. It's no big deal. I don't really wanna talk about it." *At least not with you. I'll be calling Dana and seeing Kim inside in a minute.*

"Okay. I hope it all works out and that it's not serious."

"Thanks. I don't think it is."

"So I wanted to figure out Wednesday. How about Gordon and Wallace's?"

"Sure. 6:30 still good for you?" I said.

"Sounds good."

"Okay, I'm heading in to pick up my son so I have to hang up. I'll see you then?"

"I'm looking forward to it, Kelly."

"Me too. Bye." I hung up and walked inside.

Kim was standing just inside the door. "Hey, there," she said.

"You're not going to believe my morning."

"Try me."

"I saw that knee specialist today that Dr. Oliver referred me to, and it's *Janitor Guy*."

"What?" She laughed.

"Yep, apparently that's the office that he mostly works in at the hospital."

"Oh, my God! That's so cool! You must have been in shock!"

I grabbed her arm. "The best part was that I got a blow off message from him that I read in the waiting room."

Her face dropped. "No. Oh, Kelly. Oh, that's," she paused and smiled, "that's actually kind of funny." She started laughing.

"Oh, thanks." I crossed my arms across my chest.

"And then you see him today. The very next day." She started laughing harder. "And he has to examine your knee right after rejecting you." She grabbed my arm. "Come on, Kel, think about it! This is good stuff! You should be writing this stuff down. Not that relationship crap that you write. You're so funny. You should be writing a comedy."

I looked at her laughing at me and my life. "Now you're not only laughing at me, you're telling me my book is crap? Somehow I'm not getting this joke, Kim."

"Oh, Kelly, I didn't mean that it's crap. I just mean that you're so funny, why aren't you writing a comedy? I mean, your texts always make me laugh. You know how to make people laugh. You know what's funny. Why aren't you writing funny stuff?"

"I dunno. What would I even write about?"

"I'm sure you could think of something." At that moment the kids all started walking up the stairs. Evan was the line leader today for his class.

The hard part was that he had to stay in line—even though he'd seen me—until he got the line in place by the door and until his teachers told him it was okay to come to me. This was really a challenge for him.

He got to the place where the line stopped and then squeezed his fists, scrunched his face, and tried his best not to move until finally he heard the magic words, "Evan, you may go to your mom." Then he ran over to me and gave me a huge hug which was followed by a, "Walk, please, Evan." Meredith was dismissed too, and we all walked out to the parking lot together.

"Do you want to come over for sandwiches, Aunt Kim?" Evan asked.

Kim looked at me, and I shrugged and nodded my head, "I've got plenty of stuff in the fridge."

"Does that sound good, Meri?" Kim asked her.

"Yes, go to Evan and Aunt Kelly's house." She put her hand in Evan's hand. She loved her big cousin Evan. They skipped ahead a couple steps.

"Sounds like a plan then," I said. I leaned a little closer to Kim and whispered, "Hey, has she stopped saying shit and that other stuff he taught her?"

"For the most part."

"Good."

The Glider

After Kim and Meredith left, I sat down at the computer to try to write.

I heard Kim say *write something funny*. Now that was sort of funny.

Or could it work? Could I write a funny novel? I pushed my hands on my desk and rolled my chair backwards. I shook my head,

"I dunno."

I wasn't ready to try.

I walked out to the porch and sat down. My timing was impeccable. Dana was walking by with Pepper. "Hey, get over here! I need you!" I motioned with my hands.

She headed over to the porch. "What's up? Sit, Pepper," she said. She sat down beside me on the glider, and Pepper sat down and then laid down in front of us.

"You will never believe my day. Never in a million years will you believe my day." I shook my head.

She raised her eyebrows. "Worse than usual?" She laughed.

I looked at her. "You know what? This day puts all my other days in the ring," I held my hands up making a square shape, "and kicks all their asses." I threw the fake square over my shoulder.

She patted her legs quickly. "No way! Tell me!" She smacked my leg and got a huge smile on her face.

"So I got a big old rejection message this morning from Dan."

"Oh, bummer." Her voice had lost a little enthusiasm.

"Well, no big shock there since I totally clammed up on the date. It sucked that he had to be so cute. Asshole."

"What?"

"Yeah, it was pathetic. He was gorgeous, and it threw me off. You should have seen him, Dana." I closed my eyes for a second picturing him. I opened them, looked at her, and shook my head. "God, his stupid picture did not do him justice."

"That's not fair." She shook her head and reached down to pet Pepper.

"Seriously! So in the waiting room for my new knee specialist I really ticked off this guy."

"How?"

"It was crowded, so I had to sit right in between two people, and I look at him and say, 'Tough break?' and he had no sense of humor. Anyway, that's not the point of the story."

She patted my thigh. "God, you're a dork!" She laughed.

"I said a bunch of other stupid stuff too, but that's really not..."

Pepper jumped up and started to chase a car that went by. Dana pulled the leash, "Pepper, no. Sit. Good girl."

"So to make a long story short, Dana, the janitor... is my knee doctor."

Dana, who was petting Pepper and kissing her face, whipped her head around to me, "What!"

I nodded my head.

"You have got to be kidding me."

I shook my head.

"Does the hospital know that the janitor is seeing patients?"

I laughed hard for a few seconds. "I'm pretty sure he's a real doctor, Dana. He seemed to know what he was doing."

"No, no, no, no, no. Back up," she said and sat up straight.

I smiled. "Okay." I sat up straight too.

"This guy who we've been envisioning pushing a mop around the hospital walks into the room holding your chart?" She gestured big with both hands.

"Yep. Not only the whole mop thing, but I had literally just read a message from him saying he felt no connection. I'm so glad I opened that dating app in the waiting room! Oh, my God! It could have been even more embarrassing if I hadn't known he'd rejected me." I shuddered. "That could have been awful!"

We both leaned back into the glider and slid back and forth a few times. "Holy shit. I'm blown away. Seriously. I'm blown away." She reached over and patted my leg. "And that sucks, by the way, the rejection part."

"Eh, whatever. But he did look really cute when he was getting all medical on me—pointing stuff out on my x-rays and twisting my knee around and making notes about how far it could bend and stuff. Oh, my God. It was so sexy. And he was kind of flirting with me a little bit, but I'm pretty sure it was just nervousness on both our parts. I mean, what are the odds, right? It had to have been just as awkward for him too. At one point we both just started giggling and couldn't compose ourselves, and then he took a deep breath and turned on doctor mode again."

She grabbed my arm, "Oh, Kelly."

"Oh, well. Right? Easy come, easy go. I'm seeing Tom on Wednesday."

"See that?" She smacked my thigh.

I looked down at her hand. "Why do you keep hitting me?" I laughed.

She laughed too. "I dunno. I'll try to stop." She paused. "Where was I?"

"Um, I said I was seeing Tom. You said, 'See that.'"

"Oh, yeah! I think I was going to say that you don't wanna date two guys at once anyway, right?"

"Why's that?"

"You wouldn't get your book done! Plus, you'd be too exhausted."

I rolled my eyes. "I'm so stressed out about this book that I doubt I'll get it done at this rate, anyhow." I paused. "Kim said I should try writing a comedy."

Dana laughed.

At the same time I said, "I know, right!" And Dana said, "You'd be great at that!"

"Wait, you think?" I squinted my eyes.

"Hell, yeah! You're hilarious! If you can't write a comedy, I don't think it can be done."

I elbowed her. "About what?"

"About anything. Write one about me and Pepper," she said as she leaned forward and started to pet Pepper and kiss her face again. "I just love this girl! You're so kissable, Peps!"

"About you loving your dog? Yeah, that's funny as hell, Dana."

"Sure, it is. I'm sure you could put a funny spin on it!"

"I'm not sure I could get a full novel out of you sitting on my glider kissing your dog. I could get maybe a page or two about Pepper taking a dump on my front lawn and everyone tracking it through my house. Now that was funny in a *you don't ever want it to happen again* sort of way."

"See, you have two pages," she smiled. "You just need what?"

"I don't know… About 300 more. That should be no problem. I'll use a big font. Any other brilliant ideas?"

"Are you mocking me?" Dana said.

"No!" I looked out toward the street. "Not at all."

"Not at all?"

"Maybe a little. Not much though." I laughed and leaned into her.

"Just write a toned-down version of your real life, Kelly."

I laughed loudly. "Toned down, huh?" I leaned away so I could see her face.

"Kelly, like, way toned down. The real stuff is, well, stranger than fiction. No one would believe that someone could get dumped in the waiting room by the same doctor she was about to see. That stuff doesn't happen. I mean, not to normal people."

I started laughing. "Stop. You're simultaneously cracking me up and depressing me. When did my life start to be so bizarre?"

"I'm pretty sure it always has been. But your recent foray into the dating world has really highlighted that fact nicely."

"I know. I think I give up. Well, after my date on Wednesday. I mean, I might as well get another free meal since it's already scheduled. I'm trying to stick with a budget, and at least that'll help as long as he offers to pay again."

She laughed. "You can have dinner with us any time you want."

I smiled at her. "I'll keep that in mind once I drive away all my suitors."

"Okay, I'm leaving."

I grabbed hold of her arm. "No. Don't go. Then I actually have to go back inside and try to write, and I'm not ready to do that yet."

"Look at me," Dana said.

"What?"

"Just look at me."

I turned and faced her.

"Sit up straight."

I laughed. "You sound like my mother."

"I know," Dana said. "This is what my mom used to tell me. You can talk yourself into—or out of—doing anything." She raised her eyebrows. "Now which would you rather it be? So stop telling yourself that you have writer's block and that you can't do it and that it's going to be horrible, Kelly. I'm sick of hearing it. Do you know how many people actually want to be writers—to get published? You already have a few books to prove you can do this, an agent, and people granting you money to make it all happen. You're a writer, Kelly Ramsey. Remember that and go be one." She stared at me for a couple seconds and then looked down at Pepper. "You ready, girl?" Pepper jumped up and wagged her tail. She was always ready. She didn't care what it was for. They walked away.

I slouched back into the glider and sat there until Evan came out and found me. "What are you doing, Momma?" He climbed into my lap. It was starting to get dark out.

I squeezed him tight. "Trying to talk myself into doing something."

"Can you help me with something?"

"Sure. What?"

"I had a little spill in the kitchen," he said.

I leaned my head around to look at his face. "Oh, boy." Considering he had come to find me, I was scared to see what I was going to find in the kitchen. Typically he let a little spill go. "Let's go see."

I started to get up. "Promise you won't get mad before you get up," he said as he tried to pull me back into my seat.

"Oh, boy," I said again. "I think we both may be in big trouble."

SIXTEEN

The Therapy Session

I sat in the waiting room and felt a bit out of place and a bit silly. I didn't want to be one of those people who couldn't get her shit together on her own. I liked people to think of me, and my life, as being together and perfect. I knew it was the farthest thing from being either of those things, but as long as I could convince other people that it was, I was doing okay.

Being in a therapist's waiting room made me feel a little like I wasn't pulling that off so well. Luckily the waiting room was empty so at least I wasn't dealing with whether or not I should talk to anybody or just mind my own business.

After about 10 minutes the door to the office opened and a woman who looked to be in her late 40s or maybe early 50s peeked her head into the waiting room. She was a round woman with short reddish hair. "Kelly?"

I nodded. "That's me."

"I'm Brynn Follow me," she said, and I got up and followed her down a long hall and into an office. The office was fairly cluttered with books and paperwork. There was a loveseat that I ended up sitting on across from a wingback chair that she sat in. The bookshelves were full of books and there were a few end tables that had books and knickknacks covering them.

"Are you comfortable?" she said.

"Yes, I'm fine." I straightened my skirt.

"So what brings you in?"

"It's a long story. It really is. I don't necessarily feel like talking about it, but I guess that's why I'm here, so..."

She smiled at me. I liked her, I think. I mean, I felt like I could trust her. There was a warmth about her smile that made me feel like I wasn't going to fully let my guard down, but that I could talk—at least a little—and that she wouldn't tell anyone that my life wasn't, in fact, put together and perfect and that I was actually a hot mess.

"I guess the main problem right now is that I'm a writer, and for whatever reason I just can't seem to write anything. I'm stuck or something."

"Tell me a little bit about that—why you feel stuck."

"I got this grant a few months ago. And recently my sister sort of crunched some numbers to see how long I could comfortably live off the money. Basically, I have six months—well, closer to five months now because it's been a couple weeks since she gave me my budget."

She was smiling and nodding so I continued, "I have five months to write something that I don't even know what I'm writing about at this point. And it's just been so stressful because," I paused for a long time. "What if I fail? What if I can't get it done? And it's not like I can't write. I know I can. I have a few things published. They sold okay—okay enough that every once in a while I get noticed somewhere random."

She laughed.

And I continued to talk about everything that I was doing instead of writing. Then I opened up and started to talk about Sam—about how he left me on my birthday almost a year ago. I talked about my marriage, family life, and how that compared with being a single mom. It all poured out of me for the next 45 minutes or so. I paused and looked at the clock. "I think my session's over. I'm sorry that I just rambled."

She asked me if I wanted to come back.

I nodded. I did. Talking about things had felt good—and safe. We scheduled my second appointment for next Wednesday morning. I stood up and hugged her. "Thank you," I said.

The MRI

I had arranged for Kim to pick up Evan at preschool, so I went straight from therapy to my MRI appointment. I showed up with my phobias following closely behind me—fear of spiders, fear of shark attacks (in swimming pools, specifically), fear of the world in general, and fear of tight places and being trapped. The fourth phobia was on my mind the most at that moment.

The receptionist greeted me. "Hi, Kelly, how are you this morning?"

"Not exactly happy to be here. I'm not looking forward to being put inside a tube."

"Ah, it won't take too long." She smiled at me. "Do you have your insurance card?"

"Yep." I dug through my wallet and found it.

She made a copy of it and then keyed my address and birthday and some other information into the computer. "Okay, follow me." She led me into a small dressing room. "Take everything off but your panties, and put on this gown, and this robe on top of it, and these slippers." She handed me a key. "Put your clothes and purse in this locker and then come out to the waiting room that we just walked through. Someone will come and get you there."

"Okay. Thanks."

She left, and I got undressed. My gown was blue with several different colored stripes on it, and my robe was an ugly shade of gray. "You'd think they would have matchers," I said as I sat on the chair and pulled on my slippers. Then I stuffed everything in my locker and walked out of the dressing area, but I couldn't find a room that looked like it was supposed to be a waiting room.

Wasn't it supposed to be right outside this door? A place we had supposedly just walked through? God! I wished that I paid better attention sometimes! A few people wandered past me, and I looked at them expectantly because I was hoping they were the person who was looking for me for my MRI. No one seemed to want to claim me. This was getting to be embarrassing because everyone else was dressed, and I was wandering around in a mismatched gown and robe with only panties underneath. The least they could have done was given me a cute outfit to hyperventilate in. I looked hideous! And for some reason, that really bothered me at that moment even more than the fact that I was about to be stuck inside a tube that was essentially the same size I was. Well maybe the tube thing was bothering me more again now that I'd thought of it.

I took a couple deep breaths and tried to calm down. Good

freakin' God! I was about to be inserted into a tiny tube, barely bigger than I was. I couldn't get that thought out of my head. I wanted to curl up in the corner and hide—or die. Death would probably be better. Another person walked past me, "Where's the waiting room?" I snapped at him and then immediately wished I hadn't.

"Are you Kelly Ramsey?"

"Yes," I whispered and felt my cheeks burn a little.

"I'm Brian. The waiting room is just around the corner, but you can come with me. I'll be doing your test." He looked half amused and half annoyed with me. He was a really little guy, small and scrawny. The kind of kid who you would picture always getting picked last in gym class. Why was I mentally picking on the poor guy—especially since he had just essentially found me and saved me from wandering around lost in these mismatched pajamas? God, I hated myself sometimes!

I smiled at him and followed him into what looked like a holding area. "I'm sorry, Brian. I don't normally snap at people—not that you'll believe that. It's just... I'm really scared, and I've been wandering around in these hideous pajamas, and I couldn't find the waiting room, and I sort of took it out on you—well, you know that part, and now I'm rambling because, like I said, I'm nervous."

He smiled and pointed to a chair. "It happens," he said and sat across from me. "I need to ask you a few questions."

"All right." I sat down and adjusted my robe.

"So how old are you?"

"I'm 34."

"Do you have any metal in your body anywhere?"

"No."

"Are you claustrophobic?"

"Extremely!"

"You're in the wrong place then." He laughed and looked up at me. "But at least since I'm looking at your left knee, I can put you in feet first. Your head won't even be in the machine. Does that make you feel any better?"

I put my hand up to my chest, and I almost jumped up to hug him. I squealed a little—an odd noise that just sort of popped out. "I can breathe again for the first time since Monday!"

"I'll take that to be a yes. Let's see." He smiled and looked back at his sheet of questions. "Any chance you're pregnant?"

"No. Not even a slim one." Why did I always feel the need to elaborate on that question when a simple no would do? Brian didn't need to know I hadn't had sex in ages.

"Did you ever work in a mill?"

"No?"

There were a few other odd questions and then, "Okay, can you sign this for me?"

"Sure."

"Now comes the fun," he raised his eyebrows and smirked. "Come on."

"Can't wait." But it wasn't going to be so bad. I was going in the tiny tube feet first, and my head wouldn't even be in the machine! Life was good!

It still wasn't the most fun test because I had to lie perfectly still in an uncomfortable position, but I was relieved to not have to be in a machine with my face pressed up against the capsule. What a relief!

The First Second Date

When I got home and got Evan settled, I used my date with Tom as an excuse to not work and started to figure out what I could wear that would be appropriate for dinner at Gordon and Wallace's. I had decided not to sweat it anymore on dates with Tom. This probably wasn't going anywhere so I really didn't care much about what I looked like. I mean, I wanted to look cute, but I wasn't going to make myself puke again stressing about it.

At 6:14 p.m. the doorbell rang. "Daddy!" Evan bolted past me and opened the door. "Mom, Daddy's here! I'm leaving."

"Just wait one minute," I walked over to him. Sam was behind him. "Hi, Sam."

"Hey, Kel." He smiled. "You look," he paused and took a second look, "you look really cute."

"Um, I think that's a compliment. So thanks." I scooped Evan up and gave him a quick hug and kiss.

"I love you, Mommy."

I squeezed him for a few seconds longer. "You are the sweetest boy, and I love you so much, Little Man. I'll see you later." I put him down.

"Here," I handed Sam a key.

"What's this for?" he said.

"I'm going out. You might beat me home."

He raised his eyebrows.

"Good-bye, Sam," I said.

He nodded and they left, and I got my things together and left for Gordon and Wallace's. "Here we go again."

The drive there was pretty quick. But I enjoyed having the windows down and listening to a few good songs. I pulled into the parking lot and parked as far away from the restaurant as I possibly could without actually making it seem like I was trying to park far away. But I liked those few moments where I could get my head together as I walked up to the restaurant. I took a deep breath, opened the door, and stepped inside.

Like the good date that he was, Tom was already waiting for me.

"Hey, how are you?" I said as I hugged him.

"Not too bad. How about yourself?"

I cringed a little and mentally corrected his grammar. But he had that adorable smile on his face, so I could forgive him. "I'm doing great," I said.

"You look great, Kelly," he said.

"You look pretty good too." That was very much an understatement. How could he not tell that I was nine years older than he was? He was so damn cute!

It wasn't at all crowded in the restaurant because it was a Wednesday, so we were seated immediately.

"How many?" the hostess said.

"Just us two," Tom said.

"Okay, follow me," the hostess said.

Tom motioned for me to go in front of him. "Just us two

chickens," he said quietly as I passed him.

I closed my eyes and shook my head.

We got settled in our booth as the hostess told us the specials and then walked away.

I watched her go and then looked at Tom. "So what's been going on in your world?" I said.

"Same old stuff. Work. Running. Nothing too exciting."

The waitress came over and took our drink orders. We both ordered a beer. "What are we having to eat?" I asked. "Are we splitting a pizza, or what do you want?" God, I felt like his mother all of the sudden.

"What do you wanna do?"

"Let's split a pizza. I just want cheese on my half, so figure out what you want on yours, and you can order it when she comes back."

"Cheese is good." And there was that amazing smile that made me forget all about his bad grammar and other shortcomings.

"You know you have a great smile," I said.

He looked out toward the restaurant and shook his head a little.

"Don't get all shy on me. You do. You probably hear it all the time though."

He shook his head again and looked down at the table. "Thank you," he said. "So how's your son?"

"He's great. He's with his dad tonight, so they're probably doing something amazingly fun because I'm the boring parent. He's a character. He tried to help me by doing the dishes the other afternoon, but he ended up overflowing the sink. What a mess! It was nice that he was trying to be helpful, but I honestly would have re-washed the dishes anyway. I'm not quite sure I trust a wash job done in cold water by a five-year-old boy."

"Not too thorough?" He shook his head.

"Not up to my standards."

"Gotcha."

"So what degree did you get that you're choosing not to use? I should have asked you that last time instead of who you loved in the past. Sorry about that by the way."

He laughed and leaned back into his seat. "Secondary Ed. Math is, um, the degree I'm not using."

"So you never tried to sub or find a teaching job?"

"I tried, but I got promoted at Gabes, and I stopped trying."

"That's sad."

"I don't know. Maybe. Or maybe I decided teaching wasn't really my thing." He shrugged.

"Is that true, or is that just something you say? I have some of 'those.'" I put air quotes around the word those.

The waitress came back with our drinks, and Tom ordered our pizza.

When she walked away Tom said, "Some of my friends are heading to Barney's later on, and you're welcome to join us." He raised his eyebrows.

"Barney's? My God! I haven't been there in years."

"Yeah, well, my one friend's girlfriend is 20, so she can get in there."

"Oh," I laughed. "God, those were the days, huh? Seems like

such a long time ago." And then it hit me. It wasn't that long ago for Tom and his friends.

We smiled at each other for a few seconds. God, I hated feeling old. "Yeah," I said. "I think I'm up for that. In fact I'd love to."

"Cool." We both took long drinks of our beer.

"So what do you want to talk about now?" I said.

Tom laughed and shook his head.

"Can you tell I'm very uncomfortable with silence?" I said.

He nodded and smirked. "Kind of."

"Growing up my family never shut up unless everyone was mad at each other so I can't help it. Silence creeps me out. It's just me."

"I like it." There was that smile.

I was okay—at least for a couple seconds until the silence became uncomfortable and awkward. God, he was making me work too darn hard to keep this conversation going. Or maybe if I would just shut up for half a second, I'd give him a chance to think of something to say. *Try that approach, Kelly.* I took a breath and smiled back at him as I willed him with my eyes to say something to me.

"What's that?" he said.

"What?" I said.

"I said, 'What's that?' It looked like you were about to say something to me."

Damn! Why did men have to be so extremely challenging? "So aside from flirting with old ladies outside of Gabes, what else do you do for fun—well, aside from all the other things you've already told me you like to do?" I said.

"Did I say I flirt with old ladies?"

"Didn't you?" I squinted my eyes.

"I can't remember, but I don't think so. Sometimes they flirt with me, but..." His voice trailed off. Good. He passed my *I'm not an old lady* test.

"So what are your parents like? Did you have a good relationship with them growing up?"

He shrugged. "They're okay. They act like I ruined their life sometimes because they had me when they were 16, so it's been this whole grudge thing with them off and on. I'm not gonna have kids for a long time. Not until I get everything figured out, you know?"

"Sure. Makes sense—except for the having 'everything figured out' part. That might happen the moment before you die—or the moment after, probably. But I do understand. No one wants to feel like a burden. My mother lays a guilt trip on me every time she sees me. She didn't have a clue how to raise a creative child. She's a doctor, and she's very scientific. My dad's a psychologist, so he was always trying to analyze us growing up—not step on our toes and respect our boundaries. It was so obvious though that it was funny—well, once I had him figured out. They're both great—just so opposite. Are your parents still together?"

"They are, but sometimes I wonder why. Maybe when my sister graduates from high school, they'll finally just split up and get on with their lives."

I nodded my head and felt bad for bringing up a sore subject. I wanted to cry because Tom had to grow up in that house where he felt like he had ruined his parents' lives and for his sister who still had to live there. And for Evan who had to grow up with his parents separated—will he feel any of those feelings? "I'm sorry, Tom. That must be really hard on you and on your sister."

"Thanks."

I took a long drink of my beer and finished it. The waitress walked by our table. "Excuse me. Can I have some water, please?" I said.

"Sure, I'll bring some right over," she said.

"Are you always this quiet, Tom? Or is it me?"

"I'm kind of a quiet guy, but you kind of make me nervous, Kelly. You do on some level."

I put my face in my hands for a couple of seconds. I just wanted him to be at ease with me. "Why? Why do I make you nervous? That can't be good."

"You're great, Kelly. You're funny. I dunno. Maybe it's that I don't know what's going to come out of your mouth next, and that's what makes me feel nervous. You ask these really intense questions. But at the same time, I like that."

"What do you mean?"

"I dunno…" He shook his head and looked out at the other tables.

The waitress set glasses of water on the table, and we thanked her.

I took a drink and then glanced around at the other tables. "Hey, what couples here do you think are going to make it?"

"What?" He had no clue what I was talking about.

"Look around. What couples in this restaurant do you think will actually make it?"

"Make what?"

"Survive as a couple. Who's not going to break up?"

"Oh," he said. He leaned toward me and then looked around for a little bit. I looked around too. "The couple at the bar—the one with the woman in the red shirt—definitely not making it."

I looked and found the couple he was talking about. "Why?"

"She won't look up from her phone, and he doesn't seem to care." He looked at me. "I don't think they really like each other much."

"I'd agree with that. Okay. Who else?"

He tilted his head to his right. "Two tables over," he whispered. I looked in that direction. There was a couple that looked to be somewhere in their 40s. The woman had short, auburn hair and the man was blond. They seemed to be having a fairly animated conversation and were leaning in toward each other and laughing off and on. I watched them for about a minute—maybe two.

I looked back at him. "What about them?" I whispered.

"Splitsville in under a year."

"Really?" They seemed happy to me—happy enough that I didn't want them to break up.

"What the hell do I know?" He shrugged. "You can't tell just by looking at someone what'll happen." He leaned back. I guess he had a point on some level. "And how do you know they're not just brother and sister or friends?"

I hadn't thought of that.

The waitress came and put our pizza and some plates on the table between us, and Tom grabbed a plate and put a piece on it. He set the plate in front of me and then put a piece on the other plate for him. "Thank you, Tom." I was impressed that he had done that. I took a drink of my water and set it down. Then I looked back over at that couple. "I sort of wanna ask them. I'm curious." Plus, I was somewhat drawn to them. They seemed to be having an enjoyable conversation.

Tom was chewing and set his piece of pizza down. "What?" he said.

I tilted my head in their direction. "The Splitsville couple," I said. "I sort of wanna ask them if they're friends or dating or what..."

Tom looked at them for a couple seconds and then back at me. "Do it."

I shook my head.

"Why not? Do it." He nodded his head slowly a couple of times.

I'm not sure what came over me—maybe it was just feeling like I was being challenged by Tom. Maybe it was that I wanted to be part of the fun they seemed to be having. I stood up, and Tom's eyes got a little bigger. "I'll be right back," I said and walked toward their table and looked back at Tom who was watching me with a slight grin on his face. I leaned over toward the couple.

They stopped talking and looked up at me.

"Hi, I'm sorry to interrupt. I need to ask you a question. Do you mind if I sit down for a minute?"

They looked at each other. The woman looked up at me. "Sure," she said and pushed out the chair beside her. "Join us."

"Thank you." I sat down. "This is silly, but I need to ask... Are you married?"

They looked at each other again and the woman let out a laugh. She looked back at me.

"Yes. We're married," the man said and nodded his head.

The woman grabbed my arm and leaned closer to me. "Just not to each other." She winked at him.

I looked from her to the man. "Oh... Um. I didn't mean to pry. We were just trying to figure out what couples would last. I'm not sure why I came over here exactly. My impulse to do weird things gets the best of me sometimes," I smirked and shrugged my shoulders.

"You and me both," the woman said. "Relax. We're not married to each other because we're cousins," she added and looked at him, so I did too.

He tilted his head back slightly and smiled.

She looked back at me. "How about you?" She nodded her head toward Tom. "He's really rather cute, you know."

I started to laugh. She and I waved at Tom who sheepishly waved back. Then she and I leaned toward each other and touched our heads together for a second. *Why the hell was I over at their table again?* I think it was mostly just to give Tom and me something to talk about, or I needed to get away for a minute or something. I looked at Tom and then back at her.

"We're not married either... or cousins." I leaned in closer to her again and said quietly, "It's probably not going to work out, but he is adorable. I'll give him that."

She grabbed my hand and squeezed it. "Well, you never know," she said.

"I better get back over there. I'm sorry to bother you two."

"No bother," the man said. "You just gave me a story to tell."

"Just not to your wife," the woman said and laughed.

I laughed and stood up. "Enjoy your 'date,'" I said and walked back over to Tom and smiled at him as I sat down.

"And…" he said. "And are they going to make it?"

"You were right. Not as a couple. No."

"They said that?" He leaned closer to me.

I nodded my head, "Pretty much."

He nodded his head and put another piece of pizza on his plate.

I shrugged. "She said you were cute though."

His cheeks turned pink.

"You are."

He shook his head and took a bite of his pizza, so I picked up my piece and took a bite too.

We ate quietly for a few minutes. I was trying to remember what Sam and I were like out at a restaurant. Would anyone who had noticed us have thought that we were doomed? Weren't we the animated couple who was always laughing, leaning together to share a secret or a joke that only we got? Didn't we have the relationship that all our friends envied? No one was having as much fun as we were.

I looked up and realized that Tom was saying something. "I'm sorry. What?"

"You looked a million miles away there. Where'd you go?" He took a drink of his beer.

"It's been a long day. I'm sorry. I was just thinking about how much I liked that couple." I glanced from him to the couple who were standing up to leave. They smiled at me, and I mouthed 'bye' at them and smiled.

"Are you one of those people who talks to everyone everywhere you go?"

Am I? I guess I never really thought about it much. "Maybe. I don't know."

We finished our pizza, paid the bill, and got out of there. In the parking lot I told Tom that I would follow him to Barney's. He walked me to my car. "You have the worst luck with parking spots, Kelly," he said.

I laughed. "Yeah, I know."

He walked to his car, and I was really happy to be alone in my car to regroup and collect my thoughts.

This dating thing was really hard, and as Lisa had pointed out it wasn't supposed to be. Sam and I spent hours hanging out and talking non-stop and having the best time.

Before I was ready to be back out on this date, I was pulling into a parking space and getting out of the car at Barney's. "Oh God! Help me through this," I whispered then immediately decided that I would just tell Tom I was going to pass on Barney's and head home. This obviously wasn't a love connection. But then he walked over to me and smiled his *Tom smile* and winked.

Grabbing my hand, he said, "Ready?"

My stomach flip flopped. I swallowed hard, nodded my head, and started walking. My God, I was so easy when it came to cute boys! But it felt really nice to be holding his hand again, and I kind of leaned into him a little bit.

We walked through the door, and he steered me through a crowd over toward the bar. "Let's get a couple drinks," he said. "What do you want?"

"Whatever you're having. I mean, I guess I should ask what you're having. I don't want to end up passed out in the corner."

He laughed. "I'm getting a beer."

I smiled at him. "That'll be good," I said and bit my lower lip. As Tom ordered our drinks, I glanced around and wondered if any of the groups already hanging out were his friends. Were they watching us? Checking me out?

It seemed like it was taking Tom years to get the drinks, so I told him I was going to use the ladies room and we'd meet up wherever.

It was loud in the ladies' room too, but it gave me a chance to think again. Not necessarily a good thing on a date with Tom. I got the whole *what the hell am I doing here* attitude going again. In the mirror I could see the years of maturity on my face compared to his. I mean, he was absolutely adorable, but there should be another reason than that to keep me at Barney's—meeting his friends. Shouldn't there be?

I walked back out into the bar and started to wander through the crowd as I looked for Tom. This was one of those times I wished I had Lisa's height, especially when she wore four-inch heels and never got lost in a crowd.

Anyway, I finally spotted Tom and started to head over toward him. He noticed me and nodded and smiled. He reached his hand out to me, I took it, and he pulled me into the group. He put his arm around my shoulder. "This is Kelly."

And I looked at his friends' stunned, young faces. I felt like their school teacher. Why didn't Tom see it?

"Kelly, this is Jim."

"Hi, Jim." I shook his hand.

"And this is his girlfriend Abby," Tom continued.

"Hi, Abby," I shook her hand. I guessed she was the under-aged one because she looked really, really young!

"And her friend Caitlyn," Tom said.

"Hi, Caitlyn," I shook her hand.

"And this is Steve."

"Steve," I shook his hand.

"And Phil."

"Hey, Phil," I shook his hand. He was really adorable too, like Tom. And he looked like he might be the closest in age to me.

"Tom said you're a writer," Steve said.

I smiled at Tom and then looked back at Steve. "I am."

"So you're, like, for real?" Abby said. "You have stuff published and stuff?"

"Um… I guess I'm 'for real.' I have a book of short stories and two novels published."

"So, like, what's your name?" Abby said. "I mean your writing name."

I laughed. "Kelly Carter Ramsey."

"No way!" Caitlyn said and seemed suddenly interested in the conversation. She grabbed Abby's arm. "My mom has your books. She loves you!"

"Aww, that's nice to hear," I said. "Tell her thanks."

"She's always hoping that maybe she'll run into you someday since she knows you're from around here."

I laughed. "Well, I guess that could happen," I said. "Tell her to say hi to me if she does."

"Get a picture with her," Abby shouted to Caitlyn. "So you can show her."

"Can I?" Caitlyn said and looked at me. "My mom will be so jealous!"

"Um, sure." I said and laughed again.

I posed with Caitlyn and Abby while Caitlyn took a selfie of us. The guys looked kind of amused and kind of like they were watching a sideshow of sorts. I hoped I was just reading too much into their concerned-looking stares. Caitlyn gave me a quick hug, and then I pointed to one of the full glasses of beer on the table and looked at Tom. "Is that mine?"

"Yep," he nodded and handed it to me.

"Good." I took a long drink and hoped that by the time I was done we'd be talking about something other than my writing. I noticed Caitlyn texting someone and assumed she was sending her mom the picture.

"So where did you two meet?" Phil asked.

I looked at Tom and raised my eyebrows. *What is with the third degree!* I was going to let Tom take the lead on this one. He could make up a fairy tale for all I cared. I wasn't going to say anything.

Tom glanced at me and then looked at Phil. "We met at work," Tom said and then looked back at me.

I nodded at him in agreement.

"Kelly was having trouble with a rug she was buying, and I helped her put it in her car. Right?"

"Yep, you did. You folded it up all nice so the bottom was on the outside, and it wouldn't get dirty in my trunk." Now I remembered the whole thing. He was nice to me when no one had been. That was how I had gotten into this whole Barney's mess. A man had been nice to me—a man with an incredible smile—right after Kim had told me I should put myself out there. I looked up at him. God, there that smile was again. That thing should be illegal.

He squinted his eyes at me. "And then didn't you ask me if I was gay?" Tom said.

I laughed and put my hand on his chest and put my head on it. I shook my head and then looked back up at him. I had completely forgotten about that part. "I'm sorry. My mouth gets me into trouble sometimes. I was just really happy that you had folded up my rug. And I dunno. I just say things..."

"So what did you say?" Steve asked Tom.

"Did you come clean?" Phil added.

"I said yes. I was relieved to finally have it out in the open," Tom shrugged.

"No, like a true man," Caitlyn said, "he probably promptly asked you out to prove his manhood." Her phone beeped and she looked at it.

"Not quite," I said. "He waited a couple days."

They laughed.

"So it gets better," Tom said. "When we met up for coffee, the first thing Kelly does is she calls me a cock while we're waiting for a table."

Phil almost spit his beer mid-sip, and I bit my lower lip. "What!" Caitlyn shrieked.

"I did," I nodded. "But it was something to do with chickens. I wasn't really trying to insult him." I looked at Tom. "And I think you sort of liked it."

He shrugged his shoulders and smirked. "I might have."

"Okay, can we talk about somebody else?" I said.

But then that was the problem; they did talk about something else. They rambled on and on and on about stuff that would, could, only interest people with the life experience that they had up to the point of early 20s. And I found myself zoning out, looking at my watch, nodding politely, but not really enjoying being there even with Tom's great smile.

About an hour later I pulled Tom aside and told him that I needed to get going. Like a gentleman, he offered to walk me out to my car, and I agreed. I said goodbye to Tom's friends and followed Tom outside of Barney's.

We took a few steps away from the building, and the silence of the night surrounded us. "It's gotten chilly," I whispered and hugged myself rubbing my arms.

Tom put his arm around me and squeezed my body to his a bit, and I wished I hadn't said that out loud—although maybe he was going to do that anyway. Maybe it was just the kind of nice guy thing that he did. "How about Caitlyn?" He laughed. "Is that the first time that's happened?"

"No, but it doesn't happen too often because most people don't know what authors look like. I think I have a very small following in the area though—like maybe Caitlyn's mom and about three to five of her friends."

Tom laughed again. "It's kind of cool though," he said.

"I mean, it was awkward there in front of you. But don't get me wrong. I'm glad there are people who like what I write and buy my books."

We stopped in front of my car—complete with a child booster seat in the back, and I turned to face him. I took a deep breath. "I'm not sure this is working," I whispered and pressed my lips together.

The smile faded from his face, and he nodded his head. "I thought you might say that."

"You did?"

"Yep." He put his hands on the sides of my face, leaned down, and kissed me. We're talking *kissed me* kissed me—really, really well too I might add. *Wow!*

"What the hell was that for—were you not listening?" I laughed.

"I was. But, Kelly, you're so pretty. I wanted to kiss you all night, and even though you said it's not going to work, I thought you probably wouldn't mind so I figured what the hell. I was just going to go for it." We both laughed. "I should have asked you though. I'm sorry."

"C'mere," I said and hugged him. "Oh, my God. You're adorable, and you crack me up, Tom." I pulled away from the hug and pushed the button to unlock my car.

"The feeling is mutual, Kelly."

"Thank you for this evening." I reached over and squeezed his hand. "Take care," I said and got in my car. I started it and opened up my window.

Tom was standing on the curb watching me.

"By the way, you kiss fantastically well!"

He rolled his eyes and shook his head.

"No, I'm being completely serious here. I'd put you in my top three."

"Go home!" He smiled.

I winked at him and pulled out of the parking spot and was sort of relieved that the date was over. He wasn't right for me, right? I looked back in my rear-view mirror as I drove away, and he was just standing there looking at the ground with his hands in his pockets. That image made me feel really sad.

At home Sam was sitting on the couch twiddling his thumbs.

"Hey there," I said when I shut the front door.

"Hey," he said.

"Is Evan sleeping?"

Sam looked toward the stairs. "He called for me a few minutes ago, so I'm not sure," he said.

"Okay." I turned and put my jacket in the closet.

"How have you been, Kelly?"

Okay… What's going on here? "I've been," I paused, "okay." I shrugged. "How about you, Sam?

"Could be better. I dunno. The past couple days I've just been thinking a lot about everything." He looked at me, and I met his gaze for a couple seconds and then looked away.

"I'm thirsty," I said as I walked toward the kitchen to get something to drink.

He followed me. "Kelly, I guess I'm trying to say," he paused, "that I miss you."

"You want some water?" I pulled a glass from the cupboard. "Wait, what was that?" I sat my glass down and rubbed my eye.

"Do you ever think about us, Kelly?"

I wanted to say that pretty much since the second that he left me that *us* was all that I had thought about and that I had desperately wanted him back for so long—desperately wanted my family back. But lately because of his recent actions, and especially after seeing that therapist, I'd been starting to reframe all my thoughts. I shook my head for a couple seconds and didn't turn around to face him because I wasn't sure I would have been able to say these words to his face. "I think about us, Sam. Pretty much constantly. About how much fun we had. About what a great team we were." My voice broke a little. "And it always leads to me trying to wrap my mind around how you could leave me. How at the end you could give up on our family and then just leave me. And lately that's led to remembering all the bad times, so, yes, I do think about us, Sam."

He was quiet for a few seconds. "You weren't roses either, Kelly," he said to my back then walked out and shut the door.

"That's why you miss me so much," I whispered and blinked my eyes to stop the tears. I picked up the glass and thought about throwing it down on the counter because seeing it shatter into pieces would have given me a lot of satisfaction on some level. Instead I filled it with water, took a long drink, and went to bed.

SEVENTEEN

The Phone Calls

I wasn't sure what time Evan had woken up, but he must have risen and shone at a very early hour. By the time he did his puppet show at the foot of my bed to wake me—a show about a lazy mom who never took care of her son, by the way, he'd pretty much trashed the rest of the house.

He was in a pretty agreeable mood though and helped me get things straightened up. We did all that before I tried to sit down to write. I couldn't muster any creativity if the house were a mess, right? That little private joke was starting to really simultaneously amuse and annoy me.

But, for a change, when I sat at the computer, I dove right into the book. Screw social media. Screw online dating. They could wait for me. If I wanted drama in my life, I'd put it into my book. I had no pending dates with men to distract me. In fact, I'd just gone from two suitors to zero in a matter of a couple days.

It was time to write.

Didn't Dana tell me that I needed to remember who I was and write? She said something like that, anyway.

Maybe I should call her and ask? No, that would make me lose focus, and focus was something that I thought I had for a change at the moment. And it was obviously just about to slip away so I needed to make good use of it before it was completely gone.

I read for about 10 minutes while trying to figure out where I needed to add something in my novel. I started to type a couple sentences, and my phone rang. I noticed it was Tom, and I almost didn't answer it. After the fourth ring, I grabbed it, "Hello."

"Kelly."

"Hi, Tom," I paused. "What's up?"

"I've been thinking about you and wanted to make sure you got home okay last night," he said.

"Aren't you sweet? I did. How about you? How was the rest of your night?" I grabbed a couple slips of paper that were lying on my desk and put them in a pile.

"It was," he paused, "it was okay."

"Did you and your friends close out Barney's?"

"Nah, I pretty much went home after you drove away."

"Oh," I said.

No one said anything for several seconds.

Then Tom said, "Kelly, you freak me out, but being with you makes me feel something. I know you said we're not going to work out, and you could be right. But I wanna see you again."

"Tom, I don't know what to say."

"Just think about it, Kelly."

I leaned back in my chair. He had such a gentle, sweet way about him. I truly didn't think it would be a love connection, but, for whatever reason, he seemed to be really drawn to me, and I didn't want to hurt him again in that moment. "Okay, I'll think about it."

"Can I call you this weekend?"

"Okay."

"I'll call you," he said.

"Bye." I hung up the phone. "Oh, my God." I pushed my leg off the ground to let the chair spin around a few times.

I picked up the phone and called Dana. "Kelly, what's up?"

"Oh Dana…"

"What, Kel? What's up?"

"So Tom and I went out last night and met up with some of his friends at Barney's, Dana. We hung out with his friends at Barney's. When was the last time you were at Barney's?"

"About 15 years ago. Maybe more," Dana said and laughed.

"It was very, well, boring. I have nothing in common with any of them. Probably not even with Tom."

"Well, you weren't convinced you had a lot in common with him already, right?"

"No, I know. Anyway, the point of the call is that I told him I wasn't sure it was working out, and I thought he agreed even though he kissed me right after I told him that." I pushed off to spin my chair again.

"Oh?"

"Yes, and kissed me really well, I might add. And then he called me just now and asked me to reconsider."

"Oh," she said. "You must have kissed him 'really well' too," she added.

I snickered. "So when he called just now he said something fairly sweet about how I make him nervous but also feel good or something like that… I can't really remember. It's sort of all a blur because I so did not expect to hear from him again."

"What did you tell him?"

"That I needed to think about it. And he asked if he could call me this weekend."

"Well, that is interesting."

"Is it? I mean he is sweet, and he's cute. And I like him as a person and all. But it's not going to work. Oh! He said that even if I'm right about it not working out, he still wants to see me! What's that about?"

"Well, he's young and probably not looking for a life partner so if he enjoys you now, that's enough—even if it's not going to work out long term," she paused. "Actually, that may be one of the reasons he does like you. There's no pressure for the long haul."

"Oh, okay. I hadn't thought about that. I just sort of freaked out a little."

"So if you like hanging out, then keep hanging out. If you don't want to deal with it, then don't."

"Yeah, that makes sense, but I'm not sure what I wanna do."

"Well, you don't have to decide today, so you can get back to your writing, or cleaning, or procrastinating, or whatever you were doing when the phone rang."

"Um, thanks. I will." I put my hand on my forehead and then ran it along the top of my head and further back until my hand hit and landed on the chair behind my head.

"Talk to you later." She hung up.

I spun the chair again. "Evan!" The house was quiet—which was never a good sign with my son. "Evan!" I got up to find him.

He wasn't in any of his normal spots—his room, the kitchen, the living room, or bathroom. My heart skipped a beat. "Evan!" I shouted a little louder and started to re-check all those locations and hoped that I had somehow missed him.

As I was walking through the living room, I noticed the front door was slightly open, so I rushed to the door and went out onto the porch. He was lying on the glider and was flipping through a book and laughing.

"Evan!" I shouted.

"Ahh!" He shuddered and dropped his book. He looked up at me with wide eyes. "Mom!"

"Evan! You scared the heck out of me. When you leave the house—even just to go on the porch—you need to tell me first."

"Mom!" he shouted again. "You're mean. Why did you scare me?" He hid his face.

"Evan, you scared me. I just ran around the whole house and looked for you—twice. I didn't know where you were. I don't wanna lose you, Buddy. You're the best thing in my life." I sat down beside him. "I'm sorry I scared you though."

He picked up his book and tried to hide behind it. "Hmmp." He peeked over the top. "Hmmp."

I reached over and tickled his foot.

"Mom!" He laughed. "I don't wanna be happy. I'm mad at you."

I tickled his foot again. He swung his legs off the glider and leaned his body into my chest. "Don't scare me," he said.

I hugged him and kissed him on the top of the head. "I'm sorry, Evan."

After a while I sat at my computer again. I started reading my story for about the millionth time. I pushed my chair away from the desk, "I've got nothing to say." I put my face in my hands and started to cry. I didn't want to be that stupid character that I felt so much like lately—a flighty girl who couldn't focus on her book. I didn't like being so distracted by dumb things—men and Sam—so much that I had lost my ability to support Evan and me. "I refuse to fail at this." I breathed in sniffing and shook my head.

I got up and went to the kitchen to make dinner. Maybe just a quick break would help me get my creativity back. I had no clue where it had been hiding for the past few weeks, but I was praying that I would find it soon.

EIGHTEEN

The New Neighbor

My phone rang shortly after breakfast. It was Tom. My first impression was, "Not now." That really could only have meant one thing. "Go with your gut, Kel," I said quietly and let the call go to voicemail. I seriously needed to write this book. Tom was too distracting. As kind and sweet as he was, he wasn't worth the potential failure of not finishing this project.

I looked at my phone and shook my head. I could have the final goodbye conversation with him later. I had too much to get done before I had to be at my friend's wedding.

I dropped Evan at the play space and started through the aisles of the grocery store silently cursing myself for deciding to shop on Saturday. If I hadn't been on my last roll of toilet paper, I would have somehow pushed off the trip until Monday. I made a mental note to grab an extra package of toilet paper this time (and to get something larger than the four-pack that I grabbed the last time) so that I wouldn't run out so quickly. I told myself that when I opened the second package, I'd remind myself to buy another. But who was I kidding? I knew I'd wait until I was on my last roll of the second pack to get more. With my luck, that would also be a Sunday night before a major holiday.

"Hey, I thought that was your cute kid in the play center," I heard someone say as I was putting the second 24-pack of toilet paper in my cart. I looked over and saw a man walking toward me with a smile on his face. His face didn't register for a second, and then it hit me. He was the guy from the zoo.

I laughed a little and touched the toilet paper package. Why had I picked this moment to buy 48 rolls of toilet paper? "Hi," I said. "How are you?"

He pushed his cart over to mine. "I'm good." Several people were pushing past us. "Well, as good as you can be when buying food on a Saturday morning. Are we getting a blizzard or something?"

"Exactly. I hate shopping on the weekend!"

He pointed to my cart. "Looks like you're set on toilet paper if we do get a blizzard though. Make sure you get some milk and bread too." He smiled at me.

I laughed and then maybe blushed a little. I touched the package again. "It's a long story." I laughed again. "But it is April though, so I think we're done with snow." I adjusted my purse strap on my shoulder and tried to think if there were any good, quick reasons to explain why I was buying 48 rolls of toilet paper at once. I glanced at the shelf—it wasn't even on sale. So I changed the subject. "So do you live out this way, or are you just stalking me?"

Then he laughed. "Yeah."

"Yeah to what?"

We both laughed. This could go down as the goofiest conversation I ever had... or maybe just most awkward—or endearing. I wasn't sure yet.

"I live about two minutes from here, so I think you're stalking me," he said.

"You win. I'm more like six or seven minutes away. Ten if I get stuck at the light."

"Hmm. Small world," he said.

"Definitely is at that." I didn't want the conversation to end. "So how were the rest of the animals? Did you get any good pictures?"

"Of Michael?" He laughed. "No. He wasn't playing along. Too serious for a three-year-old," he paused, "but he's been through a lot."

I nodded my head although I had no clue what he meant, and we weren't close enough for me to ask. I mean, we were essentially strangers. So why was he still standing here and talking with me?

I didn't want him to walk away, but I wasn't sure why he was staying. And what did I want to happen? For us to exchange numbers? For us to all go and get lunch together? Hadn't I just decided that men were too distracting for me right now? I wished that I could make a decision and stick with it for longer than half a day. I could. "Well, it was nice to run into you, Jack, right?"

He nodded and pointed to me, "Kelly."

If I hadn't blushed earlier over the enormous amount of toilet paper that I was putting in my shopping cart, I knew I did then over him remembering my name. My stomach flip flopped a little too. "So I guess I'll see you around the neighborhood, Neighbor," I said.

"I hope," he said. We both smiled at each other, and then I looked down at my cart. I looked back up at him. He was still smiling at me.

"Okay, Jack. I'll see you." I pushed my cart around the bend and into the next aisle. "Oh, my God," I said quietly. *Oh, my God.* I mouthed again. People probably thought I was crazy. Well, this was assuming anyone was actually paying any attention to me. It was way too busy in the store for that.

I was almost to the end of the next aisle when Jack pushed his cart around the other corner toward me. "Hey," he said.

"Hey," I said.

"This may be a little strange, but if I leave here without trying to get your number, I'm going to kick myself in the head the rest of the day. And to be honest, I'm really not that flexible."

I laughed at the image then said, "So you're not married?"

He laughed. "If I were, I'd feel bad for my wife right now." He shook his head. "No, I'm not married anymore."

"Okay," I paused. "I'll give you my number."

He pulled out his phone and typed it in. My phone rang. "And now you have mine too."

I smiled. "Okay," I said quietly. "Have a good day."

He nodded his head, and I pushed my cart past his into the next aisle. *Oh, my God!* I mouthed again.

When I got home, I got serious about my book. I mean… really. I had to.

There were closer to five months than six, and I had about 70 pages written. Some of them weren't even all that great—most of them, really.

Write something funny kept going through my head in Kim's voice. I wished I could write something funny, but I wasn't exactly sure how. When I talked, funny things came out of my mouth, but I hadn't really thought much about how I'd come up with them. They just seemed to be there. But thinking about and actually writing funny things didn't seem quite as simple as that. *Write a toned-down version of your life* popped into my head in Dana's voice. I laughed out loud.

Then I started typing more of the usual stuff. I was leaning toward a back story of one of the extremely minor characters. What other choice did I have at this point?

Write something funny. "Shut up, Kim!"

The Wedding Guest

At about 3:00 I had to stop working so I could get ready for the wedding, drop Evan at Kim's house for a sleepover, and get to the ceremony about 30 minutes away by 4:30. I didn't leave a whole lot of time to get ready, but I didn't really care too much about how I looked. And my options for dressing up were pretty slim. There was only going to be one person there aside from the bride and groom who I knew. I hadn't seen this friend (or the bride and groom) since before Sam and I separated. I wasn't too excited about going alone. But I really didn't have any other choice aside from skipping it all together, I supposed. In a moment of nostalgia, I had accepted the invitation without really thinking through the whole going alone to a wedding thing. Since I said I was going, I felt like I should go.

I sniffed my armpits (*passable*), put on a basic black dress, straightened my hair, brushed my teeth, put on a little extra makeup, and had Evan out the door at about 3:55 to take him to Kim's. I knew I was going to be a little late for the ceremony, but there was nothing I could do except hope that no one would really notice.

I pulled into the church parking lot about 4:45 p.m. Was it possible that the wedding hadn't started yet? Some weddings started a little late, right? I parked my car and walked toward the entrance of the church. When I went inside, I could see that the bride and groom were at the front of the church already. It looked like they were about to exchange vows or rings. I glanced at the empty pews toward the back of the church. Would I be able to sneak into a seat without anyone really noticing? Or would it be better to just stand back here and watch?

I heard the outside door of the church open, jumped a little, and turned to see who was catching me being late. It was a man I didn't know—of course it was since I didn't really know anyone. He had dark blond short hair and freckles across his nose and cheeks. He was smiling at me and looked friendly, so I tapped my watchless wrist a couple times and whispered, "You're late."

He walked over and stood so close to me that our arms were touching. "How long has it been going on?" he said quietly.

I shrugged my shoulders. "I just got here." I elbowed him.

He tapped his wrist and shook his head.

I smiled at him and put my hand on his forearm. "Do you think we should try to sneak in there quietly, or is it better to just stand here and watch?" I looked at him, and he shrugged. "That's what I was trying to decide when you walked in," I paused and then added, "late."

Someone started singing a song, and the bride and groom moved to light the unity candle.

He leaned into me. "So how do you know Bill and Holly?" he said.

"Holly and I worked together many years ago." I linked arms with him and steered him out the front door. "We're too late." I said in a louder voice once outside. "It's better just to wait until they come out. Don't you think?"

He nodded his head.

"How do you know them?" I added.

"Bill's an old friend."

We walked over and sat on a bench.

"My flight was late," he said.

I straightened the skirt of my dress and smoothed it with my hands. "That's good—you've got a good excuse."

"What's yours?" he said.

"I don't have one—at least not a good one." I raised my eyebrows and shrugged, "Time got away from me?" I smiled.

"Well, you're screwed then. They'll probably never forgive you." He leaned back and crossed his left ankle onto his right knee.

I laughed. "We're not that close anymore so I don't think Holly will even care that I wasn't here. My friend Sherry is supposed to be here. How about you? Will you know a lot of people?"

"I don't know. I'm not sure who's coming. I flew in basically just for the wedding. I have a flight out early tomorrow morning."

"That was nice of you. I only drove over from the next town. You probably brought a better gift than I did too. Show off!" I leaned toward him and smacked his shoe.

He started to say something. I pressed my hands to my ears, "La, la, la, la. I don't want to know." I stopped doing that and looked at him.

"I wasn't going to tell you." He smirked and laughed. "I was just asking if you knew how to get to the reception."

I shook my head quickly. "Oh, sorry. Yeah, it's not far. You can follow me there if you want. Or you can just put it in your GPS." I looked toward the door of the church. "Should we be sitting here when they come out, or will that be awkward?" I looked back at him.

"You worry a lot, don't you?" he said.

I shrugged. "A fair amount, I guess." The church door opened. I shrieked and jumped up. "Come on!" I grabbed his hand, and we started running toward my car.

We got behind my car, and I crouched down. I breathed hard a few times and then laughed. "Do you think anyone saw us?"

He bent down beside me and put his hands on his thighs. He shook his head and started laughing. "What just happened?"

I straightened a little and put my elbow on the trunk of my car. "Basically, I freaked out and did something really embarrassing in front of a stranger."

He laughed. "I like you. You're kind of a hoot."

Then I laughed. "I'm Kelly by the way." I reached my hand out to shake his.

He straightened up. "I'm Brad. Do you wanna get out of here? Your jumpiness is making me nervous. You realize we're stalking the church right now."

I pulled my keys out of my purse and pushed the button to unlock my car. "This is my car. Jump in," I said. "Well," I paused, "as soon as I clean off the seat a little bit."

I started the car and backed out of the parking spot. "Where do you wanna go?"

"I don't know. What's around?" He buckled his seatbelt. "We have about an hour to kill, right?"

"I guess, about that. Are you hungry? Or would that be stupid since we'll, in theory, be eating at the reception?" I glanced over at him. "Well, unless the food sucks. I definitely don't want to start drinking at 5:00. I'll never last. And then there's the driving home part too. So I won't be drinking much at all really."

He laughed.

"Yeah, I ramble too," I said.

He laughed some more. "I don't care what we do. I put you and all your rambling quirkiness in full charge of my schedule for the next hour. After all, if it weren't for you, I'd probably be sitting and watching my friend getting married."

"That is such a lie!" I said loudly.

"How so?"

"You heard the church door open. That wedding is over. You can't watch a wedding that's already happened, Brad."

"Well, I'd be shaking their hands and wishing them well in the receiving line."

"And then doing what? Being bored for all that time until the reception starts? I'm saving you!" I laughed. "By the way I hate those!" I added.

"Hate what?" he said.

"Those receiving lines and forced hugs and handshakes. I hate being forced to talk to people. I'm just not good in social situations."

He started laughing.

"What?" I said.

"I was just thinking, 'Who the hell are you?!'"

"I told you. I'm Holly's friend, and you know my name. That's all you need to know for now, Brad." I laughed and turned into the mall parking lot. "Don't get all worried on me. You're in good hands."

"You're taking me to the mall?" he said. "Are we 15 again?"

I laughed loudly. "Pretty much. Don't you feel like it right now?"

"Not until you pulled into the mall," he said. "But, yeah, I guess I do now."

I reached over and smacked his thigh. "I don't know. What else is there to do if we're not going to eat or drink for an hour." I pulled into a parking spot and turned the car off. I looked at Brad and shrugged. "You ready?"

"I was just mentally fast forwarding to the part where you ditch me in a mall in a strange town, and my rental car is back at some church that I can't even remember the name of." He smiled and shook his head.

"Do I seem like someone who would do that?"

"Well," he paused. "Yes, actually." He laughed. "And yet I've gotten myself into this somehow so now I'm wondering what's wrong with me?"

"Hmm," I looked out the front window. "I can see why you might think that, but I promise I'll behave." I tilted my head from side to side and tapped my thumbs on the steering wheel as I tried to think of a solution. "I got it," I said and pulled my phone out of my purse and handed it to him. "Here."

"What are you doing?" he said and took it.

"If you have my phone, I won't ditch you, right?" I nodded my head and smiled at him. "Promise."

He started laughing. "It would probably be easier to exchange numbers."

"No, you're not thinking this through, Brad. If we just exchange numbers and we somehow get separated, there's no guarantee I'll answer." I put my hand on his hand that held my phone. "But if you have my phone, well, I'm not going to ditch you."

He looked down at my hand on his, then he looked back up at me and smirked. "You've thought about this before."

"Let's just say this isn't the first wacky situation I've gotten myself into." I opened the door and got out of the car.

He got out and followed me. Getting into step beside me, he said, "I'm placing my bets. Three out of four sentences that come out of your mouth are totally made up."

"Wait, what? I haven't told you any lies." I adjusted my purse strap. "Well... except the drinking by 5:00 thing." I laughed. "Obviously right there—that was the lie."

"Like I said." He patted my back.

"Just shut up and walk... silently."

"Yes, Ma'am."

I shook my head. *Ma'am!* If I had the energy for a fight, I would have had one about that.

My phone started to ring. "Just let it go to voicemail," I said.

Brad pulled it out of his pocket. "You sure?" He looked at the screen. "It's Tom. You don't wanna talk to Tom?"

"Nah, I'm good. Put that thing away."

"Sounds like you're avoiding Tom?" Brad said. "I'm sorry, Tom," he said quietly to the phone.

"It's rude to answer the phone when you're hanging out with someone, Brad. I'm just being polite." I picked a piece of lint off my dress. "And, yes, there's probably a little avoidance there too."

"Why? What'd he do to you?" He sort of tried to elbow me, but we were walking too far away from each other.

I looked at his elbow and laughed.

He shrugged and shook his head.

"Nothing. He's sweet. But I'm just not feeling it. Well, except when he smiles. He's adorable when he smiles, but, otherwise, we have nothing in common."

Brad laughed a little. "You are kind of adorable when you smile, Kelly. I'll admit that."

I felt my cheeks get hot. "Don't make me tell you to shut up again."

"You were the one who said you had that in common with him."

"Wait, did I? That wasn't exactly what I meant if I had." I elbowed him and made sure my elbow made contact with his arm— and also made sure that he noticed.

He rolled his eyes.

"But thank you. I'll take the compliment," I said then laughed.

"You're welcome. Maybe you should have just answered and told him. Don't leave the poor guy hanging." He pointed my phone at me and then put it back in his pocket.

"Whose side are you on? I told him on Wednesday," I gestured with my hand. "And Thursday he asked me to reconsider. I said I'd think about it. I'm with you right now, and, no matter what your opinion of me is, I'm not rude. Unless that says 'Kim,' we can let it go to voicemail."

"What's up with Kim? Is she okay?" He reached up and scratched the back of his head.

I laughed. "She's fine. She's in charge of my son right now, so really that's my only worry," I laughed again. "I mean, I'm not worried about the care. Just worried about what it could mean if she would call. She's a much better mother than I am."

"Huh," he nodded and kind of smirked. "You have a son?"

"Yes, for five years now. Evan. He's pretty adorable."

He gestured toward me. "Well, obviously."

I laughed.

"Okay, so if Kim calls, you get your phone back. That seems fair enough."

"Thanks. How about you, Brad? What's your story? Any kids?"

"Nope. No kids."

I shook my head slowly. "I'm sorry. That must be so boring."

Brad laughed, and I smiled at him. "Well, maybe someday," he said. "There's time."

"I'll cross my fingers for you. Hey, what time is it? You have my phone."

He pulled out his phone. "5:34. You got plans?"

"Well, sort of. But we have a little more time to kill before we have to be there."

My phone rang again. "You're popular."

"We could put that on silent," I said as he pulled it out of his pocket again.

"This time it's Jack from the zoo," he looked at me and laughed. "Why do you have the zookeeper's number in your phone?"

I started laughing too. "He's not the zookeeper," I laughed some more. "But that's hilarious. I'm not that weird though."

"Did you have some sort of customer service issue there? You have to tell me why you have someone from the zoo's number in your contacts."

"He's not from the zoo. It's just that's where I met him. So if he calls me, I'll see that clue and remember."

"Oh," he paused. "Well, he called."

"Thanks for the information." I laughed. "So, like, if we would exchange numbers, you'd be Brad from Holly's wedding."

"Thanks," he rolled his eyes.

"I'm kidding. And we won't be exchanging numbers. You have my phone, remember? That's our safety. No numbers needed."

"That's right," he put my phone back in his pocket. "I have your phone. Your very noisy phone."

"Put it on silent. Seriously. If for no other reason, it'll save me from more embarrassing contacts popping up. Come on," I gestured my hands toward the pocket he put it in. "You don't need to know all the weird places I meet people."

He laughed and handed it to me. I switched it to silent and handed it back to him.

"We could probably start to walk to the car. By the time we get there and drive to the reception and park and walk in and find our tables, it'll be about 6:30."

"I'll trust you. Lead the way."

"Well, let's finish this loop around the mall first. We're almost to the end, and I guess we do have a little more time to kill."

"Makes sense," he said. Brad pulled out his phone and started typing? He laughed a little and put it away. We walked in silence for a little bit.

"Are we done talking? You're being quiet," I said.

"How do you know how I'm being? You've known me for less than an hour," Brad said.

"You don't seem like the nervous, silent type."

"How do you figure that?" he said. "And why does it have to be a nervous silence? Why can't it be a comfortable silence?"

"Have we known each other long enough for a comfortable silence?"

He shrugged. "Is there a timeframe required for that sort of thing?"

I shrugged. "When you got to the church, you came right up to me and stood touching arms with me. I was a stranger—a stranger who had just scolded you for being late. Someone shy wouldn't have done that."

"Well, maybe I'm not shy, but can't I be the quiet type?"

"I mean, you can. But you're not."

"Because, again, you know me so well," he said.

"Why are you being so difficult all of the sudden? Let's just shut up again and enjoy the silence. I shouldn't have brought it up," I paused. "I don't like awkward pauses I guess. It's more about me than you."

"Kelly," he said.

"What?"

"You're rambling again." He smiled and pulled my vibrating phone out of his pocket. "Don't you hang out with anyone who knows how to text? Are we taking calls from Dana?"

"What do you think?"

"No?" he said.

"Yes, no. I told you, if it doesn't say Kim, voicemail." I pointed back to his pocket. "Put that away."

"Just making sure there wasn't some mystery clause where on Saturdays at about 6:00 all bets are off."

I shook my head. "Nope, I'm pretty predictable. No surprises here."

He stopped walking.

I walked a couple steps and turned around, "What?"

He started walking again and caught up to me. "Says the woman who ran me through a church parking lot to hide behind her car."

I laughed out loud. Did I seriously do that? *What is wrong with me?* "Just you wait, Brad. We'll be at the reception soon enough, and then you can give me back my phone and ditch me. Won't you be glad?" We walked a couple more steps silently. "Hey, I should probably drive back to the church so you can get your car, right? Otherwise, you're screwed after the reception when I've already cut out early." I elbowed his arm.

"Good point." We were quiet for a few more steps. He stopped again. "But don't leave early."

I grabbed his wrist and pulled him along a little. "Once you're back to your car, what's it to you when I leave?" I looked up at him as we walked. I realized I was still holding onto his wrist and let go.

He looked ahead for a while and then glanced at me. "I just have a feeling that the reception will be a whole lot more fun with you at it."

"Oh, please," this time I stopped. He turned and looked at me, so I started walking again. "You're going to ditch me as soon as a friend shows up. Plus, I'm gonna hang out with my friend Sherry. I haven't seen her in ages."

We walked quietly for a while longer. "I hope the food's good," Brad said. "I'm starving."

"You want me to stop and get you some fast food? Or we could swing by the food court."

"No. I'll wait."

We were almost to my car, so I pulled my keys out of my purse.

"Here we are," I said. We got in and buckled our seatbelts, and I started the car and started backing out of the parking spot.

"Hey, we should have some sort of code," Brad said. He kind of turned his body toward mine.

I glanced at him and put the car in drive and started driving down the aisle of the parking lot. "A code? What do you mean?" I glanced at him again.

"Something we say or do if someone boring is trying to talk to us too much at the reception," he motioned with his hand, "to get out of the conversation."

I laughed and hit him on the thigh. "Brad, you're probably going to be sitting across the ballroom from me. We'd need a flare gun for that sort of code. Or maybe sparklers would work depending on how far apart our tables are. Should we stop and get some on the way?" I laughed.

He didn't say anything, so I glanced at him again. "So you're really ditching me as soon as we get to my car?" he said.

I looked at him, and then pulled out of the parking area and into the circle that looped around the mall.

"No, I mean, I said you could follow me to the reception if you don't just wanna use your GPS. I wasn't lying about that," I said.

"Okay." I could see out of my peripheral vision that he turned away from me and was looking out the window.

No way! Ignore that dejection and do not get wrapped up in the drama, Kelly. Don't do it!

I was quiet for about a minute. "So where do you live?" I said. "In Boston still?"

"How'd you know I lived in Boston?"

"You said you were old friends with Bill. I guessed."

"Oh, yeah, I did." He twisted back to face me again. "I live in Connecticut now."

"Well, at least that's a little closer." I turned on the radio. "I don't even feel like going to this thing." I stopped at a red light and looked over at him. "You're a good friend for flying in. You know that."

"We used to be best friends as kids. I couldn't miss it."

"Well… except you did. Sorry about that." The light turned green, and I started driving again.

"Yeah, well. He probably didn't notice. Wedding days are a blur for the bride and groom."

I nodded my head. "That's true." I started to think about my wedding and my reception and the fun, chaos, and excitement about that whole day. And then here I was now—in my car driving a stranger around town, and Sam was God knows where. I shook my head a little.

"At least the weather's nice today," I said. I didn't want to think about my wedding day or Sam anymore. "One less thing to worry about, right?"

He laughed a little.

I pulled into the church parking lot. It was empty.

Brad pointed at the only car left. "That's my rental."

"No kidding."

He shook his head.

"All right, get out." I laughed. "Do you have a GPS or did you seriously want to follow me?"

"I'll just follow you, so I don't have to pull out the invitation and type in the address," he said.

"Okay, I promise I won't lose you."

"Here's hoping," he said and got out, and then he leaned down and tossed my phone onto the passenger seat. He smiled at me. "I should hold onto that until you get me safely there, but in case Kim calls, you can have it back."

I smiled at him. "Nice. Thanks."

He shut the passenger door, and I watched him walk over to the car and get in. I picked up my phone and looked to see if anyone had left a voicemail. There was a message from Dana and one from Jack. I listened to Dana's message. "Are you home, Kel? I'm going to walk over and give you something. I'll leave it on the porch. Look for a bag when you get this message." *Okay.* And the message from Jack, "Hi, Kelly. This is Jack. It was nice running into you today. What are the odds? I'll try you later." I tossed my phone on the seat, made sure Brad was ready to follow me, and pulled out of the church parking lot.

NINETEEN

The Par-tay

I made sure that Brad was behind me the whole way so that he couldn't say that I intentionally ditched him (not that I would ever talk to him again). But when I got him to the parking lot, I figured he was a big boy and was on his own at that point. I put on a little lip gloss and looked in the mirror. "Eh," I said and got out of the car.

It was a really lovely evening outside, and I didn't really want to go into the venue. The air felt really warm, and it was still light out. I felt like holding my arms out and twirling around a few times. Instead, I laughed at the image and started walking toward the hall and hoping that Sherry would already be there so that I wouldn't have to awkwardly stand around or try to mingle. I hated doing that. God, I hated talking to people when I wasn't in the mood to socialize.

I walked over to the name plate table and found my name. *Kelly Ramsey, Table 10.* I saw Sherry's name tag so I must have beaten her here. "Boo," I said quietly and turned around to survey the lobby for a ladies' room. I could hang in there for a bit and hope that she would arrive shortly.

I killed some time primping in front of the mirror, but after about 10 minutes I walked back to the name table. Sherry still hadn't claimed her name, so I walked into the banquet hall and found table 10. "Hi, I'm Kelly," I said as I pulled out one of the two empty chairs and sat down. There were two couples at the table. They told me their names, David, Linda, Sam, and Jenna. I figured I'd forget them in about 10 minutes, but I tried to do mental associations to hang onto them for at least a little bit. "I'm waiting for a friend," I said and patted the seat beside me.

Like they care. I glanced at my phone.

They smiled and went back to their own conversations—each couple with themselves. I figured we must have been the mismatched table of people who really didn't have other connections and hoped that Sherry would arrive soon.

I looked over toward the entrance and willed Sherry to walk through it. Instead I saw Brad walk through the entrance. He was holding a drink and talking with a man who looked to be about his age. It was so weird to see him here. He was essentially a stranger, but I felt connected to him. I almost got up and walked over to him. But it looked like he found a friend, and I didn't want to interrupt.

Did this afternoon even really happen or had I made all of that up? And were we now obligated to continue to chat if we bumped into each other throughout the evening, or did we just pretend that we were what we actually were to each other? Strangers.

Stranger danger, stranger danger! I thought and then started to chuckle a little but didn't want to seem like the weirdo who was sitting and laughing about nothing. Linda looked up at me and smiled and then looked back at David—or was it Sam? God, why did his name have to be Sam!

I picked up my phone and looked at it for a couple minutes. The DJ started announcing the wedding party so I set my phone down and watched.

Good. Something to do.

Holly and Bill came in and danced and cut the cake and the meal started... And still no Sherry.

We'd eaten almost our full meals when the newly married couple came over to greet our table. "Congratulations," we all said.

"You look so pretty, Holly! I'm so sorry I was late and missed the ceremony," I said while I was hugging her.

Bill laughed. "Oh, you were the Kelly who hung out with Brad at the mall?"

"Well, we ended up being late together," I said as I hugged Bill. I patted him on the arm. "You clean up nice," I added.

"Thanks," he said and laughed. "Whatever you did, you made quite an impression on Brad." Bill smirked at me.

I laughed and choked on my spit a little. "I didn't do anything... special."

Bill smiled at me and nodded his head.

I shook my head, shrugged my shoulders, and said, "I swear." Then I turned to Holly. "Where's Sherry? I was looking forward to getting caught up with her."

"She's not here? I don't know. I thought she was coming. I wonder if she got sick or something," she said.

"Yeah, she hasn't come yet. Hope she's okay," I said then thought, *Oh, crap! I am so out of here as soon as I'm done eating.*

A photographer came and took our table's picture with Bill and Holly—with me standing right in between them, I might add, and then they moved on to greet the next table.

I quickly finished the food that was on my plate and picked up my purse. I smiled at Jenna, who had glanced over at me, and I walked away.

I was in the parking lot when I heard someone call my name, so I turned around.

Brad was running toward me. "Where are you going?" he said when he reached me.

"Home," I said.

"Already?"

"Yeah, my friend didn't show up, so I don't have anyone to talk to."

"You have to stay," he said.

"Why?"

"You can talk to me. I don't really have anyone to talk with either so you can't leave. We need each other in there."

"That's a lie. I saw you chatting with someone when I first sat down. You were walking in with a drink in your hand talking with someone. Go be with your friends, Brad."

"That was just some guy who was getting a drink the same time I was. He's not even at my table," he said and put his hands in his pockets. "I don't know why I came."

"You said you didn't want to miss it. You're here for Bill." I put my hands out palms up.

"I mean, aside from that. There isn't really anyone I care to talk to here," he pulled his hand out of his pockets and gestured toward me and shrugged, "except for you."

I crossed my arms across my chest. "You care about talking with me?"

"Yeah, I mean," he crossed his arms across his chest too and looked at me for a few seconds. "I was having fun earlier," he paused, "when we were hanging out." He looked back toward the hall and then back at me and blew his breath out. "I don't know. Honestly, I haven't had fun since you dropped me off at my car." He looked down and kicked at a small stone. "And then I saw you walking out the door a minute ago. I came to the lobby and hoped I'd bump into you again and saw you walking out the entrance." He looked back up at me and shrugged. "So I chased you." He smiled and laughed and held his hands out palms up toward me. He shook his head and shrugged. "It's not the first time I've run after you through a parking lot today."

Remembering my panic as I pulled him through the church lot to hide behind my car, I laughed and looked up at him.

He was smiling at me.

I closed my eyes for a couple seconds. "I don't want to be here anymore though."

His smile faded, and he pressed his lips together. "Please don't go," he said and smiled again.

"I don't want to stay here," I shook my head, and his face dropped a little. "It's a long story, but it's just too hard for me to be here today."

He nodded and crossed his arms across his chest again.

We stood there and stared at each other for a few seconds, and then I said, "But do you wanna come over and hang out for a while if you'd seriously rather hang out with me? I'm probably not much more exciting though. I was just gonna sit on the couch and, I dunno, read or something."

He was quiet for a couple seconds and then said, "Okay, sounds good." And nodded his head and smiled.

"Okay, then. You have everything?"

He patted his pockets. "Let's go," he said.

"Where's your car?"

The Conversation

I made sure Brad was behind me, again, and started driving before calling Dana. "You are not going to believe this," I said when she answered.

"Hey, did you get the bananas?" she said.

"What? No! What are you even talking about?" I said.

"I left some rotting bananas on your porch."

"Why?" I laughed.

Dana laughed too. "Didn't you get my message? I called you earlier."

"I did but that still doesn't explain why you left some rotting bananas on my porch."

"Kelly, they're for Evan."

"Why are you giving my son rotting bananas?"

"So you can make him some banana bread. Remember he and I were talking about it last week? Did you get them?"

I laughed. "Okay, Dana, that makes way more sense. I'm glad it's not some new trend in our friendship where you've taken to leaving me your rotten fruit."

She laughed. "You are so weird."

"You love me this way," I said and laughed. "But I'm not home yet. I'm headed there... with some guy I just met. Am I an idiot?"

"This time I'm going with yes. He must be, like, super hot?" She laughed.

"No, it's not like that. He's my friend's husband's friend, and he's harmless, I think. But, if I go missing, tell Kim to get in touch with Holly and tell her Brad did it." I laughed.

"Kelly, that's not even remotely funny," she said. "What's his name again? I'm writing this down."

"Brad. Seriously, he's harmless. He flew in from Connecticut for the wedding, and he was as bored as I was. He didn't want me to leave, and I didn't want to stay so on a whim I invited him over. I know it wasn't the best choice, but I just wanted to get out of there, and I felt bad for him. He seemed so sad that I was leaving. I mean, we did sort of have a fun conversation earlier. I dunno."

"Okay, I'll trust you on this one. Call me if you need me," she paused. "Or call the police. Yeah, call them first if you need anything."

"You're funny. I'm fine," I said. "I'll talk to you tomorrow."

"I hope so," she said.

"Stop!" I laughed. "I'll be fine."

We hung up.

When I got back to the house, I looked in my rearview mirror and watched Brad pull into the driveway behind me—into the driveway of my house! Maybe this was a stupid choice. I shook my head and got out of the car.

"So you're not going to kill me or anything are you? I called someone to let her know I was with you."

"Kim?" he said and smiled.

"No, I called Dana. Wait, that's not the point though. You're harmless, right?"

"If you're serious, I don't have to come in." He took a step back toward his car. "I'll just head back to the reception. I don't wanna make you feel uncomfortable."

I stood with my arms crossed on my chest and looked at him.

"For real," he added. "I won't be offended. I don't make a habit of going home with people I just met, and I can see how this could suddenly feel like a wrong choice for you—even though I can assure you that I'm a good guy."

I looked at him for a few seconds. "You seem harmless." I started walking toward the door. "You can come in." I opened the screen door and unlocked the front door. I held it open for him.

I got us some drinks (lemonade and seltzer water), and we sat on the couch in the living room.

"So you flew all this way, and you were bored. That kind of sucks," I said.

"I didn't have anything else to do today, anyway, so it's all good. So what's your story? You have a five-year-old son. You live in this house on this sweet, quiet street. You met Holly at work many years ago." My phone rang again. It was sitting on the couch in between us. *Jack from the zoo.* Brad laughed. "You have many gentlemen callers—literally."

I laughed too and pressed decline on my phone. "I've dabbled in dating recently," I said slowly. "It hasn't gone so well, I guess." I leaned my head back and sunk into the couch a little bit. "Worse than these two phone callers is this guy who I met on a dating app. I went out with him last Sunday. He rejected me via email because he didn't feel a connection. Monday morning I had an appointment with my new knee specialist. Turns out it's him. I read the rejection message in his waiting room." I laughed. "He'd been all vague about what he did and said he worked in a hospital so I kept joking with my friends that he was a janitor. Then he walked into the exam room to check my knee." I shook my head and rolled my eyes.

Brad laughed. "Seriously?"

I nodded and laughed. "Yes, right after rejecting me. You can't make this stuff up," I reached over and smacked his knee. "Tell me something stupid that you've done. I can't be the only one embarrassing myself here."

"On a date?" he said.

"Oh, I don't care. On a date, at the grocery store, wherever."

He nodded his head and leaned back into the couch a little deeper. "Okay, let me think."

He was quiet for a couple seconds and then laughed. "Okay, here's something." He shook his head. "A couple weeks ago at work, I walked into the conference room for a meeting, and my boss was in the middle of firing a coworker. It was pretty awkward."

"Oh, that's bad." I squinted my eyes. "Oh, my! I hate stuff like that. Were you close with the person getting fired?"

"Not exceptionally, but he was on my team. And I walked in all,

'Hey, Jim, Dylan, what's up?'" He swung his arms like he was walking.

"You're a dork," I said.

"I know." He looked at me for a couple seconds and then leaned toward me.

At first I gave him the benefit of the doubt and thought maybe he wasn't leaning in to kiss me, but, nope, he kept coming toward me.

"What are you doing?" I said and put my hand on his mouth and pushed his face away.

He opened his mouth like he was going to say something but then looked at me and raised his eyebrows.

"Did you think I invited you over here to sleep with you? I felt bad for you because you were pretending, I guess, to be so bored." I shook my head. "I'm not sleeping with you." I crossed my arms. "You live in Connecticut. Where did you think this was going?"

"I don't know," he said. "Somewhere. Nowhere. I don't know."

"That's even worse. You just wanna have sex with me." I stood up. "Yuck! I'm not like that." I took my glass to the kitchen, and he followed me.

"Kelly, I'm sorry. I like you. You're fun to hang out with and fun to talk to. I just felt something and went for it, and it wasn't right. I don't know. I'm sorry."

"I liked hanging out with you too. But we were just talking. Why would you try to kiss me? Tomorrow you're going to Connecticut, and we're never going to see each other again. So this is going nowhere. Contrary to what you may think by my noisy phone, I don't sleep around. So, no. I'm not sleeping with you." I leaned against the counter and thought for a couple seconds. "I mean, you seemed nice enough, and you're welcome to stay and chat." I walked over to the fridge and pulled the seltzer out of it and took the cap off. "If we can get past this awkward moment."

"Okay. I'm sorry. I'll behave."

"You better. You want more lemonade?" I glanced over at him as I poured my seltzer. He shook his head. I twisted the cap back onto my seltzer and put it away.

We walked back into the living room. This time I waited for him to sit on the couch, and then I sat on a chair across the room from him.

He laughed.

"What?" I said.

"I don't know," he said and looked at his hands for a few seconds. "I just... You just..." He shook his head and smiled. "If you lived closer, I would definitely want to hang out with you—a lot."

I put my hands over my face. "Shut up."

"No, seriously, you're a lot of fun. You're pretty adorable. Plus, you're really engaging to talk with."

I laughed. "So what do you do for a living when you're not watching your coworkers get the ax?"

"I'm an actuary," he said.

"Woo, that's exciting!" I laughed.

He smiled. "So you've heard of it."

"Yes, I have a general idea about it all. Enough that I know I don't wanna ask you to tell me more details. I'm trying to stay awake."

"Ha, ha," he said slowly. "Now tell me what you do, and I can make fun of your profession."

I shrugged. "I'm a writer."

"Huh?" he said. "I got nothing on that. What kind of writing?"

"Fiction. I'm working on a novel right now, but it's not going so well. I have a big deadline, and time's tick tick ticking away." I put my feet up on the coffee table. "I actually don't know if I'm going to finish it in time." I raised my eyebrows then added barely above a whisper, "And I'm kind of terrified to be honest."

"That doesn't sound good."

"I know. I've let a whole bunch of stupid stuff distract me lately." I pointed to my phone. "Men, mostly, which is ridiculous when you think about it. I mean, no offense, Brad. But you guys just aren't worth it."

"Generally, I'm going to agree with you there and not take offense." He laughed.

"Thanks. I don't know what I've been thinking lately. My sister... you know Kim, right?" I smiled at him.

"Yeah," he laughed.

"I dunno, recently she encouraged me to just sort of put myself out there, I guess. Then I met Tom... and Jack ... and Dan. Let's just say it's getting a little out of control."

"It sounds kind of busy, yeah." He picked up a squishy ball that had been wedged between the couch cushions and started tossing it from hand to hand.

"And don't even get me started on my ex," I made a big gesture. "He left about a year ago. Well, almost exactly, actually, since my birthday's next week, and I found…"

"Wait. He left on your birthday?" He stopped tossing the squishy ball and looked at me.

I stopped talking for a second. "Yeah," I said quietly. "Who does that, right?"

We just sat and looked at each other for a few seconds.

"Anyway, I was saying that I recently found a note that he left me when we were together." I shook my head and rubbed my forehead with my right hand for a couple seconds. "I guess I'm just letting all these stupid things distract me. And I'm rambling—yet again. I'm sorry."

"That part doesn't sound stupid, Kelly. I have an ex-wife so I know how something that seems like it should be a little thing can floor you. I'm sorry you're going through that."

"Yeah, me too. Yeah, the notes he called time capsules. And the one I found recently started with something about our son being born," I sniffed and covered my face. "God, I'm sorry." I leaned forward and put my face in my hands and sobbed for a couple minutes then just sat there with my face in my hands.

After a while Brad sat on the floor beside me and handed me a box of tissues. "Here," he said.

"I still love him," I said quietly. "He treated me like shit in the end, but I still love him." I took a tissue and wiped my eyes and nose. "I know I need to get over him and move on. But it's hard to let go when you believed that you're going to be with this person forever."

"Of course, you still love him. You said it's been a year, right?"

I nodded and blew my nose.

"It took me a lot longer than that to get over my wife, and we didn't have any kids."

I looked at him for a while. "Well, this is fun, right?" I patted his arm. "I bet you wished you were at the reception."

"Eh," he said. He patted and then squeezed my hand. "Not really." He stood up and walked back toward the couch. "So what's wrong with your knee?"

"I don't know. I go back to see the janitor on Monday."

He laughed. "Hey, c'mere."

"What?" I said.

"I didn't get a chance to dance with you at the reception."

"No," I shook my head.

"Yes, c'mere," he smiled. "No funny business." He shrugged. "It'll give us something to do." He pulled his phone out of his pocket and put some music on. "Let's get warmed up with a couple fast songs."

He tapped his phone for a couple seconds, set it on the couch, and then started dancing right there in my living room. I watched him for several seconds and then laughed and shrugged. "Okay, I'll dance with you." I stood up.

It was actually great, the dancing. We didn't talk aside from a few goofy comments back and forth. It was just fun. There were about 10 fast songs, and then a slow song came on. "No, we can't get sappy," I said. "I'm having too much fun." I pointed to the chair and shook my head. "You don't want to see me cry again."

He held out his hand. "You won't cry. I promise. I'm not that bad of a dancer. Plus, they're playing your song. You have to dance with me." He nodded.

I laughed. "My song?"

It was "She's Always a Woman." I put my hand in his outstretched hand.

"Shall we?" He said and led me over to the other side of the living room. He twirled me under his arm and twisted me into him. Then he wrapped his arms around me, and I looked at him for a couple seconds and put my head on his shoulder and closed my eyes. I took a deep breath and relaxed into him.

We stood there swaying back and forth to the song. He held me really tightly. I could feel one of his hands on the center of my back and one at the small of my back. I felt at peace—even my mind felt at peace for the first time in a while.

The song ended and another fast one came on. He twirled me out and dipped me.

"Oh, wow," I said. "Fancy!" I smiled at him.

"Thanks for the dance," he said. "My night's complete."

"Well, that was lovely, Brad. Thank you." I reached out and patted his arm. We looked at each other for a few seconds and then started dancing fast again.

"I'm not all bad," he shrugged.

"No, you're not bad at all," I said and nodded. "That was a misunderstanding earlier, and you've been great since."

He laughed.

"Plus," I added, "who wouldn't wanna kiss me? I can hardly

blame you." I laughed, put my arms up, and twirled around a few times.

He smiled at me, and we danced for a bit longer—maybe an hour, maybe 20 minutes. I lost track of time.

After a while we got more to drink and then sat on the couch and talked. He told me about his ex-wife. I think he felt obligated to open up a little after my sob session from earlier. We talked for hours. It felt easy and natural and like old friends getting caught up after not seeing each other for a few years. It seriously was one of the easiest conversations that I've ever had.

At about 4:00 I said, "What time do you have to be at the airport?"

"I guess around 7:30. Well, 7:00 because I have to drop off my rental."

"I guess we have some time to go and get some breakfast then," I shrugged my shoulders. "I need coffee. I'm going to be so tired today."

"Yeah," he agreed. "I'll probably spend the day sleeping once I get home."

"I'll be spending the day with Evan. Hope he didn't have any other plans than sitting on the couch and watching his shows. This is where I'm going to be." I patted the couch then stood up. "Come on. Let's go get something to eat."

"Okay," he said and smiled at me. "I have to ask you first. If I didn't live in Connecticut…"

"You do though," I said and shook my head. "So no what ifs. Come on."

At breakfast he asked for my phone number. "Come on," he said. "We have to keep in touch. You're like my long-lost friend… that I just met." He laughed. "This was too much fun."

"Keep in touch for what purpose, Brad? I know how this is going to go. I can see the writing on the wall. You're excited about the night we had now." I paused. "But you go home tomorrow—today, I mean. And we get back to normal life." I reached over and put my hand on his. "And this was fun. This was great, actually. I had so much fun with you today. I agree. You feel like an old friend. But tomorrow we have our own things. And if we exchange numbers, it's just gonna kill what happened today."

"Why?"

"Because there will be expectations from one of us that the other person can't fulfill."

"I promise there won't be any expectations from me," he shook his head.

"But there will be from me. I know there will be. I know myself." I let go of his hand and picked up my coffee cup. "I mean, I won't want there to be. But then I'll think, 'Why didn't Brad call me?' even as just friends, you know? And then I'll obsess about it. And I won't get any writing done."

He picked up his coffee cup. "You can write about me," he smiled.

"I'm not trying to be rude, but you'd be about 30 pages out of a 300-page book." I took a sip of coffee.

"That's 10 percent." He shook his head and shrugged. "I'm okay with that."

I laughed and rolled my eyes. "This was so much fun today, and I don't wanna ruin it."

"Okay," he said. He drank some coffee.

"She's Always a Woman" started playing in the restaurant.

He looked at me and rolled his eyes. "They're playing your song."

The waitress put our check on the table, and he grabbed it. "This is on me."

"Thank you," I said and listened for a while. I finished my coffee and fished through my purse for nothing really. I was just killing time. Finally, I pulled out my lip balm and put some on. "Okay, I guess I'm ready to go when you are." But, suddenly, I wasn't ready at all. I swallowed hard.

We walked to the register, and he paid.

We hugged goodbye in the parking lot. "I'm going to miss you," Brad said.

"For today. And maybe tomorrow." I tried to pull away from the hug, but he squeezed me tighter. I took a deep breath and squeezed him back just as tightly. We hugged for maybe a minute like that. "Okay," I said. "You can have my number."

He stopped squeezing me and held onto my shoulders and looked at me. "Are you sure?"

"I'll probably regret this." I waved my hands in front of my face. "Don't make me cry again."

"Okay," he smiled and pulled out his phone. "I was gonna get your number from Holly, anyway. So just getting it from you will be easier."

I laughed. "Okay, promise me that there isn't going to be any drama. I need to finish this book." I put my hand on his chest. "This is just phone numbers and friendship." We held each other's gaze for a couple seconds.

He nodded his head. "Friendship. I promise," he smiled again.

"You're pretty adorable when you smile," I said and punched him in the stomach.

"I guess we have that in common."

I hugged him one more time after putting each other's numbers in our phones, and he left for the airport.

"That was weird. Kind of nice, but weird," I said quietly as he drove away, and I wondered if there would ever be another occasion in my life when our paths would cross.

I had two and a half hours until I needed to leave for church where I was meeting Kim to pick up Evan. I went home, put on a pot of coffee, and got in the shower. I got dressed and ready, got some coffee, and sat at my computer for a little while.

For the first time in a long time, I didn't have an adverse reaction to my butt hitting my office chair. I almost felt... creative. But my brain was too tired to write, so I got up and plopped onto my bed, set my alarm for an hour, and went to sleep.

TWENTY

The Service

I got to church about five minutes late and headed into the sanctuary.

They were on the part where they were standing to greet each other and shake hands. I made a U-turn out of the sanctuary and headed over to the water fountain. If I waited a few minutes, I could avoid the awkwardness of the forced greeting. I hated that part. It just felt so unnatural to be forced to say hello to everyone and shake hands with everyone seated in the rows in front of and in back of me—for no other reason than that we were sitting near each other. I took a really long drink and walked back toward the sanctuary.

They'd moved on to the opening hymn. It seemed a safe enough time to enter until I almost cut off the acolytes. "Sorry," I said quietly. I motioned my hand for them to go ahead. "Go... go, go." They started down the aisle, and I followed them until I reached the pew Kim and Doug were sitting in. I squeezed past them. "Pardon me. Hello." I squeezed past my parents and stood beside my dad.

"You know the service starts at 9:15," he said in my ear and then looked at his watch.

"Your watch must be fast." I knew he was teasing.

He put his arm around me. "I'm glad you're here. Is Evan in Sunday school or with Sam?"

"He's here. Kimmy brought him. I was at Holly's wedding last night."

"I don't think I know Holly," he said.

"It doesn't matter, Dad."

"Well, we'll take you to lunch afterward," he said and squeezed my shoulder before letting go.

"Okay," I said and immediately thought that should help stretch my budget a tiny bit. I could never pass up a free meal—even one where I'd be scrutinized by my parents. Free breakfast, free lunch. I mentally calculated the couple of extra days I now had to finish my book.

Then I thought about Brad for a few minutes and wondered if his flight had left yet.

As the service was ending I said to my dad, "I'm going to get Evan and make him wash his hands. I'll see you in the parking lot." That way I could avoid waiting in the line to shake the minister's hand. It was another forced greeting that I wasn't thrilled about.

Evan's class wasn't quite done, so I stood outside his classroom and waited. He could see me and at first he smiled, but then he made a goofy face at me. I ducked out of his view. I didn't want him to get in trouble for not paying attention. After a few minutes the door opened and Evan flew out first. "Phew, I'm glad that's over," he said and ran into my arms. "I missed you last night."

"Yeah? I missed you too. Did you have fun at Meri's?"

"Yep! We ate popcorn in sleeping bags and watched a movie," he squealed.

"That sounds like lots of fun." I patted the top of his head.

"Guess what?" I said and knelt down beside him.

"What?" His eyes got bigger.

"We're going out to lunch with Grandma and Grandpa."

"Yes!" he said and did a fist pump. "Can Meri come too?"

"I think so, but I'm not sure. I couldn't really talk a lot during the service." I stood up and grabbed his hand. "Come on. You need to wash your hands before we leave."

"No, they're good," he said. He slapped them together a few times and put them in his pockets.

"No, you're washing them." I pushed him into the boys' bathroom and waited outside the door.

A couple minutes later, he came out with water all over his shirt.

"I don't even want to know," I said.

"Good," he said and shook his head. "I don't even want to talk about it."

"We're meeting them in the parking lot. Let's go."

My dad was standing by my car. "Grandpa!" Evan yelled when we were almost to him.

"Evan! Hey, what happened to your shirt?"

"Mom said we didn't have to talk about it." He shook his head quickly several times and looked up at me for approval.

My dad looked at me too and squinted his eyes. "It's all good, Dad," I said and put my hand on Evan's head. "It's only water. Where are we eating?" I opened the door for Evan.

"Is Meri coming?" Evan asked as he climbed into the back seat and got into his booster seat.

"Yes, she is. So are Aunt Kim and Uncle Doug," my dad said

and then shut Evan's door.

"Double yes!" Evan yelled.

"Where are we eating, Dad?"

He opened the passenger door.

"Am I your ride?" I said.

"Yes. Mom will meet us there."

"Did you think I was going to bail on you or something, Dad?"

"No, we just thought you'd like to have someone ride there with you." Again, my family didn't think I could take care of myself.

I pointed to the backseat. "I've got Evan. You're my co-pilot. Right, Ev?"

"That's me!" He said as he fastened his seatbelt.

"Okay. Really, where are we going, Dad? I have to know if you want me to drive us there."

"Just up to the diner. They're getting us a table."

I nodded and hoped we'd have a different waitress from the one Brad and I had a couple hours ago. "So how's life treating you, Dad?" I pulled out of the parking lot.

"I have nothing to complain about."

"Not even Mom? That's unusual." I glanced over at him.

"Well," he deadpanned.

I laughed. "Clients keeping you on your toes?"

"The practice is going well. No complaints on my end. How about you, Kelly? How's the writing?"

I took a deep breath. "It's going great, Dad! I'm really excited about it." So maybe that was a slight exaggeration, but no woman wanted her dad's pity. I mean, I was already the daughter with the failed marriage. I didn't also want to be the daughter who was failing at making a living and supporting his grandson. I pulled into the diner's parking lot.

"I'm glad to hear it, Kelly."

"Me too." I almost giggled but kept my composure as I pulled into an open parking space.

We got out of the car and followed Evan as he galloped into the restaurant.

The diner was crowded. I mean, lunch on a Sunday wasn't an original idea, and we had to wait in line with the rest of the after-church crowd. But, fortunately, since my family hadn't waited for me to pick up Evan, my dad, Evan, and I didn't have to wait quite as long.

Evan played "Rock, Paper, Scissors" with my mom while we waited.

"Mom, rock doesn't cover paper. It's not a paperweight."

She'd been trying to let Evan win even though he had rock and she had paper.

"Paper covers rock," I said as I put her hand on top of his.

"Mom!" Evan said sternly.

"You're not a cheater, Evan," I said.

"My grandson and I can make up our own rules."

"That is true, but you're setting him up for disappointment when he plays it legit with someone at school in a couple years." I turned and faced my dad. "Aren't I right—psychologically speaking? Plus, she never let me win. Why's Evan so special?"

"With your mother, just let it go. You can't win," he said quietly to me.

"Amen, Dad." He and I both laughed quietly as I leaned into him.

Kim walked over to us. "What are you two laughing about?"

"One guess," I said.

"I don't even have to say it out loud. Why do you think I have Meri sitting with Doug?"

"Good choice. Of course my Doug is missing. So there's no dad buffer for poor Evan with this family."

"True," she said.

"Grace, party of 7." The hostess said a few minutes later.

We followed her to our table. Evan sat by my mom and Meri, who sat by Kim and Doug. My dad sat by Doug leaving me between... my parents. "Oh, fun," I said quietly as I pulled out my chair. I looked over at Kim who was noticing the seating arrangements.

Sorry, she mouthed.

"It's all good," I said quietly and squinched my nose up at her.

"What's that, Dear?" my mom said.

"Nothing, Mom." I opened my menu and tried to find my happy place. *Breathe in. Breathe out. I am. Relaxed.*

"So when is your appointment with your ortho?" she said.

"Tomorrow." I looked at Kim. "Should be so much fun!"

"Can't be more fun than today," Kim said.

I laughed, but she really had no clue. I imagined that Brad was sitting in a plane on his way home.

"Grace, Kelly said her writing's going great." My dad leaned over toward my mother.

"Oh," I could see out of my peripheral vision that my mom was trying to look at Kim who was staring at her menu. "That's wonderful, Kelly," my mom said.

I patted my dad's arm. "Thanks for bringing that up, Dad."

"Well, I'm proud of you."

I smiled at him. Was he pulling some sort of reverse psychology shit on me? I looked back at Kim for help. She had started talking with Meredith about what she was going to order.

"Hey, Ev, what are you going to order?" I leaned forward so I could see him.

He had his crayons out of the package, and he was circling the things he wanted on his placemat menu. It looked like he'd pretty much circled everything.

"Well, just look," he pointed to his placemat.

"You pretty much have to narrow that down, Kiddo," I said.

He put an X over most of the original circles and then pointed to the things that were left. "Hot dog, fries, applesauce, apple juice."

"That sounds more manageable for your belly," my mom said.

"And my wallet," my dad said.

I looked at him. "Is money tight, Dad? I'm sure Doug will treat us."

"I've got it covered," my dad said.

"Good because I'm hungry," I said. But I really wasn't all that hungry. I was mostly reaching the point of exhaustion. I couldn't wait until Evan and I could go home, and I could lie on the couch and snooze for a bit. I wasn't even going to pretend like I was trying to work until I got a good nap in. Plus, my brain needed to decompress.

Our waitress came and took our orders, and I stood up. "I'll be right back."

I headed toward the bathroom. I took my time washing and drying my hands. I also brushed my hair and then put on some lip gloss. I figured my family wouldn't miss me too much and that would give my mom a chance to clarify with Kim whether I actually was or wasn't having success with my book.

The lobby waiting area was still very packed with people waiting for tables, and I was navigating my way through the crowd. "Excuse me," I said as I patted a woman on the shoulder. "Can I sneak past you?" She stepped aside which revealed Michael and then Jack. Jack and I made eye contact, and his eyes got bigger for just a split second. "Hi," I said and turned to look at the woman who had stepped out of the way. She looked a lot like me, actually. Long blond hair, thin build, 30s. She was holding Michael's hand.

"How are you?" Jack said.

"Great." I looked at the woman he was with and back at him and smiled. "Enjoy your lunch," I said and proceeded to walk through the crowd back toward my family.

"You too."

He'd said he wasn't married. I hadn't asked him if he was dating anyone. Maybe she was his sister or something, but it didn't really matter. I'd played around too much. After that nap today, I was going to get serious about my book. Well, at least I was going to try.

My family was laughing when I got back to the table. "Kim was just telling us about you diving into a dumpster," Doug said.

"You're funny, Mommy," Evan added.

"It was a paper dumpster." I sat down. "Did Kim explain why I was in the paper dumpster?"

"Mommy could see your undies!" Meri shrieked.

"Could she, Meridee?" I laughed. I had been wearing a skirt that day. "Nice, Kim." I looked at her and rolled my eyes. "You're lucky I was wearing some."

"You girls," my mom said. "I wish I'd had a sister."

"Do you want mine?" I said and looked at Kim.

She laughed.

"Mommy, tell Aunt Kim you're sorry!" Evan said. "You're going to hurt her feelings."

"She's only kidding, Evan," Kim said. "She loves me just as much now as she did when I helped pull her out of the dumpster."

"To be honest, I loved you more in that moment." I took a drink of my water.

"You were so stuck." She laughed loudly. "Her feet were kicking. It may have been the funniest thing I've ever seen."

"I wish I was there!" Evan shouted.

"Honey, settle down," my mom said. She leaned in to mock whisper in his ear. "I'm sure there will be plenty more funny things that your mom does that you'll get to witness."

"Nice, Mom." I looked at my dad. "Now she's ganging up on me with my own kid. Can't you stop her?"

"I've tried, Honey. She's unstoppable."

The waitress brought our food as the hostess sat Jack, Michael, and their lady friend at the table beside ours. Jack didn't notice right away that we were so close because he chose to sit in a chair that was directly opposite mine. Our eyes met for a second, and then I turned to my dad who was asking me to pass him the ketchup.

Our conversation changed from my dumpster dive to what Evan and Meredith were doing in school. Both kids had a lot to say, so I was pretty much safe for the rest of the meal and could sort of zone out since I was also half asleep and already knew what Evan was doing at school. Lunch ended with Meredith leading the table in a rousing group count to 30. At about 25 I noticed Jack watching us, but, to be fair, most of the tables within earshot were. Meredith was very adorable in leading us in our count. I shrugged at Jack as I said, "26, 27, 28, 29, 30."

"And... That's about all the higher we're going up to right now," Doug said.

"Yay!" I said loudly, and we all clapped. And some of the older people at the tables around us clapped too.

We all started standing to leave. "Bye," I said quietly to Jack as we were walking away.

"What was that, Kelly?" My mom said because I think she may have noticed his small wave in my direction.

"Nothing, Mom. Just someone I know at the next table."

She turned to look at him. "Oh?" she said.

I pretended I didn't notice the way her voice went up at the end of the word and kept walking. "It's nothing, Mom. Compose yourself," I said.

Later that evening after a long nap, I picked up my phone and looked at it. No missed messages or texts from Brad. See… That was what I was trying to avoid by not exchanging numbers. Was I going to start looking at my phone and wondering if Brad was going to be in touch? I didn't want to become that woman. I'd had a great time on Saturday, and I wished we had left it at that. Why did he have to squeeze me so tightly when he hugged me good-bye?

I'd said we were just friends, and I was serious. But the whole situation reminded me of what Lisa said about dating the wrong men versus the right men—nothing felt forced or awkward with Brad. A little part of me wondered if he didn't live so far away if this would have been the start of something.

But he did. And that was that. I threw my phone down on the couch and put a pillow over it. "I will not look at you again while waiting on a man," I said.

Yeah right.

TWENTY-ONE

The Appointment

After dropping Evan off at Kim's house so she could take him to preschool, I signed in at Dan's office and sat quietly this time. I was feeling nervous about the appointment—and not chatty nervous like the last time.

I picked up a magazine and flipped through it without really looking at any of the photos. It could have been porn, and I wouldn't have even noticed.

A teenage girl hobbled by me on crutches—her right foot was wrapped in a bright purple cast. "Do you need me?" her mom (I assumed) said.

"No. Please, no," the girl said.

I looked over at her mom and smiled. She closed her eyes and shook her head. "You can come in with me if it makes you feel better," I said. "I'd like the moral support."

"It seems like yesterday I was wiping her tears and kissing her boo-boos, and today she wants nothing to do with me. I don't know when she grew up." She shook her head again.

I closed my eyes and thought of Evan. Eventually, I won't be able to make everything better for him either. "Kelly." I jumped.

"Sorry," I whispered and stood up.

"How are you today?" The nurse or whoever she was asked me.

"Scared."

"Oh, you have nothing to be scared of. Dr. Peterson is great. He'll take good care of you."

"I hope," I squeaked out.

She led me into an exam room. "Have a seat. The doctor will be in shortly."

"Thanks." But that was the part that terrified me—seeing the doctor again. Well, specifically this doctor again.

I closed my eyes and tried my deep relaxation breathing. But I still sort of felt like my insides were counting down to blastoff.

There was a knock at the door. "Come in," I said quietly.

Dan opened it up slowly and peeked his head in. "Hey, Kelly." He smiled at me.

"Hi there," I said.

He logged into the computer and pulled up my MRI. "Let's see what we have." He automatically popped into doctor mode, and it helped—well, a little bit.

"Okay, I see what's going on here." He started pointing.

"You can tell what all that blurry stuff is?"

He turned around with a big smile and nodded at me.

I laughed. "You really love your job. Don't you?" I stood to walk over beside him.

He nodded. "Yes, I do. Anyway, see this?"

He pointed at the scan at some... well, to be honest, I couldn't really see anything, but I said, "Yes."

"That's some torn cartilage."

"And you recommend that I?"

"Well, you have a couple options. Come over here, and I'll tell you about them."

I sat up on the exam table.

"Surgery to cut out the tear is one option," he said and leaned against the table beside me.

"What are some of the others?"

"Pain. Pretty much constantly." He laughed. "Kelly, I'm joking. I could drain it and give you a steroid shot. It's not a permanent fix, but it'll hold you for a bit." He nodded. "You're young though. I'd personally lean toward a long-term fix if it were my decision."

I took a deep breath and grabbed his arm, "Okay, let's do this."

His eyes moved from my face to my hand resting on his arm.

I let go. "Let's do the surgery option. I'm sick of hobbling around like I'm an old lady."

"Well, if it helps, I hadn't noticed the hobbling when we met. And," he glanced at my chart, "you look about 10 years younger than you are." He smiled at me and patted my hand. "Okay," he straightened up and walked toward the door. "I'll send Jenna in to schedule and give you the details. Take care."

"Thanks, Dan," I said.

He shut the door.

I scheduled the surgery for the end of the following week which was the soonest appointment available. I figured I might as well get the slicing and dicing part over as soon as possible so I could heal and start walking normally again.

When I was walking to my car—or rather limping toward my car—my phone started buzzing. I pulled it out of my purse and answered it before registering that it said Tom. "Hello," I said.

"Hi, Kelly," he paused. "How are you?"

"Oh, just dandy. I'm leaving the doctor, and I have to have surgery. How about you?"

"I guess I'm better than that. What's wrong?"

"My knee. Torn cartilage. It should be a quick fix to make me not hobble around like an old lady anymore."

"You're not old," he said.

"I know. But I'm limping around like I am, and it hurts like hell so…"

"I hope the surgery helps," he said. "Hey, did you give any thought to what we talked about?"

I took a deep breath. "Honestly, I don't think it's gonna work out."

He didn't say anything.

"Tom, I'm not sure we're very compatible." I got into my car and started it. "Listen, I've gotta go. You take care."

"Good-bye, Kelly."

"Bye." I ended the call and put my head on the steering wheel.

I sat like that for a few minutes and looked at my watch. I had about two hours before I had to pick up Evan.

I put the windows down and turned off the engine. I picked up my phone and called Dana.

"Hey, you're alive!"

I laughed. "Brad was harmless. We actually had a lot of fun just hanging out. Nothing weird happened."

"That's good."

"Well, he did try to kiss me, but I nipped that in the bud right away." I put my elbow on the door and rested my head on my hand.

She laughed. "Okay, so what's up?"

"Did I ever tell you about the time capsules that Sam would hide for me?"

"Hmm. No, I don't think."

"So, recently, I was looking for a picture frame, and I found one of the time capsules behind the frame."

"Ew, that doesn't sound fun," she said. "What was it?"

"They're letters. He used to write and hide love letters for me. But he would write on the envelope 'Time Capsule #1' and so on. This was number five. I think there were seven in total. I hadn't found three or five until the other day. Well, three is still hidden."

"Wow, that must have sucked to read."

I pictured myself sitting on my bed with the letter. "I didn't read it yet. I started to, and I couldn't. He wrote it the day Evan was born. I can't go there. That was the best day of my life, and I shared it with Sam—a man who could leave me."

"I'm sorry, Kelly. I'm sorry he hurt you."

I put my hand over my eyes and closed them. "I think that's one of the things that makes me angrier than anything, Dana." I took a deep breath. "I gave birth in front of him. That's so personal. He was my support. We had a baby together." I was crying. "And then he left me." I leaned my head back against the headrest.

"Kelly, I'm so sorry that he hurt you."

"We stood in front of our families, our friends, in my church and promised to be together forever. I meant that!" I hit the steering wheel with the ball of my hand. "What a joke," I said quietly. "He made a joke of our vows."

"You have every right to be mad. I'd be mad too."

I sat there looking out the window for a couple seconds. "I'm so mad. I mean, I try to pretend like I'm getting over him because I feel like I should be. But it's getting harder, not easier. Each day gets harder. And I wouldn't admit this to anyone else, but I equally want him back and hate him because I never could go back at this point because he made a joke of me. I'm a joke."

"No! No, no, no, Kelly," she paused. "That is so not true. Nothing about you is a joke. You can't control other people's actions. You can only control how you react to them."

I was quiet for a few seconds. "I feel like I'm not doing a very good job of that lately."

"Nobody's perfect," she said. "You can't expect to have perfect reactions every single moment. You're human. Give yourself a little slack."

I sat and cried for a few more seconds. "I guess I just feel really stupid for trusting my heart with someone who would just step on it."

"How could you know," she paused. "Are you going to rip up the letter?"

"I want to. But I also wanna read it." I closed my eyes. "I'm not sure what I'm going to do."

"Well, you don't have to decide today, or tomorrow, or the next day."

"True. Thanks for listening. You're a good friend, Dana Newman."

"You are too, Kelly Ramsey."

I smiled and started to cry again. "I better let you get back to work," I said. "Oh, by the way, I'm having knee surgery next Thursday."

"Oh, my! So you're going to let the janitor operate."

"Yeah, I guess I am." I laughed. "Hey, can you drive me? I need to find a ride."

"Sure," she said. "That way I get to see him. I love that idea actually."

"Yeah, that'll pretty much be the only way. And then you can see how he undersold his photo. No lie. The man is stunning in person."

"Well, I can't wait then."

"Okay, I'll let you go for real this time."

"Call me if you need anything," she said.

"I will. Thanks." I ended the call.

I started my car and drove home.

The Longest Hour

I still had an hour to kill, so I went home and sat at my computer. I opened my document and started to write. Well, I mean, I scrolled to the end where I should be adding something.

Instead of writing though, I kept thinking about how I was going to lie unconscious and naked except for a thin hospital gown while Dan operated on my knee. He seemed fairly professional so I doubted that he'd sneak a peek. Although, if it were the other way around, I can't say I wouldn't be tempted. I hoped that he was a better person than I was.

I stared at my last page for a while longer then looked at the clock. Fifty more minutes. Was it even worth it? Of course, it was. I used to be able to get a lot accomplished in 50 minutes of writing back when Sam and I were together. I'd put Evan down for a nap when he was a baby and type non-stop. It wasn't always good, and, obviously, it needed to be edited and reworked, but at least there was material to work with. I looked at the page numbers.

Sixty-eight pages.

The fact that I'd only added eight pages in the last few weeks was pretty much unacceptable. "You have to get over this and just write, Kelly."

But nothing happened. I shook my head and stood up.

On the front porch I decided to just start looking for a job. I wasn't a writer anymore if I couldn't actually write. My phone rang. It was Tom. "Didn't I tell you no? Damn, you're persistent." I hit talk, "Hello?"

"Kelly."

"Tom," I said. "What's up?"

"I just wanted to apologize for not saying anything earlier."

"No apology necessary, but you're sweet to call. If I were a little younger—and maybe a little more over my ex…" I paused. "Did you know I'm 34?"

He was quiet for a few seconds. "No," he said.

"Would that have mattered to you?"

"No, not really. I like you. Your age doesn't change that."

"My friend said that you like me because you're not looking for a serious, lasting relationship right now."

"Well, maybe she's right. I didn't really put a lot of thought into the why. I just know what I'm feeling."

"I think she might be right. Not that I'm looking to get into a serious relationship. It'll only be a year on Thursday since my husband left me."

He didn't say anything.

"I mean, I'm not sure I'll ever be ready for another serious relationship. And I might not wanna be in one again. I mean, you were a great kisser. I think I mentioned that."

"Yeah, I think you did," he said quietly.

"But there was a part of me that felt a little guilty afterward—like I was cheating on Sam. It shouldn't feel like that, right? I mean, I just might not be ready for dating. I'm sorry. I'm rambling."

"Keep my number," he said.

"What?"

"Maybe someday you'll think about me and not feel guilty. You can give me a call then."

"Oh, you'll be taken by then," I laughed.

"You never know, Kelly."

"Okay. I'll see you around, Tom."

"All right," he said. And we hung up.

I grabbed my purse and keys and left to pick Evan up at school.

TWENTY-TWO

The Day with No Agenda

Since I spent the rest of Monday cleaning my house, doing laundry, cutting the grass, and doing some other yard work, there was pretty much nothing left for me to do on Tuesday but sit at the computer and work.

Well, I mean, I had to feed Evan and take care of him, but he was pretty easy. I'd probably take him to the park later on. However, at that moment, he'd been fed breakfast, was dressed and ready for his day, and was happily cutting and folding paper for airplanes on the floor of my office. There was really no excuse to not write—well, aside from the writer's block.

But I was determined not to get up from my desk until I had a full 80 pages written (or at least 75). Of course, giving myself that number seemed to make the panic I felt sitting down feel all the more intense as I opened the file for my novel.

"Just write a paragraph, Kel," I said.

"What, Mom?" Evan said.

"Nothing, Hon."

"You said something," he insisted.

"Well, you're right, but not to you though."

"Who were you talking to?"

"Me, Evan. I was talking to myself," I spun the chair around to face him.

He looked up at me and laughed. "Oh, Mommy."

"I know, Evan, but I do it all the time. Don't you talk to yourself? Ever?"

He put down his scissors and cocked his head. "I don't think so. Not out loud. My brain talks to me."

I laughed. "Well, I guess my brain was talking to me but using my voice to do it. Maybe that's what happened."

He thought about that for a few seconds, smiled at me, and started folding his paper again. I spun my chair back around to start working.

I'd been typing for a few minutes—describing a situation I witnessed at the grocery store a week or so ago that I thought might be an interesting scene for the novel. It didn't really fit into the part of the story where I had left off, but I just wanted to get it written out roughly and figured I could plug it in the right place, eventually.

"What's that noise?" Evan said.

I stopped typing and listened. I didn't hear anything. "What do you mean?"

"I heard a tapping. Are you tapping on something?" he said.

I said, "You mean like this." I typed a few sentences.

"That's it!" He stood up and walked over to me. "It doesn't usually sound like that when you're working at your computer."

He was standing right beside me, and I turned to look at him. "Evan, you've got to be kidding me. You've heard me type before, right?"

He leaned into my arm. "Maybe. I can't remember. Maybe a long time ago."

I guess it had been a while since I seriously wrote for hours every day.

"Well, that's what it's supposed to sound like when I work."

"I like it," he said and kissed me on the cheek. He sat back down and got his paper situated.

"I like it too."

I worked all the way until lunch time. Every time I got into a real groove with my story, Evan would say, "You're doing it again, Mom. Good for you!" He was such a sweetheart. Of course it would distract me and make me lose my train of thought a little. But I didn't want to reprimand him for being my cheerleader so I would just give him a quick thumbs up and try to get back to the line of thinking I'd been on.

About noon I stopped and stretched my neck a little and said, "Are you hungry, Evan?"

"I'm starved," he flopped back on his back and did a quick motion that looked like he was making a snow angel which seemed fairly appropriate because he'd cut a snowstorm's amount of paper, and it was all over the floor around him.

"Well, then you should clean up your paper scraps there." I put a garbage can beside him. "And you can meet me in the kitchen. What do you want me to get started on?"

"I can clean up later. I'll help you get started."

"That's a very sweet offer, but it'll help me more if you actually clean up the paper that you're done with first. I'll wait for you to finish if you want."

He started picking up the paper scraps. "Can you make spaghetti with parmesan and butter with bread?"

"As long as we throw a veggie into the mix, sure. How about peas?"

"Do you have green beans?" He liked peas more, but he also liked having a choice. If I'd said peas or green beans, he would have picked the peas.

"Sure, is that what you'd rather have?"

"Yes," he thought for a few seconds. "Well, no, I changed my mind. I'll take peas—just five, right?"

"At least five. More would help you get stronger for the monkey bars later."

"We'll have monkey bars later? At the park!"

I nodded my head and smiled at him. "If you want. It's a nice day."

"Okay, I'll take 20. Wait! No, just 15."

I started walking out the door. "Spaghetti, butter with bread, and 15 peas."

"And parmesan," he said.

"Of course! Meet me downstairs when you're done."

I went to the kitchen to get things started.

After lunch Evan said, "Monkey bar time!"

"You wanna go now? We need to clean up our dishes first." Going now would tire him out, and then I could work without feeling too guilty.

We cleaned the dishes as quickly as we possibly could and headed out the door. The weather was perfect. It was starting to feel like spring was actually here, and the park was more crowded than normal.

Evan immediately ran to the monkey bars. I started walking the path that was around the play area—started and stopped after about half a lap. I couldn't wait for that surgery and hoped that walking wouldn't cause so much pain after Dan fixed me up. *My God! I can't believe he's going to cut into my body!* Of all the orthopedic specialists, Dr. Oliver had to refer me to a man on the same dating app.

I started to wonder what could have happened if I hadn't been on the dating app and if Dan's first experience with me was as a patient? Would things have turned out differently? He was clearly looking. Plus, he was the one who'd sent the first message.

But did I really care?

I didn't. Probably just the part of me that didn't like being rejected cared a little so I figured that was why I kept obsessing about it.

I found an empty bench and sat down. And what was with Tom telling me to give him a call when I thought about kissing him and not feeling guilty about it? And whatever happened to Jack? And why did I care... about any of it?

What I did care about a little bit, anyway, was that Brad hadn't called me—hadn't texted. I mean, I get that I stressed to him that we'd just be friends only. But even still. Why hadn't he just called to say hello? He was the one who pretty much insisted that we exchange phone numbers.

And he had said that I was adorable.

Was I even adorable anymore?

I was feeling less and less adorable as I aged. Well, I guess it all started with my husband ditching me. That was a huge blow to my adorableness. Then there was the whole writer's block and recent limp. Those hadn't helped the cause either.

I looked for Evan and saw him happily playing with a group of kids. *To be five again...* Life was so much simpler to just want to play all day long. Although, that pretty much felt like my life with writer's block. Wasn't I just playing all day long, anymore?

I let Evan play for another 30 minutes while I overanalyzed every aspect of my life except what to write next in my book. I should have brought my laptop, and maybe I could have written a little bit more. Although part of me being here was avoidance, so I could see why I hadn't decided to do that.

Eventually, Evan and I went home.

After dinner the phone rang. I picked it up and saw that it was *Brad from the wedding*. He'd insisted I put him in my contacts as that. I laughed and answered it. "Hello, Brad from the wedding," I said and smiled.

He laughed. "Kelly, happy birthday!"

"What?" I laughed. "It's not my birthday."

"Aww, I took a chance. I know you said it was this week, and I thought it would be funny if I got the day right."

"Well, you're wrong." I leaned against the counter. "I'm sure it's not the first time."

"So, when should I call to wish you a happy birthday?" he said.

"This week—sometime. You'll have to try again."

"Why doesn't it surprise me that you won't easily give that information away?"

"I don't know. So how were your travels home?"

He blew out his breath. "Not good," he said.

"What happened?" I peeked in the living room to see what Evan was doing. He was sitting on the couch and looking at a magazine. He waved at me, so I waved back and blew him a kiss.

"First off, there was construction that I wasn't prepared for. I had to reroute all over creation and follow a bunch of confusing detour signs… mostly in the dark."

"Oh, my! That sounds awful." I felt guilty that I hadn't thought of that when he left. I could have sent him another way. Of course, I'd been half asleep when he left. *Oh, well…*

"I barely got to the airport in time. But I did make my flight."

"Well, that's good." I sat down at the dining room table.

"Sort of," he laughed. "I got stuck sitting beside someone who may not have bathed for a couple months."

"Yuck! At least it was a short flight."

"Yeah, that was definitely good because she was also super chatty. She wouldn't shut up, and I couldn't be rude."

"Really, I sort of picture you just saying something like, 'Listen, Stinky, I need to get some shut eye, so you're gonna have to shut up.'"

"Does that sound like me?" he said.

"I don't know, maybe. You called me 'ma'am.' You can be rude."

He was quiet for a few seconds. "I'm struggling to form a

sentence. What are you even talking about?"

"We were at the mall and you said, 'Yes, Ma'am.'"

He laughed for a long time. "You do overthink every little thing. Don't you, Kelly?"

"I wasn't lying about that." Evan came in and patted me on my arm. "Hang on a second, Brad." I held the phone away from my mouth. "What's up, Ev?"

"I can't figure out how to make the TV not buzz."

"Not buzz? Just a second, Kiddo." I put the phone back up to my ear. "Brad, I need to get going so I can help Evan figure something out."

We said goodbye, and I ended the call and followed Evan into the living room toward the buzzing situation.

TWENTY-THREE

The Therapy Session

Wednesday morning I took Evan to school and headed to Brynn's office. Her waiting area was empty when I got there. The door to the therapists' offices opened and another therapist peeked her head into the room, smiled at me, and shut the door. About a minute later someone came in and sat down. "What a day!" he said.

I nodded at him.

"Traffic is awful. I'm 30 minutes late, and my life is a mess," he snorted. "I guess I'm in the right place."

"Sounds like it," I said.

The door opened, and the same therapist peeked in the room again. "You made it," she said. "Come on back."

He stood and started toward her. "Traffic is awful out there today. It's like everyone forgot how to drive."

"I'm sorry you had to deal with all that," she said. He followed her out of the waiting room and shut the door.

Brynn opened the door a few minutes later. She smiled at me. "Kelly, nice to see you."

"Hi, how are you today?"

"I'm good, thanks. How are you?" she said as I walked into her office. She shut the door behind us, and I settled into my spot on the sofa.

"I've been better, but I'm okay."

I went on to tell her about how even though I'd written a little more this week that I felt like my work still lacked direction, and I was extremely stressed about the looming deadline. And then I told her about Sam and the time capsule that I'd found and kept thinking about ever since.

"Did you bring it?" she said.

"It's in my purse." I looked down at my purse on the floor beside me.

"Do you want me to read it?"

I reached into my purse and pulled it out. I looked at it for a couple seconds and handed it to her. I nodded.

"Should I read it out loud?"

"Maybe read it to yourself first, and then you can decide whether it's worth it for me."

She nodded and opened the envelope and pulled out the letter. She looked at it for a little while and then looked back at me. "I can give you an overview, or I can read the whole thing out loud. It's not too long."

I thought for a few seconds. "Go ahead and read it to me," I said.

"Okay," Brynn said and nodded. "If you want me to stop, please tell me."

I nodded.

She looked back at the letter. "It says, 'Kelly, our little man is here. He's gorgeous. I don't know if you're feeling this, but I can't wrap my mind around him being ours yet. We made this perfect, beautiful little person. Our love made this perfect, beautiful person. I didn't realize it was possible to love you any more than I already do, but I do. You gave me this perfect, beautiful person, and I love you so much more today than I thought was possible. Today I understand what the word family means. Thank you for this beautiful gift. Forever yours, Sam.'"

She'd read the letter without emotion in her voice, which helped, and then looked up at me.

I shook my head and reached for a tissue. "I wish he hadn't written down any of these things. They just feel like such lies—our wedding vows, every time he said I love you. All lies." I sniffed a little and wiped my nose.

"I don't think they were lies when he said them," she said.

I thought about that for a minute. I wasn't sure what felt worse—his words being lies or being the truth at the time but then his feelings changing. "I just wish he wouldn't have said any of it since his feelings have changed. I mean, he's definitely not 'forever mine.'"

We talked about Sam for a while longer. Talked about how Thursday it would be a year since he left and some strategies to deal with the day. Talked about how I could start to try to move on and get over him completely so that I didn't feel guilty when I kissed someone new. Talked about whether I was ready to do that.

I wanted to be.

I left therapy feeling better and worse, but mostly better.

As I was walking to my car, I pulled out my phone and noticed I had a missed text from *Brad from the wedding*. That was going to make me laugh every time. I'd told him to put me in his contacts as *Kelly from the wedding*. His reply had been, "I won't need a prompt to remember who you are." I opened the text.

Happy Birthday? Should I call you tonight?

I laughed again. *Nope, not tonight. Still 34 today.* I hit send and walked to my car.

As I was getting settled another text came in. *Tomorrow?*

That would probably be a good day to wish me a happy birthday.

I sat my phone down, started my car, and drove to Evan's school. When I got there, I noticed I had another text from Brad, *Who are you and what did you do to my friend?*

What? I hit send and started to walk toward the building.

His reply was, *Kelly? Giving away info so easily?! I thought you'd make me work harder for it.*

I laughed as I typed. *Maybe you caught me in a weak moment. I just talked with my therapist about Sam's Time Capsule letter.*

What did she say about me?

That response caught me so off guard that if I was someone who typed LOL in a text, it would have been true in that moment. I stopped walking and typed, *Don't take this the wrong way, but I'm thankful that we were both late for that wedding.*

I could see that he was typing so I stood there and looked at my phone. *She said that?*

I laughed and replied, *No. I did… right now… to you. You make me laugh, and you make me not hurt so much today. And for that I'm thankful that we met. Now get back to your boring job before you get fired!*

Good point. Talk to you tomorrow.

I smiled, put my phone in my pocket, and walked into the building.

An Ending

Later that evening I was in the kitchen and was finishing doing dishes when Sam and Evan came in. "Hi, Mommy!" Evan yelled. "I have to poop!" I heard him running up the steps, and I was laughing when Sam walked into the kitchen.

I jumped a little when I saw him then laughed again. "Oh, hey," I said.

"You're a little jumpy, Kel," Sam said and smiled.

"Well, I didn't realize you had come in so…" I shrugged and wiped my hands on a towel.

"I was hoping we could get a chance to talk for a few minutes," he said.

"Oh, yeah?" I folded the towel and hung it up. I turned around and looked at him. "What's up?"

Sam looked down at the floor for a couple seconds. "I dunno. I guess I'm just realizing what a huge mistake I've made."

A surge of energy ran through my body, and I could feel my hair stand up a little. "What do you mean, Sam? Mistake how?"

He looked up at me for a few seconds, put his hands in his pockets, then he sheepishly smiled and shrugged. "I know the whole situation is a mess, but I dunno, Kelly. Is there any way that we could revisit us?"

I stared at him for a couple of seconds. This exact situation was what I'd thought I wanted to happen pretty much since the moment

Sam had left. But standing across from him and listening to his words, I felt frozen—and a little trapped if I were being truly honest with myself. "I don't know what to say," I said. My phone buzzed on the counter, and I glanced over at it. There was a text from *Brad from the wedding*.

"What are you thinking? Do you think we should give things a try again?" Sam said.

I was still looking at my phone on the counter, but I could see out of my peripheral vision that Sam was taking a couple steps closer to me. "Sam, wait," I said and held up my hands and looked at him.

"Wait?" he said and stopped.

I nodded and took a deep breath. "Reconciling has been all that I've wanted for the past year. Like, you and us and our family with Evan. That is all I could think about for the past year, and I wanted us back so badly."

Sam smiled at me.

"But," I said. "I think it might be too late to reconcile."

His smile faded.

"I don't think it would work out, Sam." I shook my head. "I mean, you hurt me so badly. Like, I don't think you can begin to understand how badly you've hurt me." I glanced at the counter—at my phone. "And, recently, I've realized that I deserve to be with someone who values me. And I think you did value me at one point—a long time ago. I mean, I think we had a beautiful love story, and it helped to shape me into the person I am today, but somewhere between the first time we met and today that love between us died, and it won't ever be the same." I stopped for a couple seconds. My phone buzzed again, and I reached over and pushed it further away from me. "And I don't think it'll ever be enough for me. You won't be enough for me because I'm not sure I can forget about you leaving me, Sam. Like, I'm not sure I could ever truly get that out of my head. And you know what? I want and deserve better than being with someone who may leave me—who did leave me."

Sam didn't say anything for a couple seconds and then quietly said, "I wouldn't do it again though."

I looked at my hands for a few seconds and remembered how safe and secure I'd once felt in that relationship and then looked up at him and breathed in sharply. "I didn't think you would do it the first time, but you did. You're already someone who did leave me, Sam."

"Kelly..." He looked down at the floor and closed his eyes.

I breathed in and out slowly. "I'm going to hire a lawyer and file for divorce."

Sam looked up at me. "Wow, I didn't expect that reaction." He blew his breath out. "Divorce, huh?"

I nodded and pressed my lips together. I hadn't expected that reaction either, but I was confident it was the right choice.

"This is really happening?"

"It is," I said and nodded again.

He blew out his breath again and then nodded too. "I guess I'm going to get going then. Good night, Kelly."

I closed my eyes.

Sam left the kitchen, and I could hear him open and then close the front door. I followed the path that Sam had just walked to the door, and I locked the bolt.

I pressed my forehead into the door and stood there for several seconds and breathed in and out slowly. *I am. Relaxed. I am. Relaxed. I am. Relaxed.*

I went upstairs and tucked Evan into bed.

After Evan was sleeping, I went into my office and sat down at my computer because I actually wanted to write, which felt a little odd but very good.

I started to open my novel and shook my head because I wasn't going to finish that story. It was done. There was too much negativity attached to it, and I wanted to move on and focus on something a little more hopeful—something new.

But what?

Kim had said I should write something funny. Dana had said I should write a toned-down version of my own life. And Brad... well, he had said I should write something about him. He was joking, but maybe that could be funny. I pictured me grabbing his hand and running like hell away from that church and that wedding. I hadn't even known his name at that point.

I shook my head and laughed. I'd normally written love stories, but this wouldn't be a love story—not at this point, anyway. I was nowhere near being ready to fall in love again.

But Brad had made me laugh.

And he'd made me feel more like myself—like my old self—than I'd felt in a long time. I inhaled deeply and swallowed back a few tears that I hadn't even realized were welling up inside me and put my right hand on my heart. "Thank you," I said quietly... because I liked that person, and I'd missed her.

Maybe this new story could be about a writer with writer's block whose mind and emotions have felt out of control since losing her husband. And maybe, eventually, she could meet someone—not a love interest. Just one of those people who comes into your life at exactly the right moment and makes you remember who you used to be, which is really who you still are... And saves you from yourself.

I closed my eyes and thought about that for a few minutes. Kept my eyes shut and breathed and felt the air come in and blow out. Come in... and blow out. In... and out...

I opened my eyes.

"Okay," I said and opened a new document. I set the font and spacing and started to type.

I am capable of taking care of myself—at least I think I am. I mean, I'm 34 years old. I have a five-year-old, and I'm capable of taking care of him.

But trying to navigate my current life, I can't help but think about that stupid boy in high school—what was his name? Brian Somethingorother?—who had told me that there were two types of people in this world, people who were meant to work and people who were meant to be taken care of by others. He then said, in a not so nice way, that I was one of those in the second category. We were dating at the time, and I don't think he was trying to be offensive, but him saying it really irked me. Maybe it was just because it was a man—well, a 17-year-old man (a-hem)—who was telling me that I couldn't do something. Being reared in a feminist household, that hadn't sat very well with me.

But you know what? Within 10 years, I really wished I could have tracked him down to ask, "How the hell did you have me so pegged at 18?" Seriously? It wasn't like he was even my boyfriend. We had only gone out a few times, but he just knew.

I needed to be taken care of by others.

Well… at least, I used to.

QUESTIONS FOR DISCUSSION

Which character do you most relate to, if any?

What's your birth order? Could you relate to Kelly's family dynamic?

Kelly appears to be struggling with anxiety and depression. Do you think she realizes it? Do you think it's situational or who she is?

Have you ever felt lost and couldn't focus on what you needed to do? How did you deal with it? What helped you work through that period of time?

Have you ever held onto the idea of getting back together with someone even when you knew they weren't right for you?

Would you have invited Brad to your house? Why do you think Kelly did?

Of all the men that Kelly interacted with, is there one that you wish she would wind up with and why?

What do you think was really going on with the couple in the restaurant?

Some storylines were left unresolved. Which are you the most curious about? What do you imagine will happen?

ACKNOWLEDGEMENTS

Thank you to everyone who showed so much enthusiasm when I first published this book a little over a year ago! It really inspired me to keep going with my writing. I truly appreciate everyone who's taken the time to read any of my books! Thank you for reading and for sharing with friends and for reviewing! Reviews mean so much to indie authors and are very much appreciated!

Flirting with a New Life is my first of 3 books and continues to be my bestselling book. Thank you for loving Kelly!! Soon, I'll have my second *Flirting* book out! I can't wait to share it! It's my favorite that I've written so far!

I always sort of planned on revisiting Kelly—I was thinking maybe 10 years later, but your excitement and encouraging words encouraged me to revisit her sooner. So on the "eve" of book two's release, Heather Mihalic generously offered to redesign the cover of FWANL, so that it would match what's coming next, *Flirting with Celebrity* (as she's designing that one too!!! Thank you, Heather!!). This cover is GORGEOUS!!

Thank you to Tracy from Feathers Artist Market & Gifts in Irwin, PA, for supporting local authors and carrying my books in your shop!

As I said in the first edition of this book, it was written slowly, was put aside, and was revisited many times over a period of 15 years. I hope it never takes me 15 years to finish a book again… ever!

Thank you to my early readers, Penny Morse (AKA Mom), Wendy Frase (my sister), Patty Mooney, Jenn Wilson, Lucy Gazarik, Darcey Mamone, Lauren Oliech, and Heather Mihalic. Mom, Wendy, and Patty even read multiple drafts—you all deserve gold stars! Darcey saved me from a boring title. I appreciate all of your feedback and the time you all spent reading! I love all of you bunches!

Thank you to Eilish and Finn for making me a mom. I'm a better person for having known and nurtured the both of you, and I love you more than you'll ever know! Thank you to David Morse for always giving me something ridiculous to laugh about. I love you, Dad!

And, Of course, thank you to Lloyd for always encouraging me and loving me exactly as I am. I love you so much!

ABOUT THE AUTHOR

Jill Cullen lives in Pennsylvania with her husband Lloyd, son Finn, and their adorable pup Myrna. She has a BA in English from Point Park University and an MLIS from the University of Pittsburgh. Her day job is cataloging and acquisitions librarian for a public library just outside Pittsburgh, Pennsylvania. She loves to read, write, and spend time talking and laughing with family and friends. Other books include *Soulmates, Until, and Flirting with Celebrity* (coming very soon).

photo credit: Jennifer McCalla

OTHER BOOKS BY JILL CULLEN

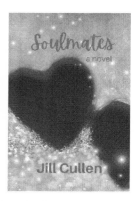

"Beautiful and captivating. I absolutely loved this book and couldn't put it down. It included vivid characters and an intricate plot. Highly recommend!" —Shavahn, GoodReads reviewer

"Jill Cullen's *Until* tells a touching love story, woven over the course of twenty-six years. It is effortlessly relatable and will quite possibly take you down your own memory lane of loss and love, like it did for me." —Leslie Savisky, author of *Other People's Words* and *Almost Too Late*

Coming February 2024…

FLIRTING WITH CELEBRITY

A Beginning

I am capable of making good choices—at least I think I am. I'm thirty-six. I've mostly successfully reared my six-year-old son Evan (no thanks to my ex-husband Sam and his abrupt departure from our daily lives two plus years ago, but that's a different story).

But trying to navigate my current life, I'm starting to wonder if maybe a certain level of chaos seeks me out and chooses me, like some creepy cyber lurker. It reminds me of that guy in high school, Christopher Reagan (I think that was his name), who stopped hanging out with me because it was too much drama for him. I mean, we only went out, like, four times. And, sure, one of them included a trip to the emergency room and another a police escort home… At the time I thought he was exaggerating and was just, well, a jerk.

But living through some recent situations, I sort of wished I could track him down and ask him how in the hell did he have me so pegged at sixteen? It was like he just knew back then that I attracted disarray like a magnet on some level… and it seems I still do.

But I'm bound and determined to break that cycle. I can do it. At least I'm fairly certain I can.

Made in the USA
Middletown, DE
10 June 2024

55433181R00201